For Joan,

ACROSS
the
MEKONG RIVER

Best Wishes,
Elaine Russell

A Novel By

ELAINE RUSSELL

MW00928695

Cover photograph by Roy McDonald
Copyright ©2011 Elaine Russell
All rights reserved.
ISBN-10: 1466338105
ISBN-13: 9781466338104
Library of Congress Catalog Number: 2011916686
CreateSpace, North Charleston, South Carolina

This book is dedicated to my mother for always believing in me and my husband for his unwavering love and support. I also dedicate this book to the hundreds of thousands of Hmong and other Laotian refugees who were forced to leave behind their loved ones and homeland to start anew in the United States and other countries.

Winner of Four 2013 Independent Publishing Book Awards for Multicultural Fiction:

Winner - Next Generation Indie Book Award
Silver - ForeWord Reveiws Book of the Year Award
Bronze - Independent Publishers Book Award
Finalist - Readers' Favorite Book Award

ACKNOWLEDGEMENTS

I want to thank my editor Dan Smetanka for his excellent and patient guidance on revisions to this story. I could not have done it without him. Also, thank you to my friends Erin Dealey, Susanne Sommer, and Marcia Freedman, who read my chapters through many versions, and Jackie Pope for a final edit. I am very grateful to Amorette Yang for reading the manuscript and offering thoughts on the story and the Hmong immigrant experience. Many thanks to Lee Yang, Shoua Thao, Ka Yang, Penny Xiong, and Chor Vang for taking time to share their families' stories and knowledge of Hmong culture and traditions with me. I am indebted to the Lao Family Community of Sacramento and the Hmong Women's Heritage Association of Sacramento for publications and information shared. And finally, to all the wonderful Hmong and Lao friends I have met through my association with Legacies of War, who also shared their families' stories, *ua tsaug* and *kop chai*.

PROLOGUE

Truth is an illusion. It is only something we create from memories and wishes and fragments of dreams. The truth is what we want to believe. And sometimes lies are so essential they become part of that truth. I realize this now, perched on a chair in the small courtroom, my mind reeling with what I am about to do. What I must do to survive.

The windowless chamber is stuffy and heavy with scents of polished wood and linoleum floors swabbed in pine-scented cleaner. My father sits alone at the scratched oak table on the other side of the aisle, a five-foot space that spans between us like a vast river. His familiar mix of stale smoke and musky aftershave drifts my way, and I want to be eight again, giggling wildly as I ride on his back across the lawn outside our first apartment in America. He wears his one tweed jacket, gray slacks shiny at the knees, and a white shirt, which is frayed at the collar if you look closely. His body remains rigid, his face impassive. He stares straight ahead at the imposing judge in his black robe behind the bench. Occasionally, the muscles around his mouth tighten and twitch as he swallows.

My mother is in the first row behind him, next to Uncle Boua so he can translate. She weeps softly and stares at me with dark, accusing eyes. I long to reach across the void, to cry out to them: *please understand.* But it is too late. They already know about my lies. And the past slips from my hands.

The judge rubs his left temple in circles. He is a portly, Caucasian man with thinning silver hair and eyes barely visible under folds of skin. The room is deathly quiet except for the low moan of his chair, as he rocks back and forth, leafing through documents. He peers over his reading glasses at me, then my father, then back to me. The clock on the back wall clicks, another minute passing. His forehead wrinkles into deep lines. His expression is puzzled, or perhaps disturbed. Does he notice my hands shaking as I crumple a damp tissue? Or the tears that blur my vision, creating halos around objects and people in the room? Can he hear my breath catch on each painful draw of air, as I dare to glance at my father?

Before long this judge, this stranger, will ask how we came to this impasse. My attorney will detail events over the past weeks and months, and Father will respond with his version. But this will not be the truth. These statements will be a fraction of the whole. For the judge to truly understand the splintered path of misunderstandings and struggles that led to this moment, I would have to begin somewhere else, far from this small room in California. Twelve years ago when I was only five.

The details of my early years remain opaque and shadowy, viewed through a window clouded with steam. I can never be sure if the few vivid images I carry rise from memory or were painted by my parents' reluctant retelling of our passage. Perhaps I invented moments out of necessity to fill the empty spaces in my heart. To justify my choices. This is what I think I know.

You see, truth is an illusion. Lies are essential.

Here is where my story begins.

A red scar in the shape of a half-circle marks the back of my left calf, a three inch reminder of the other part of me, the part I left behind. I suffered the burn one July night in 1978 as my family ran through an open field from the cover of mango trees to bamboo stands lining the Mekong River on the last stretch of our escape from Laos. We fled the reign of terror the new communist government waged against the Hmong for fighting with the Americans during the Vietnam War. The refuge of Thailand, its twinkling lights dotting the distant shore like fallen stars, beckoned across the dark divide. Flashes of moonlight glanced off swirling waters, turning the shadows into silver stepping stones. My heart raced, and my ears filled with the roar of the river as it swept past, heavy with monsoon runoff. Mother promised we would be safe when we reached the other side. And being only a child, I believed her.

Many weeks before--maybe several months, I'm not sure-- Mother wakened me in the middle of the night. "Quiet. We are leaving on a long journey," she said in a voice so hushed I barely heard her. She warned me not to disturb the soldiers who slept in the camp next to our village, as she dressed me in two layers of clothes. The mention of the bad men filled me with dread. They loomed in my mind as frightening as the tigers Mother said roamed the forest, equally capable of harm.

I blinked, sleepy and confused.

"Not a word." She put her finger to her lips.

"But what about Hwj Txob?" This was my black and white baby pig that I had named Pepper. He tagged behind me through the village and butted against my knees, knocking me down and licking my face. I loved my pig and did not want to leave without him.

"We'll get him later."

Mother and my brothers Fue and Fong, ten and twelve years old, loaded heavy bundles with clothes and food onto their backs. We slipped from the house to the edge of our village, up the steep hill through the peach and apple orchard, and past the bamboo stands where once I had seen a red panda nibbling tender leaves. We climbed higher into the forest, fragrant with pines, the ground cushioned with fallen needles. A light drizzle brushed across my cheeks as soft as corn silk.

Deep among the trees we joined Uncle Boua, Auntie Nhia, and their four children, another cousin, Choa, his wife and new baby, and seventeen members of the Yang family, all huddled together in silence. I could barely make out faces in the muted light of a single flashlight hidden under Uncle Boua's jacket.

From behind my cousin Choa a shadow moved toward me, and a man lifted me up, murmuring in my ear, "Nou, *ma petite*, it is your father."

I thought I must be dreaming. My father had been gone a very long time. Mother had told me bad men had taken him away and kept him from us, but someday he would return. Often at night, when she crawled onto the bed next to me, I heard her cry into the quilt. I had no recollection of this man holding me close, no memory of his face or his voice or the feel of his wiry arms. I only knew the photograph that Mother had hidden under her blankets, the image of a soldier standing in front of a metal building in Khaki pants and a short-sleeved shirt with ribbons and metal shapes that hung above the pocket. He wore black boots that laced up his calves, his hands gripping a wide-barreled gun so large it nearly came to the top of his head. As many times as I studied the picture, I could not make out the face, a mere shadow obscured by his cap's broad brim. Yet here he was, leading us off into the night.

That first day filled me with happiness. We crept through the forest as if playing a game of hide-and-seek, the way my brothers and I often had in our village and the surrounding fields. Father cradled me in his arms, and I drifted off to sleep. I woke to the calls of Mynah birds and the jostling of Father's steady pace, my head bouncing on his shoulder. A pale gray-green light seeped through the canopy of teak and rosewoods that towered over the pines like elder brothers. At last I could study the face next to mine with its sharp angles around the brow and chin, the sunken cheeks, the skin so pale and thin I was afraid to touch it. Bones protruded from Father's ribs and hips and arms. I had never seen anyone like this, not even old Grandfather Yang who had withered away to dust. I touched his wrist and asked why there was not more of him. His smile revealed gaps of missing teeth. He whispered that he had been hungry a very long time, but soon he would be fine, as fat as a big hog. I laughed at the idea, picturing him running around with Hwj Txob.

We stopped in a clearing to rest and ate bundles of sticky rice. The rain had stopped and up through the branches, I could see white puffy clouds sail past. Sunbeams sprinkled through leaves, casting elaborate patterns on the ground as I chased about, tracing them with a stick. Mother threw two quilts over a bed of moss and pine needles. My brothers collapsed on one, while my parents lay on either side of me on the other, smiling and whispering to one another. A woodpecker rapped on the trunk above us, and hypnotized flies buzzed in shafts of sunlight as if trapped, unable to find an exit. A string of carpenter ants gnawed at the decaying log beside us. I gasped as an enormous orange dragonfly landed on Father's leg and fluttered its sheer wings of spun gold for one pure and perfect moment.

Eventually, days and nights blurred together. Each became more difficult than the one before. The joy of Father's return became lost in the deep creases of his face and his ever tightening grip on my hand. We spoke only in whispers. We moved very quickly. Every time I uttered the slightest sound, Mother grabbed my shoulder and shook her head. I could not play with my cousins or brothers. I could not sing or laugh or clap my hands. At the slightest rustling in the bushes, we took cover behind the thickest trees or fallen logs, freezing in place, barely breathing until we were sure it was safe. No one told me where we were going. I wanted to go home. I wanted Hwj Txob. And for the first time I understood that Mother had lied to me. We would never go back for my pig.

Father and the other men took turns slashing a narrow trail with their scythes through dense thorny bushes, grasses, and thistles. The rest of us followed single file, up and down one jagged mountain after another, slogging and slipping through the mud, stumbling over fallen branches and roots. It was the monsoon season, and the rain poured down in great torrents. My clothes and skin remained damp with the ripe smell of decaying leaves and wet earth.

The first few days, my oldest brother Fong carried me on his back for short stretches. I felt safe with my legs wrapped about his middle and my arms around his neck. Soon he grew too weak for the extra weight. I walked until my calves cramped and my bare feet bled. Mother wrapped a cloth around my head and neck to block the mosquitoes that swarmed about me, searching for a succulent spot of skin. I became numb to the sting of leeches biting my legs, greedily sucking my blood until, sated, they fell to the ground.

At the end of the first week, I collapsed on the path too tired to move. "Carry me," I cried.

Mother clapped a hand over my mouth and yanked me off the ground. "Hush! You will kill us all." Her breath was hot on my cheek. Her eyes reflected the dark, roiling clouds above.

But Father lifted me into his arms. We continued on.

Some days the rain fell so hard, I could hardly lift my feet from the thick mud. Twice we built funny houses of twigs or bamboo covered with broad-leafed palms and stayed until the worst of it passed. Father remained tense and alert even when he slept, his knife by his side. I melted into slumber, snuggling up to Mother. I dreamed we were back in our house in the village and the bad men had fallen off the mountain into a hole where evil spirits had eaten them.

It must have been the third week when Mother complained her stomach hurt and she needed to stop. Father said we all needed to rest and dry out. He found a limestone cave with an entrance almost as tall as the trees outside. Toward the back of the cave, bat guano covered the craggy floor, and the overpowering stench made my stomach churn. There were traces of others before us— ashes from fires and discarded bones from birds or bats that had been eaten. Father and Uncle Boua patiently fanned twigs and wet logs into a fire that filled the cave with heavy gray smoke and a narrow radius of warmth. All at once a wave of bats burst from the ceiling and crevices; a mass of black wings whirled around us. I screamed and flailed as small creatures brushed my head and arms and legs, and a rush of wind like stale breath filled my lungs. Father encircled my body with his until the bats passed--a solid river of black, screeching and disappearing into the fading day. He held me close and whispered soothing words until I stopped sobbing. He promised they would stay away as long as we kept the fire going

My cousin Choa, Yang Bee, and Auntie Nhia had been clever to capture dozens of bats in baskets with their bare hands as they flew past. We roasted them on sticks and had our first meat in seven days. But Mother didn't eat. She lay curled up on a blanket, holding her abdomen and moaning. Sweat poured from her brow. Father knelt beside her, wiping her face with a wet rag. Uncle Boua was a shaman, skilled at guiding lost souls. He prayed to our ancestors and the spirits of the other world to help protect Mother.

In the morning, blood began to flow from between Mother's legs, trickling down the cave's grey and white limestone floor like a red ribbon. The viscous liquid pooled in cracks and crevices. Soon her face drained of color. She gasped with pain and gripped Father's hand. I buried my head in Fong's shoulder, too afraid to look as he led me away.

Auntie Nhia washed Mother down, wrapped her lower half in sarongs, and gave her a small piece of brown medicine collected from the poppies in our fields. She told me to stop crying and help her, taking my hand and leading me into the forest. We searched for dark green mint leaves that grew in the shadows of sweet-scented white orchids. When I rubbed them between my fingers, the pungent, cooling smell filled my nostrils. Next we gathered golden chrysanthemums along the bank of a streambed where water bugs skittered across a pool in a game of tag. Auntie Nhia patted my head and reassured me my mother would be fine. What a big girl I was, she said, to help her find the medicine. When we returned, she boiled the plants into a yellow-green potion. She roused Mother from her stupor and forced her to drink slow sips every few minutes. An hour passed and the bleeding ebbed, finally stopping late that night.

Mother slept a full night and day without waking as Father chanted prayers and stroked her hair. The rest of us gathered firewood to keep the blaze burning. Auntie Nhia and I washed the blood-stained sarongs in the stream and hung them to dry near the fire. At last Mother sat up, her face pale and worn. Father fed her some of the last rice and more of the herbal drink Auntie had made.

I nestled under Mother's arm, grateful she was alive and proud that I had helped to save her. She held me close. Two days later we set out again.

The rice was gone. My stomach gnawed with a constant ache. We scavenged for brown mushrooms shaped like elephant ears, the white larvae of giant ants, grasshoppers and beetles to roast, tender bamboo shoots, and if we were lucky, an occasional rat or bird--anything to stay alive. One day Father lassoed a small brown monkey with a rope. Another day we passed near a village where a kind farmer brought us a basket of rice and bitter melon from his wife's garden. I ate so fast it came back up.

The full moon came and passed, and still we walked. On a hot day when the sun filled the sky and steam rose off the ground and leaves like wisps of smoke, Grandmother Yang and her grandson stopped to fill their water jugs in a stream. They waved for us to join them, holding up bright red berries that they stuffed in their mouths.

Auntie Nhia clucked her tongue and ran toward them, warning them. "Stop. They may be poisonous. The birds have not eaten them." Grandmother Yang just laughed, her teeth stained vermillion, a trickle of juice dripping down her chin. Within an hour they complained of stomach aches and began running into the bushes to relieve themselves. Soon they fell to the ground, writhing with pain, pink foam forming at the corners of their mouths. Their eyes fell back in their sockets, and their insides emptied out. I clung to Mother and hid my face in her skirt as we stood by helpless. They were both dead three hours later. We buried them in the rich dark soil next to a stream and piled stones on top to keep the wild animals from digging them up. Father said even if we could not give them a proper burial, we would pray for their souls to find their way back to their birth place, then to the heavens with their ancestors.

I often cried, but silently, so the evil soldiers would not find us. They found us anyway.

A few nights later sharp bursts of light erupted as we picked our way across a steep mountainside nearly impenetrable with dense pine trees and clinging vines. Whistling noises and loud pops swept past my ears. At first I thought someone was throwing rocks. But the noises multiplied into a drum roll of deafening bangs and pings that caused my body to jerk. I felt the heat of bullets whizzing past and ricocheting off the trees. Mother grabbed my hand as we ran through the forest with the others. A thorn caught my arm. A twig scraped my eye. A huge earthquake rocked the ground, obliterating our path. Dirt and rocks and leaves flew through the air and showered down, hitting me about the head and shoulders. The air smelled of metal and fire and rotten eggs. And then another blast. In a flash of light, no brighter than the palest moon, my cousin Chao and Aunt Nhia fell to the ground, their faces full of surprise. A scream formed in the back of my throat, but I could not make the sound come out. We ran and ran and ran until finally the shooting and explosions ceased. And we kept running.

At last Mother stopped, and we fell on the ground. Her entire body shook as she wrapped me in her thin arms. The warmth of her body melted into mine and calmed my pounding heart. I lay there as she rocked me back and forth. Fue soon found us. We huddled together, listening for the others. Our terror settled over the hum of crickets and mosquitoes and a thousand crawling creatures living in the dark.

In the first shadows of dawn, the remaining members of our group gathered. Mother wept with relief when Father and Fong appeared. A bullet had grazed Fong's neck, leaving a red burn. Yang Shoua had a bullet in her arm. Her husband wrapped a cloth around it, and a slow trickle of blood oozed through. Four were missing. Father, Fong, Uncle Boua, and Chia crept back to look. An hour later Fong came for us. We found the men digging graves beneath the leaves and moss, gently placing my cousin Chao, Auntie Nhia, Yang Kim, and Yang Lia to their rest. We cried and prayed for their souls.

Mountains receded into rolling hills and dense pines gave way to coconut palms, monkey pod and acacia trees. Fruit orchards dotted the land. I happily gorged on breadfruit and mangos and corn stolen from fields in the middle of the night.

Late afternoon a plane buzzed over the stand of mango and palm trees where we had stopped to rest. A fine yellow film seeped through the leaves like the white clouds of mist that had often veiled our village and mountain early mornings until the sun burned through. The yellow powder seared my eyes and lungs. Father lifted me into his arms, and we scattered through the mango trees into the hibiscus bushes and ferns and away from the choking fog. We reached a stream where Father dunked me repeatedly, scrubbing my skin. The water turned pink around me, and when I touched my nose, blood covered my hand. Like many in our group, I retched for hours that night until there was nothing left in my body. My muscles quivered and convulsed. Mother gave me a small piece of the brown medicine, and I floated in and out of consciousness. Three days later I ate a bit of corn, then a banana. But my young cousin Chay was not as lucky. He had bled from his ears, eyes, nose, and mouth, and died the first night.

At last we reached the flatlands of flooded rice fields. For a week we crept along the narrow levees at night, hoping not to encounter poisonous water snakes or Pathet Laos soldiers, one as deadly as the other. During the day we hid in groves of bamboo or oleander. It wasn't far now, Father said.

Only twenty-two of our original group reached the Mekong River. Seven had died, and Youa had left with her baby for her brother's village near Luang Prabang after Choa was killed. We hid among the bushes, waiting for our chance. I knew that when we reached the lights in Thailand, we would be safe.

Father talked with local fishermen and learned there were no boats to ferry us across, no matter how much silver he offered. The soldiers kept close guard and shot anyone who ventured onto the water. So Father and the other men crawled on hands and knees through the darkness to the riverbank, cut bamboo poles, and fashioned crude rafts by lashing them together with rags and reeds. Once they were ready, Fong rushed back for the rest of us.

We ran bent low to the ground, but Yang Bee's baby girl, tied to her back, woke from the sudden bouncing and wailed. Within seconds, bright shafts of light swept back and forth across the meadow like giant sunbeams trapping flies. Gunfire erupted over our heads, followed by rockets. A swirl of yellow and blue and red filled the night sky like Chinese fireworks at a New Year's celebration. Mother dragged me by the arm, my feet tripping over mounds of dirt, my lungs burning as the world exploded around us. I never noticed the spark that set my pant leg on fire.

If I close my eyes, I can still feel the shock of cold water rushing over my body as we crashed into the river. My memory plays tricks now; those next moments stretch into endless minutes like a film in slow motion. I could not find a footing as my body became weightless. Father held the raft with one hand and grabbed my arm with the other, but the swift current caught me. I felt his grip slip down my arm to my wrist and over my palm, his fingers sliding away one by one until I sank into the depths. I could not lift my arms and legs. Water filled my mouth and lungs. Muffled screams, perhaps Mother's, drifted down. A hand thrashed through the water and pulled me up. Somehow Father caught my hair and then my shirt, grasping, lifting me to him and onto the raft, pinning me under his left arm. I coughed up water and gulped for air. Father had saved me. I believed he always would.

Father helped Mother roll onto the fragile hollows of bamboo. She cried out for my brothers to hurry, her arm stretching out to them. Ten feet away they struggled onto a smaller raft, swirling around like a top. Rockets whistled overhead and a huge wave crashed over them. A machine gun echoed in my ears, bullets bouncing off the bamboo and splashing on the water around us. A searchlight passed and in that moment of illumination, Fue jerked up to his knees, his hand flying to his chest. Mother let out a piercing wail as he fell into the river. The light brushed away and the world turned black once more. Our raft was swept into the rushing waters. I tried to keep my eyes pinned on the spot where my brothers had been, but they had disappeared into the dark expanse.

Father whipped his arms in the water, trying to guide our raft across the rushing current, avoiding floating logs and debris that bounced past. We clutched at the sharp edges of bamboo, spinning and rolling. I squeezed my eyes shut. I had no sense of how long it took-- minutes or hours--before we finally washed up on the opposite shore. I remember being passed into a strange s of arms and then sitting on sand and rocks. My body shook. My limbs felt numb, too heavy to move.

Fourteen others from our group struggled onto the riverbank in Thailand that night. My aunt, four cousins, and half the Yang family, were all dead. My brothers Fong and Fue floated somewhere in the depths of the murky, blood-stained waters, never to reach the shore across the Mekong River.

The judge shuffles the papers into a neat pile and puts them aside. The muscles in his face go slack as he lets out a long sigh. The air is filled with static, the heated anticipation of what will come next.

"We'll begin with a statement on the filing and the report from Social Services," the judge says at last. "First, Miss Lee, would you state your name as you wish it to appear in the court record. Do you want to be referred to as Nou Lee or Laura Lee?"

The court recorder, a younger woman with bleached blond hair cut into short spikes, turns to me. Her hands are poised above the keys of her machine, waiting for my response. She blinks several times with a bored indifference.

The question catches me off guard. I am confused, unsure how to answer. I am not one or the other, but a strange fusion of both. I do not know how to split apart the pieces.

Of course, I am here today because I am being forced to choose. The American flag hangs on a pole to the side of the judge's bench, an unspoken promise. A reminder: nothing is given without a price.

PART I

Chapter 1
PAO

If only we had fled Laos as soon as the civil war ended. If only I had not been lulled into complacency by the charade of peace the communist insurgents offered the Royal Lao government. If only I listened to my heart and not their empty promises. If only. So many times I have wept. *If only.*

In late February 1973, my men and I received a radio message. *Cease fire in effect. Return to headquarters.* An agreement between the two sides had been signed, yet I never believed anything would come of it. The enemy was still shooting shells at us, and that morning U.S. bombers had flown over as usual. I knew the communist Pathet Lao, buttressed by North Vietnamese troops and guns, could not be trusted.

The conflict ceased without ceremony, a candle snuffed out, leaving only a momentary halo in the darkness. The five men in my unit stood before me, shock and disbelief swimming in their eyes. For over three years I had led them on covert missions behind enemy lines. We shared the bond of fighting side by side, surviving despite the odds. I was their commander, friend, and counselor. I had tended to Xiong when he fell ill with a fever and to Nao when a bullet lodged in his stomach.

The week before, I had chanted a blessing in a *bai si* ceremony to protect us as we headed out on an assignment to track Pathet Lao movements. We still wore the strings we had tied on our wrists to keep our souls tethered to our bodies. I touched my frayed strings, brown with dirt, understanding the unspoken questions that muddied all our thoughts. What of the brave soldiers, our Hmong brothers, who had fought for our land and freedom, only to be shot or blown up and buried in unknown graves on forsaken mountainsides? What had they died for? After our sacrifices and blind loyalty to the Americans, how could they leave us to the mercy of the Pathet Lao? This time, I had no reassurances to offer my men.

My rifle suddenly felt heavy in my hands, cold and unnatural. Yet the mind grasps for hope even where there is little. In that moment, my thoughts turned to more immediate concerns. I would be home with Yer in time for the birth of our third child. I did not want to think of anything beyond this happy event.

Over the next two days we made our way back from the jungle east of Sam Thong. An eerie silence had settled over the forest. No planes. No explosions. No gunfire. I grew keenly aware of the trills of thrushes and woodcocks, the swish of a civet cat slinking through the ferns, and leaves whispering the sorrow of those who would not return from this long, bitter war.

Late afternoon we reached the airstrip on the hilltop at Lima Site 201 and caught a Huey for the short hop back to headquarters in Long Chieng. It was the start of the hot season with clear skies and warm hazy air. The helicopter's front and rear rotors whirled in competing tempos as we skimmed above the mountains. The scarred landscape below sagged as tired and worn as I felt. Faded green forests clung to the hills, punctuated by gaping pits, some over twenty feet wide, trees stripped of foliage, and swaths of barren land, the legacy of rockets and bombs and napalm. Occasionally, the crumbling remains of abandoned villages appeared. The chopper climbed over the jagged peaks of Sky Line Ridge and dipped precipitously into the long, narrow valley of Long Chieng with its single paved runway. The CIA building sprouted a forest of antennas, and haphazard shacks sprawled in every direction.

The base was alive with nervous uncertainty. Even though I was anxious to see my family, I went directly to my friend and superior officer, Blong. He would know the truth behind the cease fire.

Blong shook my hand and offered me a seat. He was a square, stocky man with a broad face and ready smile. His spirits never flagged no matter how grim the war had become. I needed his enthusiasm. He nodded his head and spoke quickly, "The agreement is good, I think--a coalition government. Both sides keep the territory they hold now. They will work for reconciliation."

"After twenty years of fighting, the Pathet Laos sings a song of peace?" I could not keep the disdain from my voice.

He lifted his hands in the air with a shrug. "The government has no choice but to accept. Since the Americans signed a treaty with Hanoi, they've been pressuring the ministers. They are leaving."

He was right of course. The desperate Royal Lao ministers had nowhere left to turn. They would wear their best faces with smiles and handshakes and endorsements for the agreement based on nothing more than prayers that it would work.

"All foreign troops must withdraw within sixty days," he said.

"The Vietnamese will never leave." The anger rose in my chest. Nothing would change with signatures on a piece of paper.

"We can hope." Blong hesitated a moment, staring down at his hands. "The Special Forces must be disbanded as well."

Here was the core of my fear. The Pathet Lao hated us. It had never been the small and undisciplined Royal Lao Army that kept them from taking over Laos, but the guerilla troops of the Special Forces made up of Hmong, Mien, and Khmu, the ethnic tribes that lived in the hills, separate from the ruling lowland Lao.

The trouble began after World War II when Ho Chi Minh's communists defeated the French and forced them to cede colonial rule. The 1954 Geneva Conventions granted Laos full independence, banning foreign interference. But this did not stop the North Vietnamese. They slipped in and out of our eastern provinces, recruiting poor farmers with no education or thoughts of their own and propping up fledgling Lao communists groups. Other countries flocked to Laos—China, Russia, the US--all vying for influence as governments came and went. The world leaders tried again with the 1962 Geneva Conventions to stop the manipulation and military aid from outsiders. But no one paid attention.

Intrigues and skirmishes turned into civil war, and we were pulled into a conflict of shadows and deception while the world pretended the fighting did not exist. The CIA recruited us to fight for them, knowing how we treasured our independence high in the mountains of Laos and that some of our people had fought with the French against the Vietnamese years before. They fed our fears, arguing the communists would destroy our way of life and force us to give up our land. The point had come when we had to choose one side or the other. While some Hmong were fooled by the communists, most understood the threat and the logic of siding with the powerful Americans. Surely the U.S. would win. The American military trained our troops and provided us with arms and air support. The conflict widened.

At the United Nations, foreign diplomats twisted and bent the truth, spinning away from scrutiny like Chinese acrobats. *No, there aren't any North Vietnamese troops in Laos. Why would anyone think the Chinese and Russians are providing arms? No, the American military does not have planes in Laos. These are private contractors delivering humanitarian aid. What bombing? America isn't bombing Laos.*

I had been a student attending the French high school in Vientiane during those days. I read the official reports in the newspapers, but they did not match the reality of what I witnessed, the hundreds of foreigners drinking in the bars, skulking around town for secret meetings, while pretending to be tourists.

"What does the General say?" I asked Blong at last. The leader of our Special Forces, General Vang Pao, the only Hmong general in the Royal Lao Army, held great sway in government circles. Or at least, he had.

"He tried to persuade the ministers against the agreement, but no one wanted to hear." Blong tamped his pipe on the bottom of his shoe, the old tobacco spilling out on the dirt floor. "The Americans are already preparing to take their planes to Thailand."

My body sagged. The Americans had forced us into defeat, their promises as worthless as those of the Pathet Lao.

My oldest son Fong, almost eight years old, held up the bamboo pole. His tongue worked at the side of his mouth with the effort, and his arms strained from the weight. I tied the pole in place around the front door of our new home. Over the past few weeks the other men in the village and I had worked together, chopping down sturdy bamboo poles, stripping them smooth, and framing each family's home. Bamboo, cut into thin slats, lined the walls and roofs. Fong insisted on helping at every step, his face serious and intent on whatever task I assigned him. My heart swelled with pride.

I stood on the threshold of our house, each side six meters long, solid and sheltering. Hmong homes had no windows, only two doors. And as was necessary, we had a sweeping view from the front door of the densely forested mountains that rose and fell across the narrow valley. Yer had already tamped down and swept the earthen floor until it was hard and smooth, but there were still many things to do. I needed to complete the loft for storing rice and the stove in the center of the room, and install the woven dividers to section off the sleeping areas. The next day we would attach thick layers of thatch to the roof to keep out the rains when the monsoons arrived.

There were other projects as well. I would spend a day felling a pine tree and sawing timber to help build Uncle Boua's shaman's bench, a simple plank sanded smooth and attached to splayed legs at each end. We would craft an altar with two shelves to hold his tools—the cymbals, gong, drum, and buffalo horns. Auntie Nhia and Yer would cover the altar with paper stamped with intricate patterns.

The following week we would light incense and make offerings to Sou Kah, the protective house spirit, and the other spirits of the front door, central post, and fireplace. We would ask them for blessings and good health.

As sweat ran down my back, I thought how happy I would be to finish these tasks. The hot season was still upon us, and we had fields to plant. I put a hand on Fong's shoulder. "Son, we are done."

"Look how much you helped!" Yer said to Fong, and he grinned. She sat under the wide umbrella of the monkey pod tree, our daughter Nou sleeping on a quilt at her side. She was weaving swaths of thatch, her quick, nimble fingers gathering and wrapping the yellow-green stalks of grass. A silky shawl of black hair hung down her shoulder. She had grown more beautiful with each child, maturity strengthening and defining her delicate features. I stared at the curve of her neck and chin that fit perfectly against my shoulder in bed. Her dark eyes shined brightly as she gazed up at me.

Through the hardships and terror of combat, her love had been the constant that kept me alive. Each night when the children went to sleep, we renewed our passion for one another. It reminded me of the first years of our marriage when even a moment apart felt too long and I could not get enough of her love. The night before she held me close and cried, begging me never to leave her no matter what happened. The intensity of her plea caught me by surprise. She never complained when I left for duty during the war, but now I understood how difficult it had been living with the constant fear and uncertainty, the pall of death hanging over their tenuous existence. I vowed to stay with my family.

Yer rose to check the pot of vegetables simmering over the fire as Fue darted past, laughing and chasing the crows that pecked at the ground for stray grains of rice. He raced in circles and clapped his hands. As he neared the tree, his bare feet kicked dust into Nou's face. She woke with a start and wailed.

"Oh, Fue, look what you've done," Yer scolded, lifting Nou into her arms and wiping her cheeks. She opened her blouse and guided Nou's mouth to her breast. "Boys, go wash. It is time for dinner."

I smiled and scooped Fue into my arms. "I'll take them to the stream."

I cherished small, ordinary moments with my family. This simple beginning was all I had dreamed of during nine years of combat. At times, I struggled to put the horrors of fighting behind me, but nightmares woke me in the middle of the night. Unexpected sounds in the forest made me quake. I could not escape my fears of what the future might hold. Yet for the time being, calm prevailed.

General Vang Pao had complied with the conditions of the cease fire and disbanded the Special Forces over the six weeks following the signing of the agreement. He urged us to go back to our lives, settle with our families, and once more become farmers. Our compensation on leaving included new tools and corn and rice seed. I rejoiced at the chance. Our family was lucky after all; we had survived when so many had not.

In early April Yer and I had left Long Chieng with Fong, Fue, and Nou, only a month old, and our remaining relatives, five households now. We were part of the Ly clan, one of the eighteen Hmong clans. In Laos we only had clan names, which we used before our given name. I ran into an old friend from my early school days, Yang Chia in Long Chieng. We had grown up in neighboring villages, and Chia married my cousin Ai. After the men in my family discussed our future, we decided to join Chia and six other Yang families to build a new village near Muang Cha.

We hiked three days to the town of Muang Cha, set on a broad plain in the mountains. It had grown into a large Hmong settlement during the war with schools through second level. I wanted my boys to have an education, to go on to the French high school in Vientiane, as I had. Perhaps even to college in France or somewhere abroad. It was the key to their future. With money I had saved, I bought six chickens, two sows, and a hog. We found a site for our village on a gentle slope near a stream, a half-day's walk from Muang Cha, and set to work.

Now the boys waded knee-deep in the stream, splashing one another and screeching at the cold drops trickling down their skin. Fue, two years younger, had a talent for drawing Fong out of his quiet reserve. Tiny fish, too small to eat, scoured the shallows around boulders and the boys' skinny legs.

"Come now. Who is hungry as an elephant?" I called. Fue trumpeted at the top of his lungs and swung one arm in the air as he raced back.

I took the baby from Yer and sat under the tree, rocking our tiny bundle and soothing her fussy cries. Yer spread the meal on a round mat. Nou's fingers grasped my thumb, and I thought I had never seen a child as beautiful. Her lips formed a little round O, and her eyes grew enormous as she studied my face.

Fue leaned over my shoulder, fascinated by this strange creature that filled his mother's days. He gently touched her hand. "When will she play with me?"

"When she is older," Yer said. "Be patient."

Fue turned to me and blinked. "Will she like me?"

I laughed. "Of course. And you can teach her everything you know."

Fong frowned and shooed away a fly. "But she's only a girl. She can't do the same things."

I shrugged. "Perhaps. But she will find her talents and be special in her own way."

Fue dove into his bowl of rice. "I'll show her how to use a sling shot."

"I'll teach her how to build a house," Fong said.

After dinner the boys and I played kickball until the light faded into deep shadows and it was time for bed. In the house, I crouched next to their bamboo platform built low to the ground. Yer sat nearby on our bed, nursing Nou. Every night I told one story of my adventures in the jungle or related one of the Hmong folk tales that had been told and retold, one generation to the next.

Fong leaned forward. "Tell the one about the snake."

I shook my head. "You've heard it many times."

Fong bounced up and down. "Please, oh please. I want that one."

Fue's face scrunched up with anticipation. "Yes, yes."

"If you wish," I said, laughing softly. "Well, I was with my men just south of Xieng Khouang. We spent the night deep in the forest." I dropped my voice to a low whisper and leaned in. Their eyes became large in the light from the lantern. "It was completely dark. As we lay on our knapsacks, noises filled the jungle like many instruments playing a song." I embellished the details to drag out the story, adding a tiger's roar and a hooting owl as their anticipation grew.

A moth swooped into the light, and the boys started. "At last I fell asleep and when I woke the next morning, I felt something heavy on my stomach like a big stone. I opened my eyes, and what do you think I found?"

Fue clasped his hands together. His shoulders hunched up as his voice slid into a squeak. "A big green snake, coiled on your stomach. Asleep!"

"Is this true, Father?" Fong asked.

"I would never lie. So I waited and waited, hardly breathing. I have to admit, I was very scared. One bite and I might be dead. An hour went by, and still the snake slept. I was so hungry, my stomach began to growl."

"And the snake put its head up and looked you in the eyes," Fong said.

"Yes. He stared at me as if thinking about what to do. I held my breath. His tongue flickered about several times. Then he slipped onto the ground and disappeared into the brush. Just like that!"

Fue scooted onto the floor, his tongue darting in and out, and waved goodbye as he slithered off. We all laughed.

Our third April in the new village, we cleared another field to plant with corn, yams, bitter melon, sugarcane, and opium. Last year's opium had provided enough cash for new tools, a horse, and another cow. Our crops had been bountiful the first year, but each season the plants leached the soil and rains eroded another layer of dirt. We were constantly shifting to new land, letting the old fields lay fallow for the soil to regenerate.

We located a mostly level site three miles from the village at the bottom of a forested hill. Over the next two weeks we cut down the pines and hardwoods, stacked the logs for firewood, and burned the remaining stumps and brush. I worked next to my brothers Tong and Shone, cousin Shoua and Uncle Boua. We threw our hoes deep into the earth, lifting great clods of dirt, uncovering rocks and old roots, and working the nutrient-rich ash into the ground. We edged our way up and down the field, carving out the last few rows. My arms and shoulders ached and calluses covered my hands, but the labor of these familiar tasks fortified me.

Fong and Fue followed behind me, removing large rocks and tree roots from the rows to make room for seeds. Fong lifted a rock almost a third his weight and struggled over to the side of the field. He dropped it onto his neat stack that came up to his chest. He kept at it without complaint as steady and plodding as a water buffalo. Occasionally, he looked up for my nod of approval.

I turned around to find Fue jumping and hopping like a frog across three rows in pursuit of a cricket. "Fue, help your brother. Look at all these rocks," I called.

He grinned and returned to his place, picking up a small rock and throwing it hard into the forest. The rock made a loud thwack as it hit a tree. "Did you see, Father? I hit the trunk."

I shook my head and smiled at his delight with the smallest accomplishment. As I continued working my hoe down the row, I wondered how it was possible that my two boys had such opposite temperaments. During the wheat harvest I had taught Fong to use the scythe. He was an apt and serious student, careful and methodical in swinging the blade. But I did not know when I could trust Fue to try this. He was only fit to help feed the cows and pigs, pulling their tails and bursting out with giggles when the poor beasts complained. Fue's mouth ran with a million questions and nonsensical stories. I only knew that when my boys stared up at me, their faces filled with awe, I was flooded with love.

I stood and stretched my sore back. Fue crouched over a fresh pile of dirt, prodding a large beetle with a stick. He ran to my side and threw his arms around my leg. "Come look. It is the biggest beetle I have ever seen. He is shiny and the color of new leaves."

How could I be mad? Each boy was special. Each a joy.

Yer arrived with lunch as the sun climbed to the top of the sky. After eating, Fong and I would pass down the rows, pounding our metal spikes into the loose dirt. Yer and Fue would follow behind, dropping corn seeds into the holes and covering them with soil.

Nou, now two, was tied to Yer's back in a brightly colored, embroidered carrier. Other parents left their little ones in the village with the elders who were too old to work the fields. But Yer refused

10

to part with her baby, still nervous from the years of war. She untied Nou and set her on the ground.

Nou spotted me and tried to toddle on her wobbly legs to my side but fell. I lifted her into my arms. Her little hands grabbed my neck as she held her chubby cheek close to mine. I pointed to my other cheek, "*Comme ca,*" I said, the way I had seen in a French film once in Vientiane. And Nou snuggled on the other side. Everyday, over and over, we played this game.

We sat under the banyan trees with our family members and ate sticky rice and roasted sweet potatoes. The boys doted on Nou, sharing their food and pretending to hide from her until she laughed so hard she got the hiccups. She attempted to chase after them, stumbling and falling and clapping her hands. Each day was a treasure, a momentary gift like a precious crystal of water languishing on a leaf until the wind scattered it dry.

Around this time, the peace began to unravel. In the evenings after dinner we listened on the short wave radio to the news reports on Lao National Radio and the U.S. sponsored Voice of America broadcasts from Thailand. Sometimes, we tuned in to Radio Pathet Lao, afraid of what we might hear, but more afraid not to know what they were saying. Details on the final terms of the coalition government in Vientiane remained unsettled. Negotiations continued, the announcers said, as the parties worked toward reconciliation. Each side blamed the other for the stalemate.

Every few weeks we walked to the market in Muang Cha to trade our produce for items we needed. I spoke with old friends here, who were closer to the truth. The news grew more disturbing. The coalition government was disintegrating. The peace agreements were being renegotiated. The Pathet Lao edged Royal Lao officials out of ministries and launched massive propaganda campaigns. The call went out to Lao workers to join the struggle for freedom and equality. *The government must purge the puppets of the American imperialists*, they said. The rhetoric echoed throughout the cities and into the countryside. Farmers and workers, caught up in the wave of change, took to the streets of Vientiane and Luang Prabang, demanding the Pathet Lao take control of the government. Rumors filtered in of North Vietnamese troops moving ever farther west.

Uneasiness settled in my middle. A friend told me of former Hmong soldiers who were organizing forces and gathering arms. If the Pathet Lao took over the country, they would be ready to fight again.

In early May, Uncle Boua received a message from General Vang Pao calling a meeting of clan leaders in Long Chieng. By now everyone had heard the chilling pronouncement on Radio Pathet Lao--*the Hmong Special Forces are the enemy of the Lao people; the Pathet Lao will duly punish or wipe them out.*

I accompanied Uncle Boua to Long Chieng and attended the meetings at the General's house. For days leaders argued and struggled over what to do, their faces lined with worry and fear. Should we take up arms again, or was it best to flee the country? If we left, where would we go? Who would take us? Many could not contain their anger, ready to fight once more to save our country. But emotions would not be enough to win a war. We needed arms and support. Being one of the younger men, I kept quiet. Then Uncle Boua, a steady voice of reason, said that without the Americans, fighting would be futile. I had promised myself never to leave my family again. There must be another solution, a way to live in peace.

Days passed, but no decisions were reached. Then I heard the devastating news. My friend and former commander Blong came to me. After the ceasefire, he had joined the Royal Lao army and stayed on with Vang Pao. His face was ashen and filled with deep lines, making him look much older than his twenty-eight years. He suggested we take a walk so we could speak in private.

We strolled in silence down the jumble of dirt lanes between hastily built houses, most of them nothing more than tiny huts. They had been slapped together with bamboo, wood, tin, cardboard boxes, whatever was available. The makeshift town had grown up around the air base over the war years as more and more Hmong were driven from the hills to seek refuge. Many of the homes had been deserted after the cease fire agreement as families left to rebuild their lives in the mountains once more. A few had stayed on. Laundry hung on ropes, and the smell of onions and cilantro and garlic wafted through open doorways mixed with the pervasive smell of garbage and open sewage drains. Barefoot children screamed and chased each other up and down the dusty paths, fighting with sticks. A group of boys played a game with wood tops. As we continued on, a naked baby girl stood in a doorway and cried. Her nose ran, and her face was streaked with dirt. I thought of my own three children at home.

At last we reached the edge of town and continued on the path to the neatly planted vegetable gardens, lush with the promise of newly sprouted herbs, mustard greens, broccoli, onions, and bitter melon.

"They have take Sala Phou Khoun," Blong said at last.

My heart sank. This was the last stronghold of the Royal Lao government. Now there was no defense left against the Pathet Lao. The communist troops would march into Vientiane and take over the capitol.

Blong clasped his hands behind his back, his head hanging down. "There is more. Yesterday, the CIA told General Vang Pao that he and his top officers must leave the country. The Pathet Lao will take them prisoner, or worse, kill them." A slight tremor filled his voice. "The CIA will fly the men to Thailand until things are sorted out."

I was speechless, trying to grasp his words. Was our country truly lost, every shred of hope gone? I could not accept this. Surely the Americans and other countries would not stand by and watch the government fall. Perhaps a compromise could still be reached.

The first rains had left narrow cracks in the dirt path. Soon torrential downpours would erode these into deep ruts and gaping holes.

I swallowed hard and glanced at Blong. "Will you leave?"

"I don't know. We're waiting to hear how many planes are coming. I wanted to tell you. Maybe you want to bring your family here. Just in case."

I talked it over with Uncle Boua. Should we rush home and bring our family back? It was a three-day walk each way. Would there be time? Uncle thought the leaders were overreacting. Surely only the top officers in the Special Forces need worry. We had been lowly lieutenants, not that important. Why would the Pathet Lao bother with us?

Uncle was the elder of our family, a wise man, a shaman of renown who drifted between this world and the one beyond. I trusted his judgment. We decided to stay in Long Chieng until it became clear what the Americans would do about the evacuation.

Fear erupted as rumors circulated of Vang Pao's departure. Hundreds and then thousands of Hmong from surrounding settlements began descending on Long Chieng, pouring out of the hills, hoping to be rescued. Men and woman pushed past one another as they hurried into town, carrying tattered cardboard boxes, bundles of clothes, and baskets filled with belongings. Children clung to their mother's skirts, their eyes wide with confusion. An elderly man collapsed on a basket at the side of a Quonset hut and gasped for breath. A lost boy, maybe three years old, screamed for his mother, and a woman stopped to help. She had a baby on her back, another in her arms, and two older girls crowding close to her, but she took the little boy's hand and hurried along. Others thought only of themselves, abandoning the weak.

Families settled in empty houses and on every bare patch of ground around the air strip. They built camp fires to cook rice and laid out quilts to sleep. A hum of muted conversations, pierced by the occasional cries of babies, settled over the town. The air filled with the stench of bodies massed together in the oppressive heat. The knot in my stomach wound tighter. And more people came.

After two days of endless waiting, the familiar roar of engines filled the brilliant blue expanse above the mountains. Expectant murmurs rose into urgent calls as families stood and gathered their belongings. One C-130 transport appeared over the horizon, the sun reflecting off its heavy metal body and whirling blades. It circled the sky, dipped into a steep descent, and landed with a jolt. At the end of the runway, it turned around, engines still running,

14

poised for a quick takeoff. I stood in the doorway of Blong's office as the chaos unfolded. A lieutenant colonel stood on a box with a clipboard in his hands and called out the names of the families designated to leave. A ring of soldiers surrounded him, holding up their guns, trying to maintain control and keep the crowds back. But people drew closer, packed tight against one another. Women and children cried out. Men begged. *What about us? What about my wife and children? Please, I'll give you all the money I have. You must help us. You must.*

The pilot dropped the tailgate of the cavernous hull. People rushed forward, tripping over one another, shoving and screaming, overpowering the soldiers. Hundreds pushed their way up the ramp. The pilot raced to the cockpit and revved his engines, blasting dozens onto the tamarack like rocks rolling down a hill. But hundreds more pressed and shoved their way toward the ramp. Somehow the pilot and soldiers managed to beat back the crowd and close the tailgate. The engines roared as the plane rushed down the runway, wobbling and straining, barely lifting off the ground and climbing high enough to clear the mountain ridge.

Silence descended. The waiting began as hopeful eyes turned again to the sky. Surely more planes would come. But only a twin engine Piper landed briefly and whisked away the wives and children of two colonels. Then two rickety C-47s took a few hundred more. The angry crowd erupted, fighting the soldiers, jumping into the side doors.

The first C-47 filled immediately beyond capacity, but somehow the pilot closed the doors and lifted the rattling hunk of metal off the ground. The crowd turned and surged toward the second plane like a flock of birds shifting directions in one seamless dip of wings. Over the mass of bobbing heads and clawing, tangled arms, I caught sight of Blong rushing his wife and four children around the far side and into the plane's hold. My breath caught in my throat with a mixture of happiness and envy that they should escape. But a few minutes later he stood at my side, tears streaming down his face. He waved as if somehow his wife could see him through the metal body of the plane. The doors jammed close, and the plane rolled to the end of the runway. It started up at full speed then screeched to a halt. The doors opened and dozens were pushed out like baby birds nudged from their nest. I cringed as the plane took off, its belly nearly dragging on the tarmac and over the mountain top. Blong sobbed, his eyes still searching the horizon as the hum of engines faded away. I had no words to comfort him. We both knew he might never see his family again.

Throughout the day small planes ferried the lucky few to Thailand, and then the skies grew silent. Blong confirmed my fears. No more flights. Even if I had returned home for my family, we would not have made it back in time. We would not have been among those evacuated.

My anxiety mounted each hour as the latest rumors spread about movements of Pathet Lao and Vietnamese troops. Then the news. In one last covert operation, the CIA had swept General Vang Pao to the safety of Thailand. His life was in imminent danger. They had given him no choice. He was shuttled out the back door of an office building into a waiting helicopter, hidden on a rise above town. No one could know. The end was that close.

Panicked families gathered themselves up and began a mass exodus on foot, heading out on the road to Vientiane and the Thai border. Thousands more arrived from the mountains, winding their way into the base, a giant stream of ants stretching over the landscape.

Uncle Boua and I left immediately for our village, weaving our way through the tide of men and women, young and old, carrying their children, blankets, cooking pots, baskets of rice, jewelry, clothes, whatever they could manage. Most people plodded steadily down the dirt road, bent with heavy loads and grasping the hands of crying children. Others became more and more agitated with each step, casting away belongings on the roadside, half-running and pushing past the slow ones.

On our walk home Uncle Boua and I talked at length about leaving. Uncle could not believe it would be as terrible as expected. He said the Pathet Lao would make a show of punishing a few Hmong officers to bring fear into our hearts and quell thoughts of resistance. But life would go on. In such a war-weary country, we would turn our energies to rebuilding. Besides, he was too old to start over. What would Thailand do with so many Hmong fleeing across their border? Would the Americans take us in? Too many unanswered questions. He would stay and take his chances. I did not share his optimism, but I hoped he was right.

We reached home to find that rumors and fear had spread through Muang Cha and to our village. My youngest brother Shone, cousin Soua, and their wives and children were preparing to leave with several members of the Yang family for Thailand. Uncle Boua urged me to go with them if I thought it best. But Yer and I talked it over that night. Uncle Boua was the elder of our family, the one who had raised me from the age of six. I could not abandon him and Auntie Nhia. It was my duty. My brother Tong insisted on staying as well.

The next week a Voice of America broadcast reported the Pathet Lao had opened fire on 10,000 Hmong as they tried to cross the Hin Heup Bridge on the way to Vientiane. The soldiers had mowed them down with machine guns and rockets and bayonets. Hundreds died. Radio Pathet Lao told another story, reporting brave soldiers had saved the Hmong from their CIA leaders who were forcing them into exile. The announcer urged all soldiers to follow the spy activities of reactionary traitors to completely eliminate the American enemy. We knew they meant the Hmong.

Another ten days went by. We heard from a passing farmer that communist troops had taken over Long Chieng, and former soldiers were disappearing. All the people had to attend reeducation classes. That evening Tong and I went to Uncle Boua to discuss the latest news, urging him to reconsider. As he puffed on his pipe, his eyes clouded with sadness. His shoulders slumped, doubt gnawing at him and eroding his resistance. I waited patiently for his answer. After a long silence, he shifted in his seat and nodded. We should prepare to go.

I needed to remove all traces of my role in the Special Forces in case the Pathet Lao soldiers came to our village. It must appear that I was nothing more than a simple farmer. As dawn spread over the mountain, I folded my army uniform into a small bundle, carefully matching the creases on the pant legs, smoothing the ribbons flat on my shirt pocket, and placing my cap on top. I wrapped them in a piece of hemp cloth tied with twine then did the same with my rifle. The boys and Yer watched in silence. As I stood to leave, Fong and Fue clamored to go with me. But for this last mission, I needed to be alone. Carrying my packages and a shovel, I climbed for twenty minutes up the hill and into the woods. My legs grew heavier with each step. A light mist still covered the ground and cooled the morning air. I stopped to dig beneath an acacia tree covered in white blossoms. Sweat ran down my back as my shovel worked through the tangle of ferns and moss. When the hole measured two feet deep, I kneeled down and gently placed the packages inside. I pushed the dirt back into the hole with my hands as white petals drifted down and grazed my cheeks like soft tears. I thought once more of the men who had died and the bravery and dedication of those who fought. Here was the legacy I left them, one of fear and retreat when I had once been so proud. I buried all hope for my country.

Yer and I left later that morning for Muang Cha. We needed supplies for our trek out of Laos--a flashlight and batteries, a new scythe, extra rice, additional salt to dry fish and pork. We could have managed without these things, but I hoped to learn more about Pathet Lao troop movements. We would head southwest toward the Thai border below Pakse, staying clear of the towns and villages. The walk would take at least three weeks, perhaps more if we had to hide along the way. We had no way of knowing how difficult our trip might be, how wide the enemy's reach might extend.

But the trip to Muang Cha changed everything. If only I hadn't insisted on going. If only we left that afternoon with whatever we had. If only we escaped while the border was still relatively easy to cross. *If only.*

Chapter 2
YER

Always war in Laos. Long before I was born. The village elders told stories. Foreigners from near and far intruded. Thai, Burmese, Khmer, and later French and Japanese. They wanted to steal the land. Then Vietnamese rebels crossed the border and stirred up even more trouble. I never understood. What made these men do this? Since I was a little girl, conflicts came and went like cycles of the moon. Small changes hardly noticed. It started with rumors. We heard from a passing villager of fighting in another province. In time the conflict grew closer until we could no longer ignore it.

We lived in the mountains of Xieng Khouang Province, in the middle of northern Laos. A beautiful place of gentle streams and green forests. On a clear day from the peak above our village I could see the broad Plain of Jars with its ancient stone jars, some as tall as two men. Lao villages and flooded rice patties dotted the valley. Beyond were the houses and Buddhist temple of Xieng Khouang town. We built our Hmong villages on the steep hillsides, working our fields and tending our animals. Only our land mattered.

Right after Pao and I married, once again war spilled into our lives. The fighting began to the east on the Vietnam border and slowly stretched from one town to another. The young soldier

Vang Pao traveled through the villages, calling on the Hmong to stop the communists before they took away our freedom. Pao was reluctant to join, hoping for a peaceful end. But after the Pathet Lao and North Vietnamese troops occupied the Plain of Jars, Pao and the other men in our family said enough. They joined the Special Forces. After the rice harvest in the twelfth month, my husband left to train in Thailand. I was only seventeen.

At first life went on as before. I shared a house with my mother-in-law and Pao's youngest sister Sri, not yet married. So it did not feel as empty. With our cousins, aunts, and old Uncle Mang, we hiked to the fields to plant and weed and harvest the crops. Evenings we chatted and laughed as we cooked dinner and sewed by the fire. I took comfort in the routines, the satisfaction of turning the soil and nurturing tiny sprouts into strong healthy plants. Long hours of labor left my muscles sore with a satisfying tiredness. The rhythm of the seasons tempered my loneliness and worries about Pao.

Every second Friday, Sri and I hiked two and a half hours to Xieng Khouang. We traded our vegetables and embroidered cloth at the market for salt, silk thread, or metal tools. I kept a wary eye on the Pathet Lao and Vietnamese soldiers. They acted friendly, but I was not fooled by their false smiles and easy words. They puffed out promises of freeing our people from the corrupt Lao government. I had to smile and pretend to agree. Inside I hated them, knowing one of their bullets might take my husband's life.

There were happy days when Pao returned home for short visits. He could not tell me what he did, but I knew he was fighting in the jungle. Not so far away. One season passed into the next for two more New Years. At last we were blessed with our first child, Fong.

By the end of the next year I seldom went to town. It was too dangerous. Bloated, green American planes roared overhead, scattering bombs along the Plain of Jars. The explosions echoed through the valley and up the hills like thunder. Huge clouds filled the sky with smoke and the smell of burning metal. I worried for the Lao villagers in the valley caught in the path of the bombs.

Communist troops expanded into the mountains like wild mustard plants spreading through a field stealing nourishment from the crops. We heard stories that the soldiers were searching for families of the Special Forces.

One morning in October, Pathet Lao soldiers marched into our village as I was feeding the pigs and chickens. Two were Lao. One was Hmong. From Sam Nuea he said. He was short and wide with large ears that stuck out and a broad flat nose. His eyes narrowed as he looked at me with a mixture of hatred and hunger. I wondered what had brought us to this, Hmong fighting Hmong. Surely he must have seen my fear as I picked up Fong and held him close. The man ran his finger back and forth over the trigger of his rifle as he spoke. *What hot weather now. How old is your baby? How are your fields? Where is your husband today?* My legs quivered. But my tiny mother-in-law came to my side, standing very straight, giving me strength. For the first time in my life I lied: *He went to another village to buy a cow. He should be back tomorrow.* The other women gave excuses for their husbands and sons. The Lao soldiers walked into our houses uninvited and poked among our things. I could hardly breathe. At last they turned to leave. The Hmong soldier stared at me, barely smiling. *We are winning the struggle, Sister. Only those who join the people's cause will be safe.*

They came again in the second month of the New Year. We were working in the fields, slicing the buds of the opium poppies and collecting the thick, milky sap. I had Fong, almost a year old, tied to my back. He bounced and kicked, babbling unformed words in my ear. Sri was telling me again about Chor, the boy from a neighboring village. He had been courting her since they met at the New Year's celebration. As soon as Pao returned home again, Chor would send his marriage negotiators.

Auntie Nhia's son Gia, only five years old, stepped into the woods to relieve himself. We heard a loud crack like an axe splitting a log. Gia ran into the field, shouting there were soldiers in a ravine. They were cutting a path up the hill. One had fired a rifle at him. I dropped my knife on the ground and raced with the others into the forest. We ran up through the trees and over the rocky peak. My sides ached. I thought my lungs would burst. We did not stop until we reached a thick grove of bamboo and buried ourselves in the middle. I put Fong to my breast to quiet his cries. That day we were lucky. They did not find us.

Two months passed. This time they caught us unaware as we harvested the last of the corn. Soldiers ran into the field yelling, firing guns. I thought I heard someone laughing. We fled into the trees once more. Sri clung to my arm, pulling on me harder and harder until I stopped. She fell slowly, first to her knees and then on her side. A bullet had passed through her middle, leaving a large, red hole in her back. Blood gushed onto the mossy ground. My hands shook as I stroked her cheek, the tears spilling down my face. She asked me to say goodbye to Chor. My mother-in-law collapsed next to us, rocking back and forth, moaning.

Smoke drifted through the trees. The soldiers had set fire to our field. When at last it seemed safe, we carried Sri back to the village to bury her. We found our houses burned and the rice and animals gone. From that day on, time and seasons had no meaning. Survival meant escape. Running away. Farther and farther away. Hiding in the jungle.

We walked through the night and half the next day. We were fourteen women, ten children, and Uncle Mang. It took all my effort to convince my mother-in-law to come. She wanted to die right there next to her youngest child. But I held her arm and led her along the path.

On another, taller mountain deep in the woods, we built small shelters, tying bamboo poles together against the trees and covering them with thatch. I think we were there six months, maybe longer. We could only plant a small vegetable patch and search for food in the forest. But somehow our husbands found us and brought whatever supplies they could carry. Sometimes they sent small planes that buzzed overhead and circled low, dropping bags of rice and baskets with live chickens that floated down in big silk umbrellas. The American pilots waved to us.

The Pathet Lao always followed. Soldiers surprised us one evening in June as we came back from gathering mushrooms and firewood. My belly was beginning to bulge with our second baby. Fong was strapped to my back. Bullets flew and rang out from every direction. I had no thoughts: I took my mother-in-law's arm and dragged her along. We ran across the wooded hill and down a knoll to a stream, crouching down in a patch of high grass in the water. I held a hand over Fong's mouth, but he seemed too stunned to cry out, his eyes enormous as he stared up at me. I smelled the soldiers coming, their sweat sour with garlic and hot peppers. Their footsteps sounded like galloping horses as they trampled through the brush. I was sure they would hear my heart pounding. Minutes or maybe an hour passed, and still they pushed through the growth. Fong fell asleep on my shoulder. My mother-in-law sat down in the stream, her eyes closed as if drifting into another world. My legs ached from the icy water. At last the men gave up, swearing vile oaths as they headed down the hill. They killed my sister-in-law Pa, Tong's wife, and Auntie Kee and her daughter Gao that day.

The following year American planes filled the skies as never before, day and night, hour after hour. Thousands of bombs rained down over every bit of land in the Plain of Jars and surrounding hills. The sky became so thick with smoke we gasped for air. The night carried a strange, yellow-red glow from the explosions and fires. The land became a giant patchwork of holes like the surface of the moon. The bounty of the earth was destroyed.

On a sunny afternoon in July we planted long beans, yams, and taro in a small clearing near to our huts. A single engine plane passed over and then circled back. I looked up, hoping for a parachute with bags of rice. Uncle Mang wiped the sweat from his brow on his sleeve and waved to the pilot. The plane dove down. A spray of bullets danced across the ground like crickets hopping through the dirt. Uncle Mang's eyes widened, his arm still lifted, his hand in the air. Blood began to spurt from his neck and chest. He collapsed on the ground. Then he let go of his last breath.

Nowhere was safe. American bombs kept falling. They did not distinguish farmer from soldiers, friends from enemies. I did not understand. Lao villagers ran into the mountains to take cover in caves or dig trenches in the woods. Thousands died. No time to bury their dead. Nothing remained of their houses, animals, fields. All blown to pieces.

23

We took shelter in a large cave with other families fleeing the madness. It was early November, the time of the rice harvest. But there was no rice. We could no longer farm at all. I felt like a plant yanked by its roots from the earth, cut off from this last shred of normal life. Many did not survive, killed by bombs or fever or hunger. One morning my mother-in-law did not wake. I understood her souls did not want to live in this world any longer.

Pao appeared one night in December after a two-month absence. I could not stop crying when I saw him. Through the years and separations, I had never complained, never told him of my terror and suffering. He led those of us who remained to Long Chieng. The Special Forces had recently won the base back from the Pathet Lao after a long and bloody battle. We lived in a small hut near the air strip. I never slept more than an hour or two at a time, afraid of what might come next.

It was my babies that kept me from giving up--Fong, so sturdy and brave, and little Fue, a child bursting with happiness and love. I kept them beside me, Fue tied on my back and Fong attached to my waist by a rope around his wrist. I never let them play farther then a few feet from where I worked. As they grew older, they helped gather plants and grubs in the forest. They learned quickly to keep quiet when we hid in the trees. There was never enough food. Many days I did not eat so they would not go hungry. I prayed to our ancestors and made offerings every morning. I know it was my father, long gone to the other world, who watched over and protected us.

Five more years passed before the war ended at last. A month later my first beautiful girl, Nou, was born. We moved to a new village and life unfolded into a familiar pattern. Two happy years passed until the Pathet Lao took control of the country. When Uncle Boua finally agreed to leave, my husband held me close in bed that night, stroking my hair. He murmured in my ear, his voice soothing and reassuring. We could stay in Thailand until the situation improved. The communists could not last long. The people would see through their lies. We would come back.

I could not imagine life in another place. Now, we would never again go to our fields. Never harvest the crops I had lovingly tended.

This was our land. The fertile earth, forests, streams. These were the source of our being.

The next morning I gathered clothes, bedding, silver jewelry, and bags of rice for the journey. I packed everything I thought we could carry.

Pao wanted to go to Muang Cha that afternoon. I left the children with Auntie Nhia and walked with Pao on the well-worn path to town. I studied the smallest details of the forest--the ferns and climbing vines, and sweet-scented orchids. Starlings and jays with bright blue feathers sang to us in the branches. Big black beetles and yellow centipedes scurried through the dirt and under the humus of leaves and pine needles. The ebony trees dripped purple and white flowers that sometimes floated onto our path. So much beauty to leave behind.

The sun had passed over the middle of the sky by the time we left the forest and crossed the wide valley. We passed a field of newly sprouted corn, but not a single farmer was in sight. The heat was great. Dust rose from the ground with the slightest movement, filling my nose and coating my hair. Wispy clouds wavered across the sky with the unfulfilled promise of rain. At the edge of town a strange quiet blanketed the afternoon. The road, usually filled with children and villagers, remained empty. We came upon an abandoned suitcase, half-full with clothes. Farther on two blankets. A photograph of a young couple. Three spoons. A tin plate. All scattered along the roadside. Rows of wooden houses sat deserted. Gardens were picked bare and chicken cages left open. A loose pig wandered into a yard. A rooster crowed somewhere in the trees up the hill.

It was a ghost village. Everyone had run away. I wanted to run as well. If only we had. But at that moment, a young Vietnamese soldier emerged from behind a hibiscus tree. He called out for us to stop.

"*Ku Thi*," he said, referring to Pao as little brother. He had a narrow, bird-like face. A rifle hung off his shoulder. "Do you live in Muang Cha?" He spoke in Lao with a heavy accent I could barely understand.

"We walked from our village. Over there." Pao pointed in the opposite direction from our home. "We are going to the market."

The soldier nodded. "You can join your comrades for a talk. I will walk with you."

"This is very interesting, I'm sure," Pao said. "But we must get home to our children. It is a half-day walk."

The muscles around the soldier's eyes tensed. "No worry. You can stay a few hours and then return. Tomorrow bring the others from your village with you. Everyone must turn in their guns. We are all brothers now. No need to fight any more."

I thought at that moment we had no hope.

The man led us down the deserted, dusty road into the town center. Maybe fifty people filled the main square and spilled into the side roads. Everyone was Hmong except for the three Chinese couples who owned stalls in the market. I recognized families we had known in Long Chieng and then Muang Cha. My cousin Bla and her husband squatted on the ground a short distance from us. The crowd remained silent. In every direction Pathet Lao and Vietnamese soldiers stood alert with their guns. Fear floated over the hot, stagnant air.

A Hmong Pathet Lao soldier stepped up on a platform fashioned from wood crates turned upside down. His uniform showed no sign of rank. He was a short, skinny man with weathered skin the color of betel nuts, a farmer turned communist leader. He stood before a microphone and stuck his lower lip out as if thinking carefully of what to say.

"Comrades," he yelled into the microphone, setting off a screech that pierced my ears. "We are here to celebrate the great national democratic revolution, a new era of equality, peace, and freedom. You have been liberated from the yoke of American colonialism. The capitalist exploiters tried to steal the gold and silver off your backs, the poor workers. They are devils, I tell you, devils!" He took a deep breath. "Those who followed Vang Pao and the American blood-suckers were wrong. How could you be so stupid?" His voice vibrated over the loud speaker. Sweat dripped from his face and stained his shirt under the arms and down the front. The speech went on this way for more than an hour, denouncing the Americans and their puppets the Royal Lao ministers.

Pao did not move. His face was slack, without emotion. The woman next to me listened with wide eyes as she bit her lower lip. Her husband dug the dirt from beneath his nails, never looking up. Another man lit a cigarette and stared at the ground, his neck muscles twitching, his face growing red. We shared the humiliation of the speaker's angry harangue. A Mynah bird landed on the roof nearby and cocked its head to one side, watching with a wary yellow eye.

A second man, this one Lao, delivered a speech as the first speaker translated into Hmong. He hurled denouncements of the Americans and those who fought with them. He repeated the words over and over. The late afternoon heat and stale air of so many people crowded together made me faint. My legs had cramped and my bottom hurt from sitting on the hard ground. I longed for a drink of water.

Finally, a Vietnamese soldier rose to the platform. The Hmong man translated his halting Lao words. "In our great new socialist society everyone will work together, sharing the land and the fruits of our labor. You can be part of this. But first you must give up your weapons and confess your mistakes, renounce the wrongways of the past. Self-criticism is the path to forgiveness and freedom." The man paused and slowly scanned the faces before him. "Who among you is ready to renounce your wrongdoing and make a new start? Step up now."

A great silence followed. People stared at the ground or eyed the soldiers surrounding us. A man to Pao's right took a deep breath and stood up. Then two other men rose and three more and another two until eight men stepped forward. They bowed their heads and offered apologies in soft, quivering voices. The speaker praised them for making the right choice. Four soldiers stepped forward and led the men away.

"There is nothing to fear. Are there not more of you?" the soldier asked. Somewhere in the crowd a man gave a sharp laugh, but no one answered. The speaker waited a very long time, the silence more terrifying than his words. He focused his gaze on several men near the front as if weighing their guilt. They shifted positions as one wiped the sweat from his hands onto his pants. One Hmong soldier studied Pao's face.

At last the speaker smiled. "Think about what you have heard today and make a fresh start." His voice was like cold metal, gliding over skin.

After close to three hours, the speeches ended, and we stood to leave. I was stiff and shaky. The Vietnamese soldier who had brought us to the meeting appeared again. My breath caught in my throat. He reminded Pao to bring the others from our village the next day.

As we headed toward the edge of town, Pao saw his friend Chai. He walked with us and whispered hurriedly to Pao. The soldiers had arrived in Muang Chai the week before he said. Many fled that day. Only the night before in the early hours, soldiers had dragged away five men who had been in the Special Forces. Two school teachers, a nurse, and three shop owners had disappeared as well. The Pathet Lao said they had been sent to special seminar camps to learn new ways. One man had been found in the woods near town, a bullet through his head.

As we climbed the path into the forest, I kept looking back, expecting to find soldiers coming after us. A few times I thought I heard footsteps or the snap of a twig. We hardly spoke on the long walk home. I tried to fill my mind with the tasks I must complete, the last minute packing. Morning could not come quickly enough.

It turned dark before we reached the village, but a full moon peeked through scattered clouds to guide us. Pao went immediately to tell the others what had happened in Muang Cha. We must be out of the village as early as possible.

I took a flashlight to the small garden behind the house and picked long beans and yams for the journey. Tears filled my eyes as I pulled a few stray weeds from around a hearty red pepper plant. I turned the dirt in my hands, mourning my garden and our fields. The fruits of my labor that I would abandon. Like orphaned children.

Neither Pao nor I slept that night. We lay in each other's arms, a string of fear binding us together. Before the first rooster's crow I built up the fire and put on a pot of water. I made chicken soup and rice for breakfast. The children wakened as if sensing our alarm. Pao took the boys to look for eggs in the hen cage that we could boil and pack with the leftover rice for a meal later in the day.

I went outside to take a few ears of corn from the bamboo bin near the house where we stored them. Nou toddled behind me. Dawn turned the sky a pale blue gray. A rustling sound emerged through the trees and caught my ear. Before I could call out, a dozen Pathet Lao soldiers, like evil spirits, descended on the village. I grabbed Nou and turned to find Pao, standing perfectly still. The boys were behind him. My body shook so badly I could hardly hold onto Nou. She began to cry as Uncle Boua and other family members gathered around.

The Hmong soldier who had made the speech the day before scanned the half dozen families gathered around and smiled. "Comrades, we are here to ask a few questions of former soldiers and to collect your guns. We know you fought against the revolution. You must make amends and learn to reform your thoughts."

Uncle Boua stepped forward. "You are mistaken. We are only farmers."

The soldier scowled and pulled a piece of paper from his pocket. "Where is Ly Pao?"

No one moved. How was it possible they knew my husband's name? They could not take him from me. Not now. The soldier's eyes flashed. Nou pulled on my hair and screeched. Then I saw the red nail marks where I had squeezed her tiny arm.

"And what about Ly Tong and Ly Boua?" the soldier continued. Silence. The soldier slowly strolled over to Pao and stared into his eyes, then turned to Fong. "And what is your father's name?" he asked.

"I won't tell you," Fong said, his voice strong and clear.

The soldier grabbed Fong's arm. "We'll see about that."

Pao raised his hands up. "Stop! Leave the boy alone. I am Ly Pao." A small cry escaped from my lips.

29

Tong, Uncle Boua and the other men stepped forward to protect their families. The soldiers searched our houses and tore apart the baskets we had packed for the trip. They lined up Pao and the other men and tied their hands together with a rope. They led them away down the path in the pale morning light. Pao vanished around a corner and into the trees like the evening sun disappearing over the mountain.

Chapter 3
PAO

The spirits of the Mekong River were angered that night by the violent assault of mortars and gunfire and blood that sullied the water and disrupted the natural balance of its flow. Awakened, the river raged with all its power and might at the evil of men, punishing unlucky souls and swallowing them whole.

I had no time to think. Everything happened too fast. I could only grasp my wife and child as we hurtled downriver. The water roared in my ears and flooded over my face until I was gasping for air. I don't know how much time passed until an eddy, created by a dead tree trunk, which rose out of the river bottom, sent us reeling toward the Thai shore. The waters slowed as we grew closer. I grabbed a branch and pulled with all my remaining strength. By some grace two men appeared in the shallows to help us. One held the raft steady as I handed Nou to the other. Yer and I struggled onto the shore, and the current carried the raft into the night. We collapsed on the ground shivering violently, as the skies thundered and rain poured down.

I was too stunned at first to understand everything that had happened. The faint crackle of gunfire echoed in the distance, and I threw myself around Nou. But the men said the bullets could not reach us. The river was too wide. Still, I clung to Nou not believing them.

The men left to help others emerging from the water or stumbling down the rocky shore like drunks who had lost their way. I settled Nou next to her mother and rose to search for my boys. My arms and legs felt heavy and my hands tingled as a vine of fear coiled in my middle and wrapped around my heart. Time stood still, as if I were detached from this earth. I told myself over and over the boys would appear. They had to be safe. But only Uncle Boua, my nephew Gia, and Yang Chor and his three sons gathered around me.

Uncle Boua hung his head and began to weep. He cried out that his boys, Nao and Blong, and daughter Lia had fallen into the water and disappeared. Tears rolled down his face as I looked on helplessly, unable to speak.

I could not catch my breath as images of our last moments filled my mind— climbing on the rafts, the crushing weight of a searchlight bearing down, Fue's scream and fall, Fong grabbing wildly. Then darkness. Only the roar of the river and bullets flying past. We were swept away. I wanted to reach out for them, but I couldn't.

Yer stared at her clothes as if surprised to find them wet. Then her head snapped up. She scanned the gray expanse and jumped to her feet. Her voice grew plaintive calling out for her sons.

A paralyzing pain seized my middle until I thought I might be sick. The truth was clear to me, but only lies escaped my lips. I touched her shoulder. "They'll be here soon."

She swung around and lashed at my arm. "You have to find them. Go back. Quickly." She began to sob.

Yang Moua staggered along the water's edge, clutching her young son and wailing for her husband and older daughter. Nou clung to my leg and buried her head as if to make the sound go away. The river's powerful flow echoed around us.

I had only wanted to keep my family safe. But I failed them. I should have realized it was too dangerous to cross the river. We should have stayed in the mountains until the monsoons passed and the river calmed. I should have found a crossing where no soldiers were lying in wait. I had put my sons in the line of fire. It was my fault. My boys were lost to the river.

The men said they were from the nearby village and pointed toward flickering lights on the knoll a half kilometer away. They had come down to the river when the shooting started. Almost every night families like ours washed up on the shores. They offered to guide us to their homes for the night and help us find the way to a refugee camp in the morning.

But Yer resisted. She splashed into the river up to her knees, still searching. I lifted Nou into my arms as I gathered my strength. I wanted to cry out as well, cry to the heavens to spare us this fate. But I had to be strong. Yer's skirt rippled and filled with water, nearly pulling her under. I tugged at her arm and forced her back, handing her Nou. "You must go with these men. Nou is so cold. I'll find..." My voice cracked, a lump in my throat making it impossible to continue.

Uncle Boua came to my side, wiping his eyes on his sleeve. "I'll go with you." Confusion followed as others tried to decide whether to stay or go with the Thai men. At last only four of us remained. Yang Chor and Yang Yee agreed to search the shore to the north while Uncle Boua and I headed south.

The night passed as a dream. We stumbled over small loose rocks along the flat shore, plodding on and on. At a curve in the river, the rocks gave way to a steep muddy bank. We slipped and slid, grasping at tall reeds to keep from falling. Then the bank widened and became flat again. The rain had turned to a soft drizzle, and the clouds began to break. I kept an eye on the shore across the water, still uncertain of the danger of soldiers on patrol. Frogs croaked in the thick grasses that grew to the edges of the rice paddies. The soft *cukoo* of an owl floated from a fig palm. A momentary hope filled my heart that it might be a sign, just a little farther, the boys were waiting for me. Sometimes we called out our children's names, but mostly we remained quiet. I scanned the shadows as clouds raced back and forth over the moon. My eyes played tricks, seeing movement, perhaps the shape of a person lying in the mud and rocks. But there was nothing. The river churned past, sweeping away broken tree branches, layers of soil washed from the hills by the monsoons, engulfing everything.

After a long time we stopped to rest, crouching down on our haunches. We would head back. There was no point in continuing. Somewhere far downstream, tomorrow or the next day, our children's bodies might be snagged by a branch or wash up on the shore, found by a fisherman or farmer or woman washing her laundry. But we would never see them again.

Dawn spread over the tree tops across the river in Laos, turning the sky blue-gray then magenta. Clouds broke apart and sent orange streaks, the color of overripe papaya, bouncing off the rushing waters and uncovering the shadows. Pale pink lotus buds swayed at the edge of the shore, slowly opening their petals to the day. The air held no sounds of gunfire or shells, only the trills of the black and yellow birds on the branches of a frangipani tree. I let out a low moan, struck by the incongruity of this beauty. My cherished boys. I allowed my tears to fall at last and prayed for their souls to find a way home to our village, the place my heart would always remain.

We had trouble finding our way back to the village, but a fisherman casting his net from the shore pointed to a small hill not far away. The families who helped us lived in wooden houses perched on tall poles. I found Yer sitting on the floor, clutching her knees to her chest, rocking and weeping. She looked at me and then turned away, and I could not bear to think of how I had disappointed her. Nou was kneeling next to a large pot of rice and greens, eating from a bowl. She turned her enormous eyes on me. I did not speak. I had nothing to tell. Instead I took the food offered by the Thai wife and ate greedily.

I slept awhile. When I woke mid-morning, one of the villagers' sons appeared with a Thai policeman. He was a large, bulky man with hair that stuck straight out from his head. In our torn, muddy clothes, our group of fourteen trudged behind the policeman for forty-five minutes to his small office in the town of Nong Khai. Beneath the gray, turbulent skies, I tried to grasp our losses. Yer stared at the ground, her expression dazed. When I touched her shoulder she jumped and stepped away from me.

The policeman asked questions about our escape and scribbled notes on a pad of paper. At last he made a phone call. We waited in the cramped room, sitting on the benches and floor. Outside the rain had begun again, a steady drumming on the tin roof. Yer and Yang Moua sat together, clutching one another's hands. Nou climbed onto my lap and after several minutes whispered in my ear, asking for Fue and Fong. My throat constricted. Finally, carefully, my voice as soft as possible, I told her they had gone to heaven to be with our ancestors. Her little brow drew into a tight furrow over the bridge of her nose. When would they be back she persisted. And I had to tell her the terrible truth. Never. She blinked several times and began to whimper, then left me to curl up in her mother's arms.

A white and green bus arrived to take us to the camp, named after the town, twenty kilometers away. Thirty-five other Hmong who had made it across the river the previous night sat in the bus, staring at us with blank expressions as we climbed on board. They fidgeted and turned to look out the windows as if they could not bear to see their own despair reflected in our faces. Uncle Boua recognized an older man he had met during the war, but they exchanged only a few words. We rode for thirty minutes in silence along the rutted, muddy road, bouncing over the potholes, past Thai farmers working in rice paddies.

A barbed wire fence surrounded Nong Khai Camp. Three Thai soldiers stood sentry at the gate, brandishing their rifles. As we drove into the compound, I did not know if I should feel afraid. Officials would explain that the guards were for our protection so no one from outside could take advantage of us. Through the barbed wire, I watched the Thai farmer we had just passed driving his water buffalo into his field. He never looked our way, as if we did not exist.

A makeshift town of long, bamboo sheds stretched across the rolling hills. In an office on the center square a Thai official took our statements and asked a string of questions. He filled out forms, assigned camp numbers, gave us ration cards, and designated a space in one of the barracks. We would live with Uncle Boua and my cousin Gia. We made our way across the square, slick with rain and mud, past a Buddhist temple, a hospital, a soccer field of patchy grass, and bamboo huts where vendors sold vegetables and basic supplies. Up the narrow, crowded paths hundreds of refugees spilled out of their rooms. We slogged along the slippery path and past the lower barracks assigned to the lowland Lao families, who had arrived first and made up the majority of refugees, and up the hill to the Hmong section at the back of the camp.

At last we found our room in a building, which like all the others, housed close to sixty families. Bamboo walls ran across the back and the far ends of the barrack. The front was open. Thick bamboo poles supported the thatched roof. Young and old, grandmothers, aunties, uncles, parents, brothers, and cousins clustered together in the tiny spaces that ran one into the other, divided only by blankets hanging from a rope or flimsy bamboo mats. Yer turned in slow circles, taking in the woven sleeping mat at the back of the room that was raised off the floor. Two stools and two plastic buckets had been left next to the fire pit at the front of the room. Everything smelled of sewage and sickness and mold.

Our neighbors gathered around, asking for news from Laos. A young woman holding a new baby told Yer where to find the trucks that came once a week to deliver rations. She clicked her tongue several times. "All they give us is dirty rice and a little fish sauce. Sometimes a bit of rotten meat."

Nou hid behind her mother's skirts and listened, her eyes darting back and forth among the unfamiliar faces.

An older woman with dirty, matted hair, rocked back and forth as she rubbed her hands together over and over. Three times she recited the schedule for filling water buckets. "I'll take you to the market for bowls and cooking pots. I know where they have the best prices. I know. I know."

A stream of complaints followed from the other women about overflowing outhouses, bad food and rude, Thai merchants who charged too much money for their wares.

A tall man with a huge square jaw cornered me and Uncle Boua. "The Thai guards cannot be trusted. They steal from us and try to get bribes if you want to go out of the camp to work." He turned away from Yer and lifted his shirt to display two deep scars, still red and raw, which ran down his chest. "Two weeks ago," he whispered, "I had to fight a soldier. He was raping a fourteen-year-old girl from the next building." He spat on the ground and shook his head. "Don't turn your back."

I could see the distress on Yer's face, clutching her middle as she slowly backed away from the chattering women. Finally, the neighbors went back to their places. Yer began to unpack the small bundle of tattered, damp clothes and a single blanket that she had carried across the river on our raft strapped on her back. After a moment, she stopped, paralyzed, clutching a shirt that had belonged to Fue. She collapsed on the ground sobbing. Nou threw her arms around her mother and cooed soothing words into her ears. I had to walk away.

As weeks passed, the rain fell, whipping through the front of the building and drenching our belongings. Sleep eluded me. I lay awake for hours, listening to the old grandfather next to us snore and moan in his sleep as he tossed and turned. Babies coughed and cried. A woman two rooms down woke screaming each night. Yer crawled into the farthest corner of the sleeping mat in a tight ball, her spine a knot of barbed wire. The tremors of her sobs rippled around me, but when I reached out to her, she shoved me away. Rats scurried in the rafters. I cradled Nou in the crook of my arm. Mosquitoes droned endlessly in the sticky, fetid air.

My heart ached with the overwhelming guilt that I had not saved my boys, a guilt that grew each day. Yer turned cold, accusing eyes on me. I wanted to hide in a corner and weep. I could not even give my children a proper burial. I feared their souls might be forced to drift between worlds never reaching the heavens. Uncle Boua and I did our best. We burned incense and candles to light their way to the heavens, provided food for their journey, and made offerings to our ancestors to assist them. Yer stood apart, her face swollen from crying. Our words seemed to float above her.

There was no comfort. Uncle Boua retreated into stony silence, walking for hours through the camp, his head down, drifting between worlds. He paid no attention to his own son. Poor Gia, thirteen years old, ran free with a gang of wild boys, sometimes going to the makeshift school, sometimes getting into trouble.

As for Yer, it was like living with a ghost. She did not notice or hear me. She shopped and cooked and filled the water buckets. She washed our clothes. But she never spoke a word. One afternoon I found her with Nou at the front gate of the camp, waiting for the buses with new refugees. She strained her neck to search the faces, starting each time a boy stepped off. I found myself looking as well, even though I knew better. Each day she seemed to slip farther away. I thought of the scenes in French films that I used to watch as a student in Vientiane where the screen slowly faded into darkness. I could not find a way to reach her. Sometimes at night I heard her whisper the boys' names as she held her hand out in the darkness. It was possible the ghosts of our boys beckoned for their mother to join them. I was terrified I might wake one morning and find she had answered their call. I performed a *bai si* to protect her, tying strings to her wrist to keep her soul safely with her body. She paid no attention.

Each morning I forced myself to go out, meeting with camp officials to learn anything, something to bring hope, to find a future for my family. Once a week I received a permit to leave camp and work in the surrounding fields for Thai farmers. It didn't matter how little I earned. If I kept busy, I could push the anguish from my mind for a few hours.

Only Nou brought moments of relief. When I returned to our place in the late afternoons, she raced into my arms, touching my cheek with hers. *Comme ca,* I would say, pointing to the other cheek. At night I played games with her to teach her how to count on her fingers and say words in Lao and French.

I could hardly bear to watch her with her mother as she desperately sought her attention. She fussed over and cared for Yer, brushing her hair and helping her dress. As the weeks slipped by, and Yer retreated into her own world, Nou tried to fill the void. Somehow she carried the heavy water buckets one at a time from the tanks when her mother forgot. She gathered wood for the fire and struggled to cook the rice and vegetables for our meals. Yer lay at the back of the sleeping mat, lost to us. Nou tucked a cover carefully about her.

In September, after two long months, at last I received good news. Thai officials had found my brother Shone and cousin Soua at another refugee camp called Ban Vinai. We could move there soon to be with them. My relief was great. When they had left our village three years before, I feared we might never meet again. Shone was the baby of my family, born when I was six, only two months after our father had died. Our mother thought he must be the soul of our father reborn. I looked after him and taught him to hunt and fish. He was an easy, cheerful child who grew into an easy, agreeable man. I never heard him speak badly of anyone. And Soua, my best friend through childhood, had given me the courage to ask Yer to marry me. All this time, they had been in Ban Vinai.

I slipped away one afternoon to a quiet spot on a knoll at the edge of camp where a thick stand of bamboo provided shelter and the illusion of privacy. From time to time I took refuge there when I could no longer continue my charade, when the veneer of strength threatened to dissolve. Alone in this place, I did not have to hide my grief. I brought a pad of paper and pen to write Shone about our pending arrival at Ban Vinai. Scattered clouds sailed across a deep blue sky. The monsoon season's blanket of gloom had at last lifted. I settled on a tree stump and gazed through the barbed wire fence at the Mekong River, a fluttering rust-colored ribbon in the distance. The turbulence had ebbed and the waters narrowed, receding from the banks and leaving a trail of broken branches, rocks, and a new layer of mud. Four fishermen had tied their long, narrow boats to trees along the shore. They bobbed in the water and cast nets into the river. Not far beyond lay Vientiane and the communist government with their ever tightening grip over Laos. The life we had once known no longer existed.

I took a deep breath, wondering where to begin, how to tell Shone about the last three years, the losses in our family, and the terrible toll this had taken on Uncle Boua and Yer. Slowly, I wrote the briefest account. I paused again and began to write the names of those who had passed to the other world--our brother Tong, Auntie Nhia, Uncle Boua's daughter and two sons, cousin Chao, and my boys Fong and Fue. The stark reality of their deaths burned on the page in front of me. My hand began to shake until the letters became scribbles and tears turned the ink into blue splotches. I put my head into my hands and sobbed. I cried as hard as I had ever cried in my life. The tears flowed until at last I was spent. The burdens and fears of the past few months lifted. We would join our family. We would start again.

Two weeks later, we boarded a bus with five other Hmong families for Ban Vinai. We bumped along a dirt road past small villages and rice paddies full of green-gold stalks swaying in the breeze nearly ready for harvest. Several farmers paused, leaning on their hoes, peering at us from under their bamboo hats. The driver stopped to let a man and his geese cross the road. Over and over he slowed to a crawl to avoid giant potholes. As we got farther away from Nong Khai Camp, a few farmers smiled and waved. My anticipation grew until I wanted to yell at the driver to hurry. After close to three hours, we climbed a steep hill and rounded a bend in the road. A huge town, much larger than Nong Khai, sprawled across the low hills in all directions.

Bamboo poles, loosely strung together fanned out on either side of the wooden gate that marked the entrance to Ban Vinai. A barbed wire fence circled the border of the camp. The driver stopped to talk to the guards then continued down the main road. The buildings and the layout were much like Nong Khai. Off to the right, dozens of long wood sheds in lines spread up the knolls interrupted by small thatched lean-tos, which had been added on the fronts and sides. On the left, two women sold vegetables, sodas, candy, batteries, flashlights, and bolts of cloth from a small thatched hut. A man walked between buildings carrying two plastic buckets of water on a bamboo pole across his shoulder. A woman with a baby tied to her back grabbed two half-dressed boys and pulled them out of the bus's path. Another woman was hanging her laundry on a rope tied between two banana trees. Everyone stopped and stared, studying our faces through the bus windows. Perhaps they too were searching for the missing.

40

The bus turned into a large square across from a field where dozens of boys and men kicked soccer balls back and forth. We stopped in front of two flat-roofed, one-story wooden offices, the first painted with *Thai Ministry of Interior (MOI)*, the second with *United Nations High Commission for Refugees (UNHCR)*. Six Thai soldiers marched up and down in front of the buildings, looking bored and tired. Our family huddled together like a flock of ducks, waving and calling out to us. I spotted my cousin Chor, who I had not seen in five years, and young children who had been babies when they left. My heart jumped.

For the first time since we had arrived in Thailand, Yer turned with a flash of recognition. The pain reflected on her face seemed to ease. We got off the bus, the women hugging and crying, the men slapping backs and fighting back tears. Nou hid behind my leg and stared at the ground, unwilling to look up or speak. When the officials called our names to check us into camp, most of the family left to prepare a welcoming meal. But Shone sat on a bench outside the building and lit a cigarette. He would wait for us, he said.

Inside the MOI office a line of Hmong waited patiently to talk with a half-dozen harried officials. A Thai man with MOI, a Dutch woman representing UNHCR, and a young translator led us to the back corner where we sat at a wooden table. We spoke in a mixture of Thai and Lao, with translations into English for the Dutch woman. Nou stared with obvious amazement at the woman's yellow hair, blue eyes, pale skin, and long bulbous nose, a sight she had never before seen.

I handed our papers from Nong Khai to the middle-aged Thai official with his carefully trimmed hair and crisp, neatly ironed white shirt. I felt self-conscious in my tattered clothes. His face remained neutral, asking the same questions we had been asked over and over at Nong Khai. We gave the same answers that were listed on the papers in his hand. He started with Uncle then turned to me as the Dutch woman took detailed notes on a pad of yellow paper. Occasionally she asked for clarification. The translator nodded at me every time I answered as if encouraging me to give the right answer. *When did you arrive in Thailand? How did you get here? Why*

41

did you leave Laos? Who did you fight with during the war? Where was the prison camp where you were held? How long were you there? Did they charge you with any crimes? How many other prisoners were there? How did they treat you? Where were you born? How old are you? Is this your wife? Do you have any other wives? How many children do you have and how old are they? How much education do you have? Do you have other relatives here or in a third country? Do you plan to apply for relocation to a third country? What skills do you have for finding work? For over an hour we circled round and round the same stories. My anger and frustration grew, but I remained calm, polite. Everything depended on these people. The Thai official's voice grew weary, as if I were trying to trick him with my answers. I thought of my endless interrogations and beatings in the prison camp in Laos.

At last, the man signed the forms once again verifying our refugee status and passed us off to the translator. The younger man repeatedly licked his lips as he pointed to a map of the camp with his pen. *Almost a 1,000 people are coming each month now so it is very crowded. You must live together here in Center 3, Quarter 2, Building 5, Room 6. It is near your family. The central market opens early each morning. Water is available in tanks at each center in the morning and evening. The food trucks come twice a week. Check the schedule. You may not leave the camp without permission from this office.* He shuffled our papers and recited the instructions in a monotone, as if recounting multiplication tables, carefully memorized and repeated every day. I wanted to laugh at the irony. Ban Vinai means village of discipline.

He assigned camp numbers, entitling us to U.N. food ration cards, and wrote the numbers one at a time on a small blackboard with chalk. He snapped our photographs as we held the board in front of us.

After an hour, we emerged from the office. Shone was pacing up and down, a cigarette burning in his hand. I thought how much older he looked, more like a middle-aged man than his twenty-seven years. Lines rimmed his eyes and mouth. His skin had turned splotchy and dark brown, his body gaunt. Weariness marked the stoop of his shoulders. He had never liked smoking before, but now tobacco stained his teeth and fingers.

He checked our building number and grinned. "Older brother, I will show you the way."

Shone stopped briefly to tell his wife Kia the location of our new home, then led us to our room only two buildings away. The long, narrow barracks were similar to those in Nong Khai only constructed of wooden poles and slats and tin roofs. We had a room, three by three and a half meters, near the end of the building, which was open to our neighbors and the front walkway. The same kind of sleeping platform, raised off the ground, filled the back half of the space. A thatched roof extension had been added on the front over the cooking pit and metal grill. The smell of urine and sweat and food cooking filled the air. A baby wailed at the other end of the building, and small children ran past, pausing briefly for a look at the new arrivals. Yer sighed and looked distraught, as if this was worse than the filthy space we had occupied at Nong Khai.

"Welcome to the royal palace," Shone said with a short laugh. "Over a hundred neighbors to share your home. I'll make you some bamboo screens to put up."

At least fifteen people, old and young, crowded together in the space to the left of ours. Blankets and clothes were scattered on their sleeping platform. An elderly man, with an oozing red eye, nodded a welcome. A young woman waved as she sat on a stool nursing her baby. A small boy wandered in and stared at Nou.

Kia arrived with a pile of wood in one arm and a water pail and large mosquito net in the other. She dropped the wood on the ground and handed the net to Shone, nodding toward the platform. He immediately climbed up to hang it over the sleeping mat.

In our village, Yer and I had always laughed at the way tiny Kia, a bundle of fire, had taken charge in her home while Shone smiled and nodded in agreement. Few Hmong husbands would allow their wives to treat them this way. I was not sure why, but it cheered me to find this had not changed.

Kia turned to Yer. "Later, I will help you unpack." She bustled about, straightening the wood. "Bring this pail, Yer. We must go to the water tanks while the pumps are open. You can wash up, and I'll show you the latrines. They are so smelly, and half the time they're overflowing, running down the road." She shook her head.

Yer looked over at me, and the miracle of a small smile formed on her lips. It was a fleeting, almost involuntary movement, one she seemed completely unaware of. I had prayed many hours for her anguish to end. This was only one tiny step, but it lifted my spirits.

Kia leaned down to Nou, who had been hiding behind her mother's skirt. "I remember you as a baby. Come and meet your cousins, my Mee and Tou, and Blia and Ger." She straightened. "Everyone come. We will eat soon."

The celebration lasted late into the night and early morning. Fourteen family members spilled onto the walkway in front of the room shared by Shone and Souas' families. Kia and cousin Yer prepared a special meal, splurging on two fresh chickens and extra vegetables purchased in the market to supplement the rations of rice. The other men and I ate the dishes of rice, chicken, mustard greens, squash, and hot chili peppers. When we were done, the women and children gathered around the plates and finished the meal. Relief flooded over me to see Yer chatting with the others and occasionally smiling. Perhaps we could resume some semblance of a normal life.

Soua winked at me and produced a bottle of whisky. His head was almost bald and two of his lower teeth were missing, but his grin spread as broad and warm as ever. After three years of malnutrition, beatings, and forced labor in the prison camp in Laos, my hair too had thinned and half my teeth had fallen out.

Yer left with the other women to wash dishes. They would go back to our place with the children to gossip. We settled on low stools by the fire. Two friends of Soua stopped by to share a drink and conversation. Everyone wanted news of Laos.

I shook my head. There was nothing but bad news to tell. "I know little, really, only rumors. Once I escaped the prison camp, we left right away."

Soua frowned. "Where were you held?"

44

"Xieng Khouang, near Phonesavanh. But there is little left there. The whole valley was destroyed by the American bombs—the villages, fields, even the animals." I took another swig of whiskey, the warmth spreading down my chest into my stomach and loosening my tongue. "Bands of Hmong are fighting again in the hills nearby."

My cousin Chor, eighteen years old, sat forward. "The resistance is strong in the camp. Support is coming from Hmong in America, and many fighters are going back and forth across the river."

Shone shrugged. "They fight small battles, but it does little good."

"Sometimes in prison we heard explosions." I took a long draw off the whiskey bottle. "Hundreds of farmers are dying from the bombs that did not explode. They try to rebuild their villages and plant fields only to find these small bombies, the size of a peach. A prisoner in my work crew threw his hoe into the ground one day. Boom! No arms. He died right there. After that I dug very carefully." I closed my eyes against the image, my head beginning to spin.

"We have heard this too," Soua said.

Chor looked at me with an eager expression. "Tell me, older cousin, how did you escape prison?"

My mind tumbled into memories of that terrible day. "Tong and I were pulling weeds in the fields. The guards sat down to smoke and talk at the opposite end. We ran for it, trying to reach the cover of trees at the edge of the clearing." I pictured Tong sprinting across the rows of tall mustard greens, not five feet from me, when shots rang out.

"Tong was killed," I whispered. I closed my eyes, seeing him fall to the ground, his face frozen in place, his eyes wide. Not another breath, not a moment to say goodbye. How many times I thought that I should have stopped. I should have carried him with me. But the bullets flew around me, and there was no time. I kept running. For my wife and children, I had to keep running.

Shone cleared his throat and spoke softly, "Uncle Boua, you are needed. There are many illnesses and unhappy spirits in the camp, and not enough shamans to help."

45

Uncle Boua nodded, but looked at me with an expression of discomfort. Before we left Nong Khai, he had performed a healing ceremony for a tiny baby, calling his familiar spirit, his *neng,* to guide him to the other world to negotiate with evil spirits for the baby's souls. He told me after how he had struggled a very long time to find the way, as if his *neng* could not hear him. At last he slipped into a trance and rode his horse to the other side, but this time he sensed his powers had been too weak. The baby died the next day.

"Pao, I know of a job translating for the French medical clinic that opened," Soua said. "I told the doctors you were the best French student in our school. I'll take you to talk with Dr. Renard tomorrow."

"Not many Hmong go to the clinic," Shone said. "They only see a doctor when they are very sick and have to go to the hospital. We had an outbreak of cholera several months ago and tuberculosis is spreading. Too many deaths."

Soua sighed. "There are few jobs, no money, nothing to do. Sometimes we work in the local fields, but the Thai pay us almost nothing and the guards steal half of it before we can come back in." He crossed his arms over his middle. "My wife earns more money than me with her sewing, or we would not survive."

"The Thai used to be nice to us, but now there are too many coming every day. They're afraid," Shone said. "Thai newspapers say we will ruin the country if they let us stay. They want the Americans and other countries to take more people. They threaten to send us back to Laos."

"Have many left for other countries?" I asked.

Shone sucked on his teeth for a moment. "More all the time, mostly to the U.S. or Australia or France. No one wants to go. We keep hoping to go back home."

"The resistance will send the Pathet Lao to their graves. Laos will be free," Chor said, puffing up like a strutting cock.

What did Chor know of fighting? He had been a small child and then a student in Vientiane during the war. Only one who had not lived through the brutality could show such enthusiasm for more conflict. I would not fight again. I already had made too many sacrifices.

Shone shrugged his shoulders. "Who knows how long before the communist government falls. I am ready to think about the chance for a new start."

Uncle Boua frowned. "You would go?"

"Yes." The answer came quickly and with assurance. "We've been in this camp over three years. What kind of life is this? I feel useless." He lit another cigarette and blew the smoke out slowly. "Do you remember the pilot Danny?"

"Yes, of course," I said. Shone had worked at the air strip in Long Chieng during the war, fueling planes and loading and unloading supplies. He had become good friends with many American pilots.

"He gave me his address in the U.S. and said to write if I ever needed help. I wrote him. He's willing to sponsor my family and Soua's." He paused a moment as if studying my reaction. "We may go when the papers come."

The news sent a shiver down my back. I had only just found my family, and already they talked of leaving. I survived one day to the next in this temporary world of the camps. After all we had suffered would we have no other choice but to leave our homeland, everything familiar and dear to us, for good? I wondered how Shone had come to this point of desperation.

His face softened. "Once we are settled, we will sponsor you."

I could not think that far ahead.

Chapter 4
YER

 Mud. All I remembered from Nong Khai were layers of red, sticky mud. It weighed my feet down and splattered my legs. It caked the edge of my sarong. It oozed into my brain. I could not see. I could not say how I spent my time. If Pao spoke to me, the words drifted over and around, never touching me. I lived in a separate place. My heart leaped whenever a boy ran around a corner. My only thoughts were of Fong and Fue. I saw their faces in the clouds. I heard their footsteps in the pounding rain. Their voices called to me in the cries of the bulbul birds. And sometimes when the wind blew in a certain direction, I smelled the warm scent of their skin.

Uncle Boua and Pao performed the funeral ceremonies, attempting to guide our loved ones to their ancestors. I could not listen. In that moment, I did not want Fong and Fue to leave me behind and travel to the other world. I wanted them close to my heart a little longer. Every day I called to them not to forget their mother who loved them more than the gods loved the heavens.

It did not surprise me when they came to me in a dream. Whispered words as sweet as honey. *Mother, we are safe. Do not cry. We will stay with you. We will wait to join our ancestors until you are happy. Come with us now.* In the dream they were younger, maybe six and eight years old. We wandered together in the mountains near our last village in Laos. The forest was peaceful and quiet, filled with the sweetness of pine needles and tiny, pink orchids. The noisy chirps of golden weavers and kingfishers echoed through the trees. A light mist swirled and played among shafts of sunlight trickling through the branches. We sang as we searched beneath the ferns and vines for mushrooms and picked bamboo shoots and roots of wild ginger. Fue soon grew bored and began chasing after the bees that were sipping nectar from a patch of yellow yarrow. Fong and I laughed to see him bounding and leaping after the wily bees. We stopped to eat rice balls under an agar tree. Fue nestled against my side and begged me to tell the story of the orphan and the monkeys. But as I began the story, their forms faded away. I reached for their hands. Only the nothingness of clouds met my touch.

Many nights the dream repeated. Sometimes they were older. Sometimes younger. Always we walked in the forest. Always I felt happy. In the last moments of sleep each morning, I savored the fragrance of mint leaves growing among the bushes. The crunch of dry leaves under my fingers. The sound of my boys' laughing and chatting. If only we could have stayed like that forever. But the roosters crowed and dogs barked. Dawn seeped into our dank space. Pao and the others stirred on the mat and jostled me awake. Then came the ache, a heavy stone resting on my chest. The glaring truth poured over me. My precious boys. Taken by the river. I felt as if someone was smothering me under a pile of thick quilts. I could not breathe.

I did not want the tedious task of living. It often surprised me to find Nou, her little face strained with worry, hovering over me, asking me questions, offering to help. I resented her presence, the way she pulled me back to reality. Pao tried to draw me to him, begging me to share my grief. I did not blame him for what had happened. All I wanted was for them to leave me alone. Let me slip into the other, happier place where my boys comforted me.

When Pao announced our move to Ban Vinai, I was terrified. What if the boys' spirits remained behind? What if they could not find me in this new camp? But that night in a dream, they promised to follow wherever I traveled. *We will always be with you, Mother. Do not worry.* There were no bounds to our love.

By the time we left for Ban Vinai, the dry season had arrived. The rains stopped. Mud turned to dirt, dissolving into thick and restless swirls of red dust. A fine film covered the camp. Grit filled the crevices in my face. Parched my throat.

Life improved in small segments. The reunion with our family was a happy occasion. I found comfort in their easy companionship and our shared losses. I was not alone. We all suffered our grief. I realized that I had been blind to Uncle Boua's pain as he mourned for Auntie Nhia and his three children. Our first night in Ban Vinai we learned of Chor's parents, who had been shot by the Pathet Lao as they tried to flee their village. My cousin Yer and Soua had lost their little Chia, only three years old. He had fallen ill with a fever and died during their escape out of Laos.

Nou, tentative and shy at first, gradually stopped clinging to me and eased into playing with her young cousins. Cousin Yer and I took the opportunity one afternoon to leave the children with Kia and slip away. We climbed up the dirt path to a hillside at the edge of camp. Great clouds of dust rose under our feet. The hot sun bore down. We sat on fallen leaves under a huge banyan tree, sheltered from the sun by the umbrella branches. Below, the barren camp stretched before us. It looked so ugly compared to our lush green mountains in Laos. Yellow and brown buildings dotted flat depressions and rolling hills, fading into the rust-red dirt. Only a few bushes and fruit trees sprouted among the barracks. Yer said more and more trees had been cut for firewood. Near the stream that meandered through the camp, small vegetable plots had been planted by the lucky few who claimed the land.

"Over there is the hospital," my cousin said, pointing in the distance, drawing me back. "By the front gate is the Thai market. Sometimes they let us go out in the morning and shop for food. Their prices are cheaper than the vendors who come into the camp." She paused a moment and let out a deep sigh. "And there, by Center 5, is the Catholic Church. The priest is French. He spent time in Laos many years ago and speaks Hmong." She played with the edge of her sarong. "I talked with him once about Chia." Her voice wavered.

A cloud washed over me once more. A small sob escaped my lips. Yer leaned against me as tears filled her eyes as well. We sat together in silence for a long time.

Yer and I had shared our lives, even as we shared the same name. She had been born a month after me, the oldest daughter of my youngest uncle. Growing up, we were best friends and worst enemies, two opposite spirits, the white and yellow of an egg, separate yet occupying a common space. We spent our early days bickering and trying to outdo one another with our sewing and cooking. If I picked four peaches from the tree in the yard, she picked six. And yet fate had kept us together. We married first cousins and moved together to our husbands' village. The jealousies and competition continued in smaller, less obvious ways, as we worked in the fields and cared for our children. But we supported one another through the difficult years of war and hardships. At times she had been the thorn of a sucker vine stuck in my side, yet I could not imagine my existence without her.

Yer wiped her cheeks with her sleeve and patted my arm. "Our boys will live in our hearts, dear cousin, but you have little Nou to care for." She put a hand on her abdomen.

For the first time, I noticed the small bump, a new life forming. We never spoke of our pregnancies out of shyness about something so personal and for fear that evil spirits might harm the baby. I wondered how she felt about having a child in this desolate place. I could not imagine caring for another child just then. A breeze drifted up from the valley outside the camp heavy with sweet frangipani blossoms and ripe papaya. The branches of the banyan softly swayed, and the leaves rattled a tune. Warm air caressed my cheeks. It passed through my body. I could not see my boys, but I sensed their presence. They wanted to assure me. They were near and well.

Each morning a line of vans entered the front gate and wound its way down the main road to deliver the foreign aid workers. The long-noses as we called them. I had met French missionaries in Xieng Khouang and Americans in Long Chieng. But still these people gave me a start with their light skin, bulging eyes, and giant, broad bodies. I shuddered at the thick hair crawling down the men's arms and peeking out the necks of their shirts. Humanitarian agencies ran the camp schools, medical clinics, and hospital. They provided counseling and aid--so many things I could hardly keep track.

One morning, I left Nou with cousin Yer and followed Kia to the donation center. We scrounged through bins of castoff clothes, looking for the best things.

Kia held up a blue blouse with a small red stain along the bottom. "This is good for Nou." I made a face, but she handed it to me. "You can wash the spot." She plunged into another pile.

I picked up a faded, green t-shirt with a turtle on the front. Confused for a moment, I thought it would fit Fue perfectly. Then I shook my head, remembering, and put it down. I squeezed my eyes shut as last night's dream came rushing back. The boys and I had been in a field picking ripe ears of corn off golden stalks. The sun was bright and warm on my back. The boys sang silly verses about a woodpecker banging on the trees. I smiled at their nonsense. Fue ran off and hid, calling out for us to find him. We reached the end of the row. He was crouching behind a cardamom tree. He giggled and threw the pungent, sweet smelling pods from the tree at Fong. Fong laughed and chased after him. They disappeared from sight. Clouds crowded past and turned the sky gray. I called to the boys, but there was no answer. The sound of a rifle shot echoed through the trees.

I woke with a start, my heart pounding. Pao, lying beside me, looked over, his expression pensive, uncertain. For the first time since we had come to Thailand, I turned into his open arms. I buried my head in his shoulder and cried. He held me tight and stroked my head, his breath warm on my neck.

Now Kia put her hand on my shoulder and guided me to another bin of men's clothes. "Look at these pants for Pao. They will have to do. Soon you will have time to sew better things."

I nodded and picked through the clothes. Later, I thought, I would go to the banyan tree and wait for the breeze.

Kia and I browsed through the central market with its noodle stands and stalls selling drinks, candy, eggs, vegetables, and fruits. Other vendors offered lanterns and flashlights, batteries, scissors, knives, tools, and cooking pots. Two Thai women called to us from a stand, holding out lengths of cotton fabric in shades of purple, green, and blue. At the markets in Xieng Khouang in Laos, I had traded our vegetables and eggs for the items we needed. Here everything was purchased with Thai baht. Kia haggled back and forth with a vendor for the soup pot I had selected. She walked away three times so the man had to chase after her. Finally, he shook his head and accepted her price.

We picked out long beans, peppers, ginger, and cilantro for the day's meals. Kia complained the whole time about the prices as she handed over coins. "We must hurry," she said at last. "The food trucks will be here soon."

We scurried up the hill to retrieve our baskets. Cousin Yer and the children joined us. By the time we reached the drop off point, a line of women and children was trailing down the road and around two buildings. The midday sun grew warm. I wiped sweat from my face and neck. Nou wanted me to hold her. But I couldn't.

The trucks pulled up thirty minutes late, and workers began the handouts. We crept along, waiting our turn. More people arrived, crowding past to get in the back of the line. The hum of women gossiping bounced between buildings. Nou and the other children chased around, shrieking as they snaked in and out of the line. I watched the little boys, so full of mischief and glee, picturing Fong and Fue when they had been small.

A mother passed by with a baby crying softly on her shoulder who looked too weak to lift his neck. His body was nothing but bones covered with skin. Mucous ran from his nose and enormous eyes. Nou appeared at my side and startled me. I picked her up and held her tight.

At last we reached the front of the line. The young Thai worker scowled and distributed the food without a word. He inspected my ration cards and measured out one large bowl of rice for each person in our household into my basket. Another worker gave me a

54

handful of dried fish and a small container of fish sauce. The meager portions were meant to last two weeks. I stared at the small pile of rice in my basket with dirty and broken grains. They had obviously been scraped off the ground after threshing. We received what no one else would eat.

We headed back up the hill past an overflowing outhouse and a stream of waste trickling down the path. I had to cover my mouth and nose from the stench.

"They treat us like dogs," Kia spit out the words. "Some people are so desperate they boil weeds and grass to eat. I see old people too weak to walk and little children with swollen bellies and arms and legs like matchsticks. We have to fight for every grain of rice."

"What about the gardens?" I asked.

Yer shifted her basket on her back. "All the spots along the stream are taken. When a family leaves, sometimes it is possible to grab a space. I watch every week."

"We have to make money to buy food," Kia said.

I nodded. "Pao will hear tomorrow about the translating job."

"We are luckier than most. But still, Soua is always searching for a way to earn money," Yer said. "Kia and I make money with our sewing. We will show you."

After lunch we settled on stools in front of their room with lengths of fabric and cotton thread in rainbow colors. Kia unfolded a quilt. "These are story cloths. The foreigners like them."

The sewing looked like a drawing. Kia had used reverse appliqué and single and cross stitches to create a scene. Hmong families danced across the blue cloth, dressed in traditional clothes for a New Year's celebration. Young men in black pants and white shirts with sashes and vests in bright patterns of red, green, yellow, and blue gathered in a line. Women in colorful skirts and jackets stood opposite them and tossed a black ball in the courtship game of *pov bov*. In another corner two bulls fought as people cheered. A man leaped in the air, playing a bamboo *qeej*. Children chased across an open field. The only traditional form of sewing was a tiger-tooth pattern around the border.

"What about *paj ntaub*?" I asked. For centuries Hmong women had made flower cloth with patterns that interpreted the shapes of plants and animals from our daily lives. A woman skilled in this art was highly prized. We sewed our best clothes, quilts, and ceremonial costumes to highlight these patterns.

"They buy this too, but they like story cloth best." Yer shrugged her shoulders. "Who can say why? We sell them in the Thai market outside camp or the aid workers take them to Bangkok. We get a good price." She held up a half-finished piece depicting the story of the origin of Hmong clans.

I ran my fingers over the bright yellows and blues. "How did you think of these? They are wonderful."

Kia smiled. "Some of the men are sewing too." My mouth fell open at such astonishing news. "They have nothing else to do."

"So many problems," Yer said, threading her needle. "The men are depressed and bored. There is a lot of drinking and smoking opium. And watch your things or people steal them." She shook her head slowly.

"Right now we need to work," Kia said, handing me a scrap of paper and pencil. "Draw a picture. Then you know what to sew."

I had never imagined anything so strange. As I puzzled over what to draw, angry voices floated from the other end of the building. The argument grew louder. I looked at Kia and raised my eyebrows.

"That is Sia's wife. They fight all the time. He drinks too much and treats her badly," Kia said.

Yer leaned in. "Everyone knows Sia trades opium smuggled from Laos. He thinks he is so clever with his motorcycle. He spends money everywhere while people are hungry." She clucked her tongue. "They say he has another woman in Center 4. What a stupid man. As if he doesn't have enough trouble at home."

I leaned over my paper once more, searching for an idea. A breeze fluttered down between the buildings. Swirling dust around our feet. I closed my eyes and felt the warmth on my cheeks. Fong and Fue danced before me. They were not lost. They were here. *Mother, tell us the story of the orphan and the monkeys.* I sat up, startled by the Kia's hand on mine. Her eyes questioned me. A small shiver snaked down my back. But I smiled and began to sketch.

56

Chapter 5
NOU

 I liked Ban Vinai. The drafty shed that served as our home, the dozens of people crowded around, none of this bothered me. I could play with my cousins and buy treats at the market. One or two evenings a week we ate with all the family, and Uncle Soua told silly jokes that made me giggle until my sides hurt. Best of all, Mother returned to me in small ways.

At Ban Vinai, she slowly emerged like a new moon growing fuller and brighter each night. Once more she brushed and braided my hair and fussed over my clothes, complaining the whole time about the dirt. The camp was smelly and noisy and full of bad spirits she said. Her chatter made me smile. Mornings, we shopped at the market and gathered firewood. She instructed me on how to clean and chop the vegetables for the soup and steam rice, as if she had forgotten that I had cooked many meals over the past months. We washed laundry and hung it up to dry. She bathed me in the tubs by the well, scrubbing my skin and hair until I was nearly raw. On special days, she suddenly crouched beside me, as if surprised to find me there, and hugged me until it knocked the air from my lungs.

Yet, her moods shifted abruptly. I never knew one day to the next when she might fade away again. Tears erupted without warning and disappeared as fast. She grew distracted by the wind, smiling to herself, as dust swirled about the room. One morning I raced back to tell her about a brown and white puppy I spotted playing under a mango tree outside the camp fence. But my voice did not seem to reach her ears. She sat on a stool, leaning against the pole and staring into the distance. Another time I found her holding my cousin Ger's slingshot that he had left in our room. She caressed it and muttered to herself. Once she yelled at me because I had not reminded her to get batteries at the market, which Father had asked her to buy. I couldn't understand when she put the plastic bucket of water over the fire instead of the soup pot. I had to tug on her arm until she realized what she had done. And sometimes when smoke drifted up from the fire, she ran her hand gently through the gray haze.

Father remained the only constant in my life. He always found time to play a game with me or tell a story or simply listen to me prattle on. But his schedule was full, and he was often out. Five days a week he translated for the French doctors at the clinic, and evenings he often met with the Center 3 council, sorting out troubles among neighbors.

When Father, Uncle Boua, and Gia returned for the evening, Mother became more attentive and joined in the conversations that accompanied our meals once more. But I think it was my aunties who helped the most. They kept her busy with their activities and drew her back to the circle of family. Almost every afternoon, Mother sewed quilts or clothes with them. My days soon revolved around my cousins--Ger who was six, and Blia and the twins, Mee and Tou, all five. We ran loose through the camp as I tried to find an opening in their tight circle. I envied them: brothers, sisters, cousins, all living together. I only had cousin Gia, a teenage boy with little patience for a young girl.

On a warm afternoon, a few weeks before my sixth birthday, we joined my aunties and cousins as usual. Mother unrolled her fabrics and neatly arranged her scissors, needles, and thread on a mat. I sat next to Blia and Mee, watching the boys play a game throwing rocks, which they had collected by the stream. I couldn't understand the point of the game as Ger changed the rules every time he took a turn.

Auntie Yer reached in a jar and pulled out coins. She handed one to me and each of my cousins. "For a treat," she said smiling. She eased herself down on a stool, holding her growing belly. She was heavier these days, and her face rounder than ever.

"I want lemon drops," Blia said, jumping up. "Come."

The boys were not ready to leave the game and handed their coins to Blia and Mee with requests for sticks of sugar cane. I could already taste the dried mango strips, sweet and tart all at once.

Mother put her hands on her back and stretched. For the first time, I noticed the round bulge in her abdomen. I ran to her side and whispered the question. Would I too have a new sister or brother? She smiled and nodded.

I clapped my hands and jumped in a circle. Mee pulled on my arm, and we raced to the lean-to at the end of the next building where an old grandmother with no teeth and a huge grin sold sweets and drinks. We placed our coins in her arthritic, bent hands. I was so excited by Mother's news, I could hardly wait. What would it be like to have another brother or sister, to hold a tiny baby?

The boys had finished their game by the time we returned. Ger grabbed his sling shot and headed out. As the oldest boy, he was the undisputed leader.

"Remember to stay together and don't go outside the Center," Auntie Kia called.

We promised, knowing very well that our adventures would take us far beyond. We crisscrossed the rutted path up the hill past a group of men playing cards and smoking. At the bathing well, two women were washing their toddlers in bamboo tubs. A volunteer cleaning crew worked its way down the path with brooms and long handled dust bins, clearing stray garbage. We stopped for awhile to watch the man in Building 12 who was making a qeej. He cut and sanded six bamboo tubes of different lengths, tied them together in an arc, and slid them sideways through the holes of a wooden wind chest. At last he attached the metal reed mouthpiece at the top. The instrument was longer than me.

Ger punched my arm. "Bet you can't catch me." I chased him and the others through the banana trees and lines of drying laundry. When we reached the latrines at the back of Building 14, Ger stopped and grinned as a man walked inside. He and Tou took off their rubber sandals and threw them at the side of the latrine.

"You'll get in trouble," I said.

"What do you know?" Ger scoffed. The man inside howled and threatened to beat whoever he caught. Ger and Tou quickly retrieved their sandals, and we raced past the next two buildings. Ger slowed down at last, laughing and panting.

"What now?" Blia asked.

"I want to play soccer," Ger said.

"They won't let you." I knew from past attempts that the older boys would tell Ger and Tou they were too little and chase them off.

Ger glared at me. "They will too!" We continued through the buildings and to the field at the center of camp. The older boys, just out of school, raced across the lawn kicking soccer balls back and forth. It didn't take long before I was proved right. Ger grumbled and scuffed his foot in the dirt as he slinked away. He glanced over at me as if it were my fault.

Blia suggested the spot behind the school on the edge of Center 1. Camp officials had designated a grove of kapok trees, palms, and bamboo off limits for cutting firewood. It was like a secret forest full of possibilities. Ger threw a rock at a branch and two doves disappeared in a flurry of wings. Ger and Tou grabbed sticks, pretending they were swords and making a loud clatter as they banged them together. Blia, Mee, and I sat down to weave pieces of grass into tiny cages. We liked to capture crickets and beetles in them, although they always escaped.

"You are lucky," Mee said as she twisted strands of grass together. "I wish my mother were having a baby."

"Our baby will be first," Blia said with satisfaction.

I shrugged. "I don't care."

Blia and Mee became bored and joined Ger and Tou for a game of hide and seek. I remained sitting, thinking about the baby. A touch of apprehension edged its way into my happiness. Would Mother give all her attention to this new little one? Would she have any time for me?

Suddenly, Ger was standing over me, his stick pointed at my face. He narrowed his eyes. "Bang!"

Three months after my birthday, everything changed. On a sweltering June morning, I dressed in the new white blouse and blue and green striped sarong that Mother had made for me. She brushed my hair smooth, wove it into a long braid, and tied it with a blue ribbon.

"You must look your very best for the first day of school," she crooned, standing up awkwardly with her expanding abdomen. In a few more months, my brother or sister would arrive. Auntie Yer had delivered a stillborn baby seven months into the pregnancy. Mother said we must never speak about it as it made Auntie too sad. I worried every day about our baby.

We walked to our family's place. As we entered, Auntie Yer patted Mother's stomach with a wan smile.

Ger scowled at me, pulling the tails of his new shirt out of his navy shorts. His face was clean and his hair plastered down with water. Tou, Blia, and Mee sat atop the sleeping mat, their legs dangling over the edge, eating bowls of noodle soup.

Ger kicked at the ground. "I don't want to go to school."

"Of course you do," Auntie Yer said, tucking in his shirt again.

"I want to go," Blia said. "Can I go instead?"

Auntie Yer laughed. "Not yet, little one. Next year."

"I'll be able to help you with your studies," I offered, proud of my status as the oldest girl and first to go to school.

Blia's face darkened. "I don't need your help. I can learn by myself."

Mee and Tou called goodbye, but Blia had turned her back to us. We left for the central square. Soldiers marched stiffly up and down in front of the camp offices. Ger began to imitate them,

ACROSS THE MEKONG RIVER

strutting with straight legs and arms until Auntie grabbed his hand and dragged him away. Across the main road three wooden school buildings formed a U-shape at the far side of the soccer field. Mother gave me a hug before Ger and I joined the orderly lines of students standing out front.

The monsoon season had started, but this day the sun was out and the air pressed hot and humid even at eight in the morning. As I waited, the girls in front of me whispered to one another, smoothing their shirts down and giggling. The soldiers across the road stood at attention as music began to blare over the loud speaker. The principal, an older man in khaki pants and an orange silk shirt, raised the striped red, white, and blue Thai flag. We filed inside.

The classroom was slightly larger than our space in the barracks with wooden plank walls on three sides. An open doorway on the left led out front, and on the right, light poured through open windows above a bamboo half-wall. Little starlings sang in the oleander bushes outside as if welcoming us to class. Five rows of long, narrow wooden tables and benches faced a blackboard on the front wall. A series of squiggly lines had been drawn in white chalk on the board. My skin tingled. Soon I would know how to read the mysterious marks.

I counted twenty students, twelve boys and eight girls. Ger plunked down on a bench in the back with the other boys. I chose a spot in the first row next to a girl with a broad, flat face and wide set eyes. She smiled at me, revealing a gaping hole where her two top teeth had fallen out. My legs hung off the edge of the bench, too short to reach the dusty, dirt floor. I clasped my sweaty hands together against my fluttering stomach.

The Lao teacher smiled and stood before us. "Sabai dee," she said.

Watching the other students, I put my hands together under my chin and bowed my head in a *nop*. "Sabai dee," I murmured.

The teacher returned the greeting once more and began, speaking first in Lao and then Hmong. "I am your teacher, Mrs. Khamvongsa. In my class you will learn to read and write Lao and do basic arithmetic. After the morning break, Mr. Boonruang will teach you Thai. As I read your name, please put your hand up." She began the roll call.

I held my breath, terrified that somehow I might miss the sound of my name. My heart jumped when she called Ly Nou, and my hand shot up. Ly Ger, she said. I turned to see my cousin hunched in his seat, his arms wrapped around his middle. He would not look up or respond. She called his name again.

"Ger, answer the teacher," I said.

"No talking," Mrs. Khamvongsa said.

I spun around to face her. "But that is my cousin Ly Ger."

She frowned. "Thank you. I will take care of this."

I slumped over the table with my face burning. My very first day, and already I had done something wrong.

Ger ran away from school at the morning break and again the next day. For the next two weeks Auntie Yer planted herself outside the school during breaks until he accepted his fate. I could not understand his aversion to class. I loved hearing the tones of the alphabet and drawing each curlicue and loop of the letters. I became Mrs. Khamvongsa's favorite, passing out papers and pencils each morning and cleaning the blackboard after class.

Father bought me a fresh pad of paper and two pencils and helped me practice in the evenings. He beamed when a few months later I read him a simple story after dinner one night. Buoyed by his enthusiasm, I raced to see my cousins, clutching the story.

I found Ger and Tou at the end of their building, shooting stones from their slingshots at a pile of sandals stacked on a tree stump. Blia and Mee sat nearby drawing pictures in the dirt with a stick. "I can read you a story. Do you want to hear?"

Mee looked up, her face bright with interest. But Blia spoke first, "I don't care about your story."

Ger glanced over. "Quit bragging. You're not so smart." He had trouble learning his letters because he didn't pay attention. It made him mad when the teacher called on me and I answered correctly.

"It's a good story. You'll like it," I tried again.

Ger stood up and pushed me roughly. "Go away. We don't want you or your stupid story."

I stared at them, stunned by the hostility. These were my cousins, the friends I played with every day. All I wanted was to be part of their group, to belong. What had I done that Ger should be so mean? And the others went along. Even Mee kept silent and would not look at me.

"I hate you, Ger. I'll never, ever speak to you again," I cried.

I ran down the path past three buildings and took refuge under a fig tree next to a small shed. I slumped to the ground as hot tears spilled down my cheeks. My breathing came in short, uneven gasps. I crumpled up my story and threw it in the dirt. Ger had tried to make me feel small. I swore to myself that I would never play with any of them again.

And I did not see Ger again until his funeral.

Two days later, as Mother fixed dinner, Auntie Kia ran into our room, wailing and flailing her arms. Mother tried to calm her as words flew like sparks burning my skin. Ger and Tou had been playing at the end of the building when their neighbor Sia, drunk, had roared around the corner on his motorcycle. The bike tossed Ger twenty feet into the air. He landed on the tree stump. All the breath squeezed from his body. He died before Auntie Yer could reach him.

Uncle Boua led Ger's funeral over the next three days. The ceremonies passed like a long dream from which I could not wake. Rain lashed at the roof and blew through the room. Ger lay on a bamboo bier, dressed in his funeral coat, hat, and hemp shoes that my mother and Auntie Kia had spent all night preparing. Auntie Kia placed embroidered pillows under his head and wound strips of white cloth around his legs. His pale, waxy face showed no sadness or anger. I had to look away.

The cold, damp room smelled of burning incense, the smoke swirling up and around into the rafters, carrying his soul to another world. I had come to know Uncle Soua by his jokes and easy laughter, but on these days he collapsed on the floor and cried like a child.

Auntie Yer wept beside him, rocking back and forth. My mother and Auntie Kia tried to comfort them as their own tears flowed. Poor Blia curled into a tight ball on the sleeping mat, refusing to speak or see her brother off.

Uncle Boua chanted and talked to Ger, guiding his spirit back to our village in Laos, the place where he was born, to where his placenta lay buried under the center post of the house. Only if he reached his placenta could he leave this world behind. Father beat a steady rhythm on the drum. The *qeej* player blew on his reed, accompanying each step in Ger's travels. Years later I would learn the names of these pieces--showing the way chanting, last breath reed music, helping the person mount the horse for the heavenward journey, and raising the body to get it on its way to the spirit world before burial.

Mee and I kneeled together at the side of the room, shivering. I kept my eyes down and tried to concentrate on saying blessings for my cousin. I offered good wishes for his afterlife, the way Father had instructed me. But a horrible guilt possessed me, pressing on the middle of my chest. Perhaps I had caused Ger's death with my angry words. Father said evil spirits who dwelled in the camp had stolen Ger's souls. It had been too late to extend the time on his life papers.

Chor helped Uncle Shone slit a rooster's throat, and Mother cooked the liver for Ger to take as spirit food. Uncle placed the dead rooster at the top of Ger's head so its spirit could guide him to his ancestors. Father motioned to me. Mee and I rose and took turns placing mangos and rice balls for Ger to eat on the trip. We added spirit money to help in passing through the gates to heaven. My gift to him was a favorite red stone that I had found by the stream. Tou parted with his best slingshot, and Mee presented a new pair of plastic sandals and three rubber bands. More chickens were sacrificed and meals prepared that we offered to our ancestors. Later we would eat the food.

On the third afternoon, Chor and Father placed Ger in his coffin. Mother and Auntie Kia had to support Auntie Yer as the procession trudged up the hill to the burial ground. The rain poured down, and our feet slipped in the red mud. We left packages of food along the way to keep Ger's souls from returning home and taking other souls with him to the afterworld.

As they lowered his coffin into the ground, my knees grew weak. The tears I had held back burst forth. I fell to the ground and whispered last words, "Please be happy."

After this the nightmares came. A giant black bird with Ger's face swooped down from the sky and plucked me from a field where I sat naked. We soared higher and higher into the air above the clouds until he let go. I spun out of control down to earth with nothing to stop me. Other nights I found myself plunging into a river, grabbing for my father as his hand slipped away. Ger was in the water, pulling me into the depths. I woke screaming for help.

Chapter 6
PAO

In September, final papers arrived from Danny in America. He had approval to sponsor Shone and Souas' families and had located jobs and housing for them. Both families interviewed with the American immigration team and prepared to leave for a place called Minneapolis. Shone said he knew nothing of this village, but if Danny lived there, it must be a good place.

Once again our family would be split apart, only this time half-way across the world. They had been in the camp for over four years without a future. Perhaps a fresh start would bring them a good life and better luck. America was a land of opportunity.

The birth of our second daughter, Moa, in late August brought joy. Our beautiful new baby delighted the family, especially Nou. Yer became more placid and content. Still, I worried how she would manage without the tempering influence of Kia and Yer. Her cloud of sorrow, though more distant, still colored our lives. At night she often talked in her sleep, and in the mornings her attention strayed. It was as if she forgot Fong and Fue had died. Once she asked me to give her extra money to buy a chicken for the boys. They were very hungry she said. I looked at her puzzled. She turned away and played with the buttons on her blouse.

On a cool October morning, with fog still hugging the ground, we saw our family off on the bus to Nikhom Processing Center, the bus to America. Others who were departing crowded up the steps and settled into seats as their families stood under the bus windows and called out good wishes. But we lingered over our goodbyes, prolonging the separation we knew could last a lifetime.

Shone surprised me with a big hug. "As soon as we are settled… I'll do whatever I must to sponsor you."

"I pray you find success and happiness," I said. "We will write often."

The driver urged them to hurry. Our family rushed onto the bus, leaning out the window to touch our hands one last time. Yer held Moa close, sobbing. Nou waved to her three young cousins with a forlorn face as the bus disappeared down the dusty road.

I sat with Nou on the edge of the sleeping mat, helping her practice five new French words. She continued to excel in school, and I had enrolled her in a private French class in the afternoons.

She wrapped her hair around her fingers and studied the first word. "Von," she said.

"It is *bon*," I corrected, "with just the faintest 'n' sound. You almost do not hear it." I pinched my nose to exaggerate the sound. She pinched her nose and repeated the word over and over with me, copying the shape of my lips, until she had it right. "Yes. That is it."

Her serious little face broke into a smile, too rare an occurrence these days. The mood in our home had remained somber since our family had departed. Life loomed too quiet, too lonely. Even before this, the shock of Ger's death had sapped Nou's cheerful nature and brought her terrible nightmares. I feared an evil spirit, or possibly Ger's ghost, tormented her soul.

"So much work for a little girl," Yer said, looking up from her stool near the fire. She was nursing Moa and stirring soup for dinner.

"She likes it," I said, smiling at Nou. I hoped keeping her busy learning French would ease the separation from her cousins. But I was also indulging my own dreams, my love of speaking this sophisticated, beautiful language. This knowledge had served me well during the war. The Pathet Lao, with their endless slogans, had declared the French language a bourgeois, elitist tool of the colonial exploiters. For me, it was the language of possibilities, the promise of the larger world.

Nou put her head to one side. "I want to learn, Mother."

Yer clucked her tongue. "What is the point?"

I frowned with impatience. "An education is important." It did not matter to me that Nou was a girl, although I had to pause and wonder. Would I have placed so much hope on her education, if my boys were still alive?

Yer stood and patted Nou's knee. "You need to fill the water buckets before the pumps close." Nou sighed and put down the paper with her new words.

"I'll go with you," I said. "We'll practice the last two words as we walk."

As we returned, Uncle Boua and Gia arrived home. They had spent the day working on a nearby farm to earn a few coins. Money became scarcer and our silver slowly dwindled. Rations grew more austere every month, and the cost of food in the market more expensive. Chor had moved in with us when the family left for America, so we had another mouth to feed. I was luckier than most to have a good job. With my pay, Yer's income from sewing, and the sporadic contributions of others, we did not suffer like others in the camp.

It pained me to see so many men languishing without work, trapped and unable to support their families. Too many went hungry. Too many fell ill and died.

Chor breezed in as Yer was serving soup and rice. We hardly saw him these days. When he was in the camp, he stayed only long enough to eat. He took off with his friends to find odd jobs or carry out activities I preferred not to know about. Evenings they spent drinking, gambling, and dreaming of girls. Some nights he did not come home at all. Now that the dry season had arrived, he would be disappearing to Laos for weeks at a time to fight with the resistance.

"What did you do all day?" Uncle Boua asked with an edge of irritation.

Chor shrugged. "I had some business."

Gia's eyes turned bright with anticipation. "What kind of business?"

"Important business." Chor winked at Gia. "But it is secret." Chor often slipped out of camp to meet with shady figures who delivered guns and ammunition financed by supporters in the camp or General Vang Pao and his followers in America. It was possible they also sold drugs to finance their activities.

Fourteen years old, Gia found his older cousin a thrilling figure, a brave hero oblivious to danger. Uncle Boua and I worried he would try to follow Chor on one of his escapades.

Chor came back from his missions in Laos reporting small successes—a road blown up, electric wires cut down, an attack on four Pathet Lao soldiers--but these skirmishes did little to change the situation. The news grew worse all the time. Hmong forces in Xieng Khouang had nearly been crushed. Casualties kept rising as more rebels were driven deeper into the forests or across the river to Thailand. It seemed futile and senseless. Still, I gave what extra money I could to the cause. I could not turn my back on my own people.

Chor finished his soup and stood to leave. "My friends are waiting."

"I almost forgot my English class is tonight," Gia said, jumping up to escape before his father could protest.

Uncle let out a long sigh. "These boys have no manners. They pay no attention to their elders anymore."

Yer surprised me by speaking up, "They have lost their mothers, Uncle, and Chor his father as well. We must not be too harsh with them."

I decided to change the subject. "They've called a special meeting of the camp leaders tonight. Perhaps you will come, Uncle?"

"What has happened?"

I sat back as Yer and Nou cleared the dishes and stepped outside to wash them. "MOI says the new arrivals from Laos are fleeing because of flooding and ruined crops, not the Pathet Lao. They have threatened to send several thousand back for repatriation.

We must discuss how to dissuade them." The population at Ban Vinai had almost tripled in the past year and a half, despite the thousands leaving for resettlement in other countries. The Thai grew increasingly nervous that the influx would ruin their economy. This latest threat was most likely a ploy to pressure the U.S. and other countries into accepting more refugees.

Uncle Boua shooed a fly off his forehead. His shoulders slumped, and his eyes sagged half-shut. "I am too tired to listen to any more troubles." He was the head of the family, yet he deferred most decisions to me. The loss of his wife and children and the futility of camp life had defeated him. He kept busy with his shaman practice, drifting between worlds, lost in his own reality.

"But, Uncle, you are an important voice. We could use your wisdom."

"Nothing changes; nothing gets better. What could I add?"

I did not have an answer. While the other camp leaders and I struggled to create some semblance of self-determination for our people, everything depended on others--relief workers, United Nations representatives, the Thai government, and, most importantly, the immigration agents of countries that might take us away from this place.

Uncle shook his head. "This place is full of evil spirits and ogres, disgruntled spirits of the water and dirt and air. I feel them all around us. I no longer have the strength to work against them."

I too felt the presence of evil spirits and hundreds of ghosts of misplaced souls. All the shamans in the camp could not counter the suffering they caused.

The camp celebrated the Hmong New Year in early December at the time of the rice harvest, even though we had no harvest. For four days we put troubles aside and honored our traditions. Laughter and excited chatter reverberated across the camp as people prepared for the events. The air crackled with anticipation.

On the first day, Yer swept evil spirits from the previous year out of our tiny room to make way for the good spirits of the New Year. We welcomed the New Year with prayers and offerings to our ancestors to bring us good luck and prosperity, and special meals of pork and chicken.

The second afternoon, we joined the festivities in the central square. Families paraded around the grounds, greeting each other with good luck for the New Year, proudly displaying their skills. Yer, like the other women, had spent months sewing new clothes for each member of our family, embroidering colorful *paj ntaub* patterns on vests, sashes, skirts, and headpieces. Coins, sewn to our vests and jackets, jingled as we moved about. In Laos we used silver coins, but given our current circumstances, Yer had reluctantly used coins made of tin. Still, most layers of our silver necklaces, which Uncle Boua had crafted in Laos many years before, hung down our fronts, symbols of our former wealth and position.

We each gravitated to our favorite activities. Gia went off to play soccer on the field with the older boys. Nou and Yer watched groups of young women perform traditional dances, gracefully dipping and turning, making intricate movements with their fingers and wrists to the strains of Hmong violins and flutes. Nou was particularly fond of the *qeej* competition. Each man vied to be the most acrobatic, twisting and hopping while playing his instrument.

Uncle Boua and I joined a crowd of men to bet on the bull fights. Fiery bulls, prodded on by their owners, snorted and pawed at the ground, stirring up great clouds of dust. The beasts lunged and locked horns as they struggled to knock the other down. This led to a great deal of shouting and cheering.

As usual Chor disappeared with his friends. Late in the day, I spotted him lining up to play *pov bov*. The New Year celebration brought romance and the opportunity for a young man to find a wife. Chor had turned twenty years old a few months earlier. It was time for him to settle down. He tossed a cloth ball back and forth first with one girl and then another.

Shortly after the last day of celebrations, Chor spoke to us of a girl name Lia. She was sixteen with a delicate, pretty face and eyes that reflected the sun. Her demeanor was shy and traditional.

For the next few weeks, Chor courted Lia every day, singing love poems and playing the mouth harp outside her room at night. Yer

PAO

and I laughed to see cocky, young Chor transformed into a lovesick bull. We hired a marriage negotiator, and Uncle Boua and I provided most of the bride price to Lia's family. January brought the blessing of a wedding and another member to our household.

Months moved through seasons and another New Year passed, our third at Ban Vinai. In February, Uncle Boua surprised us all by marrying a widow he had met on a committee of parasocial workers. Khou, thirty-five years old and an herbalist, had lost her husband and two children during the war. It pleased me to see him happy once more, almost returning to his former self.

A month after Nou's eighth birthday, Yer gave birth to our third daughter, Houa. We now had six adults and four children in our home. Our cramped conditions many times led to tensions and frustrations, but we managed.

Shone wrote to me every month. He reported that Minneapolis was a big city full of modern, tall buildings and thousands of people and cars. Their home had four rooms in a building where many other families lived. One month he enclosed a photograph of the family gathered in front of a tall red brick building wearing blue jeans and t-shirts as they stood next to a sickly looking tree on brown grass. Months later, another photo showed them bundled in thick jackets and standing in a sea of white.

Shone and Soua worked in a warehouse loading boxes of paper onto trucks. They were learning to speak English. With work and study, Shone assured me soon life would be much better. Other Hmong had settled in the area, so they were not too lonely. They did not like the cold weather that lasted for many months, but they had plenty of food. Sometimes he enclosed a little money. Always he mentioned his hopes for us to join them, but this took time. It was his half-way endorsements and unspoken details that gave me pause.

The summer monsoons arrived late that year, but with a strange fierceness. Relentless rain and winds turned the camp into a muddy bog, and the leaky barracks became damp and moldy. Water swirled and eddied down the paths. The stream became a raging river, washing away gardens and makeshift bridges. Flooded roads blocked the food trucks' deliveries and vans of volunteer staff. Cholera, malaria, dengue fever, and tuberculosis spread through the camp, as persistent as the swarms of mosquitoes.

I arrived at the clinic early one July morning to find a line of patients winding out the door onto the covered porch, huddling against the wall. Torrents of rain beat on the tin roof. Waterfalls poured off the eaves. A woman held a young girl of three or four in her arms, limp on her shoulder. A man had to support his wife to help her stand. She was drenched in sweat. As I edged my way in the door, a baby erupted into a deep, congested cough.

The tiny waiting area inside overflowed with families. The nurse assistant, a Hmong woman trained by the U.S. military during the war, registered patients and listened to their symptoms. Only Dr. Renard and two nurses were on duty.

I stood at the entrance to an examination room where an elderly man sat on the bed with his shirt off. Dr. Renard's forehead gathered in wrinkles as he held his stethoscope over the man's sunken chest. The doctor was a tall, wiry man with intense, dark blue eyes, a curly mass of light brown hair, and a prominent, narrow nose. He had come to the clinic two years ago at the age of twenty-six after completing his medical training. Always thoughtful and careful in his treatment of patients, I had come to trust his powers.

He turned to me after a moment. "Pao, I'm glad you are here. Can you ask this gentleman how long he has had a fever?"

The old man shivered slightly as he answered, "The fever comes and goes, for a long time. My brother performed a *hu plig*. I was better. But I am not so good now. My son brought me here." He nodded toward an anxious looking, middle-aged man sitting in a straight chair in the corner.

Dr. Renard asked questions about the man's sleep and body functions. He listened carefully to the answers, then held the man's eyes with his own and spoke directly to him as I translated, "Will you please do something for me, old grandfather? I want you to go to the hospital and get a picture of your chest. It will not hurt. Also, we need to take some blood for tests. Then I can decide what will make you better."

The man looked at his son and then to me, his expression uncertain. I reassured him, "The doctor is a good man. You can trust him." He shrugged in agreement.

Dr. Renard filled out several forms to give the man. "Take these with you to the hospital for the tests. Come back tomorrow." He patted the man's arm, and we headed to the next examination room.

"I'm sure the blood test will show malaria, but the X-ray will eliminate TB." Dr. Renard sighed. "If only they would come to the clinic sooner."

Many Hmong distrusted Western doctors and refused to go to the clinic or hospital. They relied on traditional herbs or small amounts of opium to cure physical illnesses. If these did not work, a shaman was called to determine the source of the body's imbalance. Uncle Boua had performed four soul calling ceremonies in the past month, but still two had died. A shaman can cure an unhappy spirit and restore the soul, but sometimes it is a person's time to pass to the other world. The date cannot be renegotiated. I knew we needed every means of fighting the illnesses and evil spirits plaguing our people. I encouraged families to try the doctors. I had seen the miracles they performed with antibiotics, fluid replacement, and malaria drugs.

It angered me that most of the doctors in the camp considered our traditional Hmong practices nothing more than superstition. But Dr. Renard respected our beliefs and wanted to learn about our herbs and the role of the shaman. We shared long conversations on how to compliment Hmong practices with Western medicine.

By late afternoon, the line of patients had temporarily receded. Dr. Renard and I hurried through the central market to a Lao restaurant for something to eat. Mostly aid workers and MOI staff filled the small cafe.

Dr. Renard sat down wearily and stirred sugar into his coffee as the owner brought us bowls of noodle soup. "There were two more cases of cholera yesterday, a woman and her daughter. Conditions in the camp have to be improved. There is no other way to stop the spread of illness."

"The Camp Council also works for this." I sat through endless meetings and discussions with camp officials and the Hmong representatives. Nothing ever changed.

He looked up and frowned slightly. "I have had a very good offer from a hospital near Paris. Once they find a replacement for me at the clinic, I will return to France."

The breath went out of me for a moment. I had known at some point he would leave, but not so soon. "When?"

"In a few months." He shrugged. "I have already been here a year longer than I planned."

"You will be missed."

"I will miss you as well." He lifted his coffee cup with his large, slender hands and took a sip. "Have you thought about my suggestion? Once I am in France, I could sponsor your resettlement."

On several occasions Dr. Renard had raised the possibility of helping my family move to France. This filled my heart with yearning, the way an old song raises pleasant memories. When I had finished my studies at the French-run Lycée Pavie in Vientiane almost twenty years before, I planned to go to university in France. I dreamed of becoming an engineer and returning to Laos to improve the lives of my people. My mother and Uncle Boua had been wary of sending me so far away. But it was the war that destroyed my hopes. I traded my books for a uniform and gun.

"It would be a wonderful chance," I said at last. "But it is complicated with my family."

"You speak fluent French. You would not have trouble finding work."

I could not express my confusion and anguish. Thoughts of our future constantly occupied my mind. Five years had passed since the communist takeover of Laos without any sign of the regime's collapse. As the centralized economy failed and poverty and discontent grew, the Pathet Lao tightened their hold. We could not go back to our country. We could not go on with this half-life, trapped in Ban Vinai like ghosts caught between two worlds.

Yet no one wanted to acknowledge the reality of our position. Uncle Boua said he was too old to start over. He and Chor remained hopeful of returning to Laos. General Vang Pao continued to send letters and tapes from America urging our people to remain in Thailand, to continue the struggle. It was a delicate matter with Yer as well. She often talked about our village in the peaceful hills of Laos, an ideal that had not existed for more than twenty years. She held on to the vision of a simple existence free of war and persecution and suffering. We would be closer to our boys, she said, closer to the clouds and heavens. Even I sometimes indulged in these fantasies. It seemed so near we could almost touch it. Just across the Mekong River.

I received a letter from Shone in late September. I kept it hidden in my pocket for three days as I wrestled over how to broach the subject with my family. A Catholic group had helped Shone complete paperwork to sponsor our resettlement. They had a job lined up, housing, and financial assistance. The completed papers should arrive any day. My mind reeled with the immediacy of the decision. I had heard the American team was coming next month to conduct immigration interviews. I would need to petition for a meeting right away. If I did not act now, another year could slip away.

I walked through the camp, trying to sort my thoughts. All around the impossibility of our situation confronted me. A group of eight young men, about seventeen or eighteen years old, tossed dice and yelled out bets. The speakers of a large tape player boomed with the latest Thai hit, a love song about loss and yearning for the past. Three half-naked children played with sticks in a muddy gully filled with garbage and sewage. From the rooms of one barrack after another, eyes filled with despair glanced up at me. In the photo shop near the center, a Hmong family, dressed in their best traditional clothes and jewelry, posed before a painted backdrop of a mountain landscape in Laos. This was all we had of the life we left behind, a six-foot mural of mist-shrouded forests.

I climbed the hill to a quiet spot at the edge of camp and sat on the damp weeds. Below was the sprawling camp and out through the fence the open countryside. The rains had turned the hills green and the trees heavy with leaves. Cascades of purple bougainvillea poured down a section of the barbed wire fence as if the stray vine was disguising our confinement.

My mind puzzled over our options. When Dr. Renard had departed for France the week before, he told me his offer remained open. All I needed to do was write him. I longed to grab this chance to fulfill my abandoned dreams, but there were others to consider.

I took Shone's letter from my pocket and read it once more. He wrote with urgency of his excitement for our arrival. My dear brother and cousin Soua had worked for over a year and a half to find a way for us. I did not want our family split apart forever.

Fluffy white clouds skipped across the sky, forming and reforming into indeterminate shapes. I lay my head back on the ground like a young child and imaged a tiger, then a house. Perhaps it was a fleeting dream or the spirits playing a trick on me, but as the sun formed a halo around a misty cloud, wisps of silver light curled into the features of my boys' faces. Fong and Fue smiled down on me through golden rays of sunshine. And then they disappeared to the east, swept across the river and home to Laos.

I made up my mind.

The next evening after dinner I brought out the letter. "There is good news," I announced. Yer glanced up from her sewing as I unfolded the paper. "Kia and Shone have a new baby. They named him John." Nou put down her school book and clapped her hands. Everyone smiled. Lia, now seven months pregnant, touched her large, round belly.

"What kind of name is this?" Uncle Boua scoffed.

"An American name. This is good," Chor said.

"There is more, something important that we must discuss." I pressed the paper flat on my leg and took a deep breath. I explained about the church group and the completed paperwork.

Uncle Boua studied me for a moment. "You will go?"

I nodded. "We must, Uncle. Please consider this carefully. I do not want to leave without you." Yer and Khou looked back and

78

forth from me to Uncle. Nou came over and put an arm around my shoulders.

"I cannot start over again," Uncle said, shaking his head.

"But Father, America has much to offer," Gia interrupted.

Uncle put his hand up. "We will return to Laos when the time is right. That is our home."

Uncle's stubborn refusal disappointed me. I did not want to choose between members of my family. My loyalty was to all of them.

Chor leaned close. "I'm leaving again next week. There will be a major victory soon. Perhaps you should wait until next year."

"I have waited three years. I want more for my children than life in this camp."

Chor's unwavering confidence puzzled me. What had the resistance fighters accomplished besides losing more lives? And Gia, ripe with admiration, would no doubt follow his cousin to fight.

"When would we go?" Yer asked, frowning.

"As soon as possible. It is best for our children, Yer. They will have a better life."

The papers came the following week, and I took them directly to the MOI office. The clerk scheduled our interview with the American team for the first week of November. He reminded me twice that every member of the family who was planning to immigrate must attend the interview.

My resolve wavered over the next few weeks as our home became a place of silence and unhappy faces. The conversations at meals lapsed into the perfunctory politeness of strangers. Chor could not see the reason in my arguments. His focus remained across the river. One morning we woke to find he had slipped away on another mission, while Lia wept and worried that her baby would not have a father by the time it was born.

I spoke to Uncle once more, but his answer remained the same. He asked me not to bring it up again. Gia took me aside one afternoon. He wanted desperately to go to America. Perhaps he could convince his father next year.

Yer did not challenge my decision, but her anxiety spilled into our lives. One day she snapped at Nou for letting the rice cook too long and the next for not cooking it enough. Her milk turned sour, causing Houa to become colicky and cry. Some days she was withdrawn while others she hounded me with endless questions: *How will I learn English? What will I do in America? Will I be able to work in the fields again? How will Shone and Soua find us when we get there? How big is Minneapolis? Are there trees and flowers and mountains? How will we manage? Will we be safe? Will we ever see Laos again?* No matter how grim Ban Vinai had become the unknown world seemed to scare her more. I could not identify the underlying shadow of her exaggerated fears. Something more weighed on her emotions, but it remained a mystery to me.

I thought Uncle and Chor would change their minds. But the interview date arrived, and only Yer and I with our three girls sat before the panel. We received approval for a mid-December departure date. And so we left our family behind.

PART II

Chapter 7
NOU

In the small courtroom I am surrounded by my attorney, the social services representative, and friends who support me. I gather my strength amid the morass of lies and misunderstandings, the struggles and disappointments that have shaped my story. None of us ever expected it would turn out this way. But the burden of blame is not mine alone. We are all complicit. I have washed onto a distant shore, no longer within my father's reach.

The judge asks for opening statements. Father fixes his eyes on him as if uncertain how to respond, waiting for permission to rise. His solitary figure at the opposite table sends a mixture of remorse and pity flooding over me. Perhaps he could not afford a lawyer and was too proud to ask for help. I know he would distrust the ability of anyone to speak his truth. To tell his story. More likely it is his unwavering faith in his decisions, his undeniable rights as my father, and the impossibility that the judge will not agree with him. His stubbornness defies reality.

My attorney Mr. Ross stands and straightens his blue and gray striped tie. He is tall and attractive with light brown hair, graying at the temples, and large hazel eyes. I have met with him twice in his office over the past weeks. He listened carefully to my story and the intermittent comments of Mrs. Hernandez from social services, only interrupting occasionally to clarify details. When I stumbled over my words, choked with tears, he handed me tissues and waited patiently until I could continue. He expressed his sympathy and admitted the case troubled him. He imagined my parents must be suffering a great deal from the situation as well.

Mr. Ross clears his throat. "Your honor, I am representing Ms. Lee in her petition." His voice is deep and, although he speaks softly in an even, measured rhythm, it resonates through the quiet chamber. His demeanor is determined but not aggressive, recounting his concern and respect for the weight of the matter before the judge. He concludes his statement by emphasizing certain words, drawing them out, letting them hang in the air for a moment as he glances at my father.

At last, Father turns his full, unflinching gaze on me. The lines in his face and the set of his jaw express his disbelief. But it is the anguish in his eyes, a suffering from deep within rooted in another time and place, the losses and struggles none of us can erase from memory, that finally causes me to bow my head. For the hundredth time I trace events over the years, trying to find when the fissures in our relationship first formed. I remember the confusion and resentment as I tried to bridge my disparate worlds, never understanding my parents' demands, their unbending adherence to a culture and rules that had little relevance to my life. Somewhere along this path I found my own strength. I made a choice to redefine myself and my future.

This is how Laura was born.

Chapter 8
PAO

I remember the day we came to America, as if it were yesterday. January 29, 1982. I told myself we could make a new beginning. We had our family. America offered opportunities, a better life for our children. I was not afraid of hard work. Yer would recover and return to me whole and happy as she had once been. All these thoughts--my hopes and dreams that ebbed and flowed on an underlying current of anxiety--wound a crooked path through my mind. Perhaps it is like this for everyone who comes to America.

We traveled on a flight from Bangkok. Such a big plane, larger than the American B-52s that filled the skies over Laos during the war. I had been on propeller planes and helicopters, but never anything like this. People from all over the world, Thai, Chinese, and Westerners, dressed in expensive clothes, sat in rows of chairs. They glanced up as the stewardess led us down the aisle to our seats. She showed us the bathrooms and how to hook the seatbelts and lower the tables. Later she would bring us little trays of food, and we would sit wide-eyed with amazement at the movie on a screen that folded down from the ceiling.

Yer's hands felt sweaty and shaky as she handed me Moa to hold on my lap. She hugged little Houa so tight that she began to cry. I admit to a flutter in my stomach as the plane swept down the runway, the force pushing me back against the chair. My skin tingled with a hundred caterpillars crawling up my arms. Yer squeezed her eyes shut, and a tear trickled down her cheek. I did not know if it was fear or the thought of what we left behind. Nou and I watched out the tiny window as the plane left the earth behind and floated up through puffy clouds into the brilliant blue sky.

We had spent over a month at the Nikhom Processing Center learning about our future lives. Authorities prepared our papers, using our clan name as a last name and spelling it as they thought it should be. Suddenly, I became Pao Lee, no longer Ly Pao.

Everyone had to be healthy to go to America—no drugs or TB or other illnesses. The sick had to stay at the center's clinic to be treated. They took our blood and urine and X-rayed our lungs. The ones who had smoked opium waited and worried, afraid they would be sent back to the refugee camps.

An Australian woman taught us basic words of English: *hello, goodbye, my name is, how are you, where is the bathroom*. Yer learned nothing. She said it was too difficult. Once more her attention wandered to another place.

Mr. Marshall, another instructor, showed us a map of the U.S. One member from each family, nervous and tentative, stuck a pin in the city where they would soon be living. Soon pins dotted the entire country. Mr. Marshall was fond of listing facts as he pointed to the map and the translator struggled to keep up. *Do you know the U.S. is so big it takes over five hours to fly from New York to San Francisco? Do you know that California has the largest population in the country? Do you know that the U.S. has fifty states, including Alaska and Hawaii?* None of us knew these things.

One evening we watched a movie that began with the Statue of Liberty superimposed on an American flag fluttering in the wind. A man's voice narrated as the film highlighted cities filled with tall modern buildings and hundreds of cars and people moving about like ants, followed by scenes of vast, flat fields of swaying wheat stalks that came up to a man's chest and jagged mountain peaks barren of trees. It was in English, so no one understood.

We heard warnings: *you must stay in the painted crosswalks when you cross the street and watch the red and green lights; do not be fooled by advertising on television; watch out for people who might steal from you or take advantage because you do not speak the language.* Yer said America sounded like a bad place. She had heard rumors in Ban Vinai that Americans cut out the hearts and other organs of Hmong people and ate them. I told her these were silly stories. She remained unconvinced.

Looking down from the plane window, green and brown fields gave way to blue ocean. Once I caught a glimpse of a ship, tiny and insignificant, like a toy floating on the vast sea. We chased the day into night, then night into dawn. We all slept in short spells until one of the children woke and demanded attention. Houa's nose began to run. Moa needed to nurse. Nou wanted to visit the bathroom again. I woke the last time with a jolt as the plane bounced onto the runway in Los Angeles. The sky and land ran together in a rainbow of red and orange streaks while stars still twinkled overhead.

We crowded into the immigration line half asleep, clutching the children, engulfed by the hum of idle chatter and close air. After twenty minutes we reached an older man sitting in a booth wearing a khaki uniform. He had a bald head and ears that stuck straight out. For a long time he studied our papers, then called to a Thai translator to help. No Hmong person would ever be so impolite. Not a smile or nod or greeting, no acknowledgement of my answers. This was our welcome to America.

An airline employee ushered us to the next flight. I thought I could not bear another four hours sitting in the tiny seats with our children squirming and whining as they climbed back and forth between laps. I wanted to be in Minneapolis, safe with my family. The sky grew cloudy and soon only streams of white and gray mist flowed past the window, obscuring the land below. The plane began to bounce and twist, like a hornbill searching for a perch. Yer clutched my arm. I held tight to Houa and fastened Nou's seatbelt. At last the plane's nose dipped down through the gray veil. Now I was the one with sweaty palms. We circled over flat stretches of white fields until white trees and white houses appeared. The plane eased onto the wide gray runway.

Yer held my gaze a moment with a weary smile as we gathered the children once more. Dazed, we stepped off the plane and through the gate. Bright lights shone down from the ceiling and bounced off white walls and the shiny linoleum floor. I had to blink against the glare. The air was hot and stuffy and smelled of coffee and sweat. People were gathered, waving and calling to those coming off the plane, while others lounged in chairs near the gate. A deep voice came over a loud speaker with announcements I did not understand. I searched the crowd for familiar faces, straining my neck to see over the heads of men and women hurrying up and down the long hall. Everyone was so tall. A strange, small car whined to a halt beside us to pick up an elderly woman. More passengers pushed past us, dragging bags and children, disappearing down the hall. Still no sign of our family. I had no idea what to do if they did not come. For the first time I grasped the difficulty of my inability to speak the language and communicate my needs.

Then I spotted them, racing toward us, bundled in bulky jackets and mufflers, unmistakable in an ocean of white faces. Our family. At last, our family. Blia, Tou, and Mee reached us first, stopping short as if unsure what to say or do, momentarily shy. Shone and Kia, out of breath and holding baby John, followed, then Yer and Soua. They encircled us with hugs and tears as everyone talked at once. Yer broke down with great sobs, laughing at the same time. She clung to Kia. The babies began to wail. Relief and happiness filled my eyes with tears.

Shone pulled me from the group, turning to a short, round man with wispy, blond hair and pink, chubby cheeks who stood slightly apart. "This is Mr. Martin from St. Paul's Church. He drove us in the church van to meet you."

I wiped tears on my sleeve and shook his hand. Mr. Martin bobbed and bowed his head, greeting me in Hmong. Every time he smiled, his face wrinkled up until his pale blue eyes disappeared.

It is funny remembering first impressions, the things that startled me as modern wonders, but also precarious and potentially harmful. Mr. Martin led us down the odd moving stairs like the ones we had seen in the Bangkok airport but had been too uncertain to try. Nou chased her cousins onto it, giggling. Yer and I stepped on gingerly, clutching the rail. It made me think of sliding down a muddy hill, unsteady and about to fall. I didn't expect the steps to melt into a ramp at the bottom, propelling me forward. I bumped into Shone who had stopped to steady Yer as she tumbled off and let out a cry of surprise.

Suitcases spilled out of a big metal mouth and circled on a turnstile topped by a flashing yellow lantern that buzzed in a low drone. People crowded around. The exit doors swept open without anyone touching them, sending cold air rushing through the room. At last our cardboard boxes, tied with rope, emerged.

Kia had brought jackets for us and blankets for Houa and Moa. The frozen air, the intense bitter ache that hit us the minute we stepped outside, stunned me. It cut through my khaki pants and sandals and made my scalp prickle. A light wind swirled around us and sent a shiver down my back. My ears and hands turned numb. When I exhaled, little wisps of white mist hung in the air. Dark clouds of charred wood blurred the Minnesota sky, turning the fading light flat and hazy. A gray-white film obscured the ground and collected on cars and tree branches stripped of leaves as if sprinkled with ashes.

Nou reached down and grasped a handful of dirty slush off the ground, her eyes blinking quickly against the cold. "It feels wet."

Blia laughed. "It's snow," she said in English.

"Snow," Nou repeated the sound slowly and smiled.

"The ice is slippery," Kia said, putting a hand under Yer's elbow to help her negotiate the slick asphalt. Her puffy jacket was made of a material like the American parachutes that had dropped soldiers and food supplies over Laos. "We have many things to tell you. Where to begin. But now you must get home and sleep." I marveled at the sound of the word home. Our home. Here in Minneapolis.

As we drove into the city, I thought I had never seen a place so devoid of color, so flat and bleak and stark, not even in parts of Laos where napalm had incinerated all traces of life from the land. Dusk slipped into darkness, and large lamps on long poles suddenly shed circles of yellow light onto the frozen streets. Mr. Martin pulled up in front of a three-story red brick building.

"Mr. Martin invites you to come to St. Paul's soon," Soua translated. "You are always welcome."

I nodded and said my first English words in America, "Thank you."

A tall woman with waves of brown hair tied back with a purple scarf got out of a car. A dark wool coat hung off her wide body like a tent. Her skin was the color of the rich beans from the French coffee plantations in Laos. She shifted a large black purse over her shoulder and shook hands with Shone. He introduced me to Mrs. Robinson from social services. She offered a wide smile of shimmering white as she welcomed us to Minneapolis.

In the building lobby a blast of hot, dry air hit my face like the heat of a strong fire. We climbed to the second floor and walked down a long hall with doors on each side. It smelled of old food with a faint hint of urine. Scraps of paper, cigarette butts, candy wrappers, and a stray ball littered the linoleum floor. Drawings had been scrawled across the walls. Two young boys rode tricycles down the hall and stopped to examine us, staring up with big, dark eyes.

Mrs. Robinson shooed the boys away, her voice turning harsh. At the last door, she demonstrated which keys unlocked the two deadbolts and another lock in the doorknob. Inside, she showed me how to lock them again and hook the chain. I wondered what kind of evil we needed to keep out. A strong chemical smell filled the musty, stale air. As Shone translated, she explained the beige walls had been painted a few days earlier. The floor was covered with shaggy carpet the color of rice stalks that are ripening and beginning to turn from green to gold. A small room opened onto a kitchen and held two chairs, covered in faded cloth with a print of green ferns, arranged around a low table. She explained that the people at St. Paul's Church had donated the furniture.

In the corner to the right of the door and opposite the sofa, a small black and white television with silver antennas rested on a metal frame. Blia immediately turned a dial, and Nou joined her cousins in front of the screen, her mouth gaping open. Soon Moa insisted on being put down and snuggled up in Nou's lap.

Mrs. Robinson pulled an envelope from her bag. "This is money for things you'll need right away and food stamps." She flashed another toothy smile and handed me a pamphlet written in Hmong that detailed available county services and a card with her phone number. "On Monday, Mr. Lee, I'll be here at four o'clock in the afternoon to take you to your job." She glanced at her watch. "I'm sure you want to sleep now, but if you need anything call me. There is a pay phone on the corner at the end of the block." She spoke rapidly to Shone and left.

Shone gave a short laugh. "We must tell you the rules and how things work."

"Always rules from these people. They treat us like children," Kia said. "Life is very different, but you will get used to it."

Kia led Yer and me through our new home, demonstrating how everything worked, reminding me of the stewardess on the airplane. In the second room, she plopped down on a thick, slightly lumpy mattress, covered with yellow striped sheets and a beige wool blanket with a large brown stain on the bottom left side. Yer sat down uncertainly and ran her hand across the blanket. Cousin Yer joined us and gently lowered little Houa, sound asleep, into the crib at the side of the bed. She smiled down and tucked a pink blanket around her.

Kia went to the doorway and beckoned. "Come see the bathroom." We crowded around the blue-tiled room, lit by a bright bulb under frosted glass, surveying the shiny white fixtures and slightly tattered, green towels hanging off the rack. Kia lifted the toilet seat up and down then threw in a wad of paper from the rack. With a flick of the handle, a great rush of water swirled around in the bowl and disappeared. "See? It goes away."

Yer smiled, admitting that she and Nou had been baffled by the toilets in the airport and on the plane. They did not know to flush them.

Kia turned on the water in the sink, then the bathtub. "Hot and cold water any time you want."

"The lights turn on and off." Kia reached her hand around to the switch and flashed them several times.

We trailed after her back to the kitchen. Kia opened the door of a large white box. A light flashed on to reveal shelves holding bowls of soup and rice. "This keeps food cold so things don't go bad. I made you this meal if you get hungry." She looked up and smiled. "Stick your hands in and see." Yer hesitated. "It's not a trick," Kia insisted.

Yer thrust her arm into the box. Curious, I did as well.

Kia shut the door and turned to a smaller white box. Her face became serious. "You cannot light a fire on the floor, because then the whole building would burn. This is the stove for cooking. Here on this metal grate, you put the pans. And you light it like this." She turned a knob and flames shot out. Yer jumped back. "It is easy once you know how." She turned the fire off. "They do not allow live chickens or pigs in the buildings."

"What will we eat?" Yer asked.

"You can buy the meat at a store already cut up and ready to cook."

I frowned. "What about our ceremonies?"

She shrugged. "We sacrifice the animals in the parking lot."

"I will never get used to these things," Yer said, shaking her head.

"It won't take long." Kia patted Yer's arm. "You look tired. We will go."

After the family left I slowly turned around, taking in our apartment with plaster walls that smelled of paint and a wooden door barricaded with four locks. This was our new home. Not one single thing remotely resembled our life in Laos. Yer stared at the television without registering a reaction, her face sagging with confusion. The silver and black screen flickered and cast shadows across the walls. Faint voices echoed off the ceiling. Nou and Moa had fallen asleep on the floor.

I picked Nou up in my arms. Her face was slack, her breathing slow and untroubled. Yer began to pull at the rope on one of our boxes, as if she needed to open it and find something familiar, something that belonged to us. I told her to leave it and come to bed. It would be better in the morning after a good sleep. I placed Nou in the middle of the big mattress then settled Moa in the crib next to Houa. The sounds of the city drifted through the windows. A horn beeped. A group of men were shouting at each other as if fighting, but then laughed. A piercing siren grew closer then faded into the night. A door slammed somewhere. The windows rattled. Yer draped an arm across Nou and gripped my hand. We drifted to sleep, still in our clothes, and did not wake until the sun came up.

Chapter 9
YER

 Her big supermarket. Kia had been talking about it for a week. Cousin Yer stayed with the babies as Pao had gone to English class and Nou to school. I left Moa and Houa in front of the television lost in a cartoon of a dog chasing its tail.

Going so far from our apartment made me anxious. But it seemed important to Kia, and I did not have the strength to fight her. I had passed another night with only short snatches of fitful, dreamless slumber. Exhaustion sapped the energy from my limbs. I could not find the rhythm of day and night in this new place. There were no roosters crowing before dawn. Instead, an alarm clock bleated like an unhappy goat. I had to hide my head beneath the blanket. I did not know how to sleep with the lights that burned forever just outside our window. When we finally crawled into bed, still my mind would not rest. I listened to the steam heater hiss and crackle. Pao snored next to me. Hours passed. Sirens wailed. Nou kicked her legs and arms into me. The babies whimpered. In these sleepless hours, I could not fight the longing and grief that once again pushed down on me. Ever since we had left Ban Vinai, my boys had vanished. The dreams had ceased. Not a whisper of wind carried their gentle presence. At first in the processing camp,

I had not worried. But weeks passed. Nothing. I told Pao it broke my heart to leave everything behind. He didn't understand. He said we must look forward. I had to do as my husband wished. I had no choice. When we left for America, panic began to swallow me. I had seen the map. Fong and Fue would never find me half-way around the world. I only wanted to sleep. I only wanted my children to return to me. But now I could not sleep. I could not dream.

Kia wrapped her muffler twice around her neck and hurried me outside. "You can buy anything you want at my store. You have never seen so many choices." She flashed a bright smile. "I want you to meet my friends Rosita and Mary, but they are not working today."

Tuesdays through Saturdays, from early morning until mid-afternoon, Kia unpacked boxes of food in the storeroom of the supermarket. She had learned English and taken the job to earn money to bring us from Thailand. For this reason, Shone had agreed. Now, she did not want to quit. She liked her independence and earning money for the family.

"Rosita is so funny, you will like her. She is from Puerto Rico. It's an island in the ocean somewhere. It sounds a little like Laos, warm and sunny, only with water all around."

"Why did she come here?"

"She was very poor in Puerto Rico and her husband drank too much. He used to hit her. So she took her three children and came to America."

"Alone?"

"Yes. She has an aunt who lives in Minneapolis. Now she is with a Vietnamese man, Tran. He came here right after the war."

I shook my head. This could never happen in Laos. Maybe in America people from different places mixed together this way.

Kia held my arm as we stepped carefully along the icy sidewalk. The sun sat low in the pale sky. It was not a warm, bright sun like in Laos, but faded yellow, almost white. I thought the frigid air must wash away colors in this place. Freezing fingers nipped at my cheeks like tiny pricks from a needle. Even with my gloves, hat, and scarf, I shivered. The cold seeped through the soles of my shoes and thick socks into my bones.

"We have to hurry or we'll miss the bus," Kia said. "It's only another block."

A police car roared past, siren blaring and red and yellow lights flashing. The muscles in my middle tightened. I caught my breath. I would not leave the apartment without someone to accompany me. I could not speak the language. I had no idea of the value of money or the papers we used to buy food. Even with Kia or Yer to escort me, the world outside loomed large and frightening. Many days we gathered at our family's home for dinner, talking late into the evening, filling in the pieces of our years apart. They lived in a two bedroom apartment in another red brick building like ours. I would cling to the children and step close to Pao as we walked the two and a half blocks home. I knew evil spirits lurked in the dark corners.

But it was more. I felt uneasy among the gangs of brown and dark-skinned young men that lived around us. Only a few times at the Long Chieng base had I seen American soldiers with these colors of skin. The young men pushed past me in and out of our building. They gathered on the street, smoking and staring at everyone who passed. So much anger filled their eyes. White people scared me too—the tattooed man at the corner market and the woman at the thrift store with white hair and glass frames that sparkled. Maybe they were not as rough, but their dislike did not escape me. It carried in the tone of their voices. Their lips closed into tight lines. Their eyes stared through me. I wanted to be like Fue's favorite insect in Laos, the brown walking stick that blended into tree trunks until you could not see it.

We stood at the bus stop, huddled together. Under her heavy jacket, Kia wore a sweater, a tight, black skirt that came above her knees, and heavy dark tights. Black leather boots with tall heels laced up the front of her legs. They made her sway and wobble when she walked. She had cut her hair to her shoulders, shaggy around her face like ruffled feathers on a bird. Little gold crosses dangled from her lobes. Another cross hung around her neck on a chain. It was the blue-green color she painted on her eyelids and her red lips that surprised me most. Pao did not approve. He said she looked too much like the women in Ban Vinai, the ones who danced at the café in the evenings and slipped off with men into the darkness. He said Shone should tell his wife to stop this. I did not argue with him. I thought Kia just wanted to look American.

The bus rolled up and stopped with a loud squeal. The doors popped open. Kia put coins into a box. They jingled as they dropped. The driver, a heavy black woman with bright red hair, handed Kia tickets and started up again. I grabbed a metal pole, nearly falling down as the bus lurched forward. I felt the eyes of others on us: Four old women, a man in a suit and dark gray top coat, three giggling teenage girls, and a young mother with a baby bundled tightly in a pink blanket. We collapsed onto an empty seat. Hot, sour air flowed over us, smelling of exhaust fumes.

Kia reached across me, wiping the steam off the window. She pointed. "This is St. Paul's Church. See the window at the top. It's made of colored glass and when the sun shines through, it is very beautiful. The parish hall is behind. The Hmong sewing group meets there. Yer likes to go."

We passed a drab brick building with a steep, pointed roof. Stairs led to wooden doors. A gold cross had been attached to the left wall. Pao and I had been surprised to learn that Kia and Shone attended St. Paul's Catholic Church every Sunday. There were a number of Hmong families who came.

Kia bowed her head and pulled on the edge of her knit glove. "I am starting classes next month to learn more about the church. I want to be baptized. Then I will go to heaven."

I wondered which heaven she meant. Was it separate from our Hmong heaven? When we were together with our husbands, I did not question Kia or Shone about their church. But now, I had to ask, "What about our Hmong beliefs? Do you not follow them?"

She looked up. "We do both. We pray to the Catholic God and pray to our ancestors." She laughed softly. "We all need extra help."

I nodded, although I did not understand. Perhaps it did not matter if they found comfort in this American church. Perhaps our ancestors, the spirits and gods of the Hmong heaven would understand.

"I want you to come with me one Sunday," Kia said. "You will like Father McConnell, the priest." I nodded again. But I knew Pao would not allow this. He had experienced enough of the Catholic priests and their contempt for Hmong beliefs during his school days in Vientiane. We had to keep our traditions, be true to our heritage, he insisted.

Every few blocks, the bus stopped. People got on and off. I studied the store fronts plastered with signs and pictures above the doors and windows. Sometimes there were big signs on poles with pictures of furniture or cars or buildings. One had a smiling family in front of a big house on a sunny day with no snow. This was how I learned about America, from pictures on billboards and advertisements on television.

The bus drove onto a wide concrete bridge with many lanes of traffic.

"This is the Mississippi River," Kia said. "It is very long like the Mekong."

Mekong. The name struck me the way lightening plummets from the sky. My mind muddled with memories. I could not figure out where I was. It did not look like the Mekong, not with snow covered riverbanks and little crests of silver lapping at the shore. I pictured my boys in the cold depths of the swirling gray-brown waters that rushed under the bridge. I had to save them. I had to get from the bridge to the water, but I could not see a path. Soon we would be too far away. My breathing came in short gasps, my heart pounding. Then I felt Kia's hand on my arm and heard her voice echoing in my head. Slowly, I drifted back to Minneapolis and a river called the Mississippi. But there was no name for my sorrow.

Kia shifted in her seat and put a hand over her bulging middle. "This baby kicks all day and night. It must be a boy." She shook her head and sighed. "I have something to tell you. It is very sad, and Yer cannot bring herself to talk of it. She lost two babies this year and now she cannot have any more. She was very sick in the early weeks and then the bleeding began." Kia paused a moment. "The last time it was so bad that Soua took her to the hospital. They did an operation and took out her uterus. Yer begged them not to, but they said otherwise she might die. They have been very sad."

I put a hand to my mouth. It was the worst thing that could happen to a woman. Poor Yer. So many losses piled upon our family year by year.

We passed streets that looked like the movie at the processing center. Tall buildings of glass and metal rose up from the sidewalks. Traffic slowed to a crawl, jammed with cars and buses. People, bundled in heavy coats, hurried along the sidewalks, carrying packages. Kia called this downtown. The window became foggy again from my breath against the cold glass. Everything floated by in a gray and white blur. Office buildings gave way to apartments. Then to houses painted green and yellow and blue.

Finally, Kia pulled a string above us to make the bell ring. The bus left us behind, choking on gray smoke. Dark clouds swept across the sky now and blocked the pale, useless sun. Across the street people hurried through the glass doors of an enormous square building with a flat roof and no windows.

Kia pulled me inside and stopped. "What do you think?" Her voice was full of a child's excitement for a special surprise.

I did not disappoint her. My mouth fell open. I stared at the enormous space, the whirl of bright lights, and noisy bustle. A forest of tall shelves spanned out in rows as far as I could see. People crowded up and down the aisles with metal baskets on wheels, piling in cartons and cans. Voices echoed over a background of soft music. Kia led me down rows to shelves stacked with boxes of cereal and crackers and cookies. Cans of brown beans, beets, and soups. Bottles of juice. Jars of jam and peanut butter. Of course I did not know these things. I squinted at the labels, trying to interpret the pictures, while Kia named the different items. We stopped next to the glass doors of the freezer. Kia explained the miracle of frozen dinners, already cooked and ready to warm. The strangest site was the meat counter with its little trays of beef and chicken and fish, neatly wrapped in clear plastic. Everything was cut in perfect shapes, free of flies and dust.

An older woman with silver hair and black hoop earrings stood behind a small table wearing a blue and white striped apron. She spoke to me and held her hand out to a tray filled with little bites of meat speared on wooden sticks. Whole sausages sizzled in a flat pan. The aroma made me hungry, but I could not afford to buy strange food like this. Kia grabbed two and handed me one. "They're free," she said. "Try it." It tasted a little like pig only very salty.

"You will like this best," Kia said. We rounded the corner to rows of stands displaying apples, oranges, bananas, yams, green beans, corn, and dozens of fruits and vegetables unfamiliar to me. I sighed. For the first time something resembled, ever so slightly, the markets in Xieng Khouang and Thailand. Kia pulled plastic bags off a roll. We selected onions, kale, green peppers, and shiny red apples. The corner market near our apartment had few choices, and the produce was wilted and tired. This was worth the long bus ride.

Outside again, the snow fell in cold wet flakes and settled like dust on my face. Kia rattled on about the market and her friends.

I listened and nodded. Suddenly I was so tired I could barely stand. The bus pulled up at last, and I sank into the seat. I put my head against the cool window and closed my eyes. The image of the oversized store filled my mind. This country was blessed with so much abundance, even in this bleak and barren city. But I did not care about these things. All I wanted was to be home, our true home, living in our quiet village. Working in our fields. It puzzled me that the American officials had flown simple farmers from the highlands of Laos across oceans and continents to live in a city like this. It made no sense. Nothing in this new life made any sense. And I let out a small moan. My boys would never find me again.

Chapter 10
NOU

Mrs. Wilson rose from her desk, back erect, head high, staring at the class with keen eyes that took in every movement. She was tall and angular with prominent cheek bones, a square jaw, and curly hair cut very short. Her skin matched the color of the crayon named sepia that I had found in the big basket at the back of the room. After three months at school, I was not so much afraid as in awe of her. She dealt swiftly with anyone who broke the rules or disrupted class. The rude behavior of the students and lack of respect for elders shocked me. No child in Laos or Thailand would ever act this way. From the beginning I wanted to be a good student. But nothing came easily without a common language. She was not unkind, yet her brusque, cool manner held me at a distance. Some days I heard a slight impatience in her voice and sensed her exasperation with the added burden of my presence.

When Father and Uncle Soua registered me at the school, the principal suggested I start in second grade with Blia. Father had Uncle Soua explain that I was eight, a year older than Blia, and had already completed level three in Ban Vinai. I had been a top student. The principal nodded. She understood, but education was different in America. I would have to learn English first. After I became proficient, then they would reevaluate.

For the first month I waded in a morass of confusion, trying to discern meaning from pictures and gestures and faces. The letters and numbers in the books and on the blackboard remained nothing more than scribbled marks, shapes without form. Blia soon tired of being my interpreter, and her impatience made me feel stupid. I was desperate to untangle the coded secrets of my new world.

Miss Swenson taught me to fit the pieces together. For an hour, three days a week, I joined her English class with six other students--two sisters from Cuba with rosy cheeks and big brown eyes, a shy, skinny boy from Vietnam, identical twin girls from Cambodia who always spoke at the same time, and a chubby boy from Poland. Miss Swenson was young and pretty with long golden hair and eyes the bright green of banana leaves. Her manner was warm and accessible in a way Mrs. Wilson's was not. I felt safe and capable in her presence. She showed us alphabet flashcards with pictures of animals and demonstrated how to shape our tongue and lips around the vowels and consonants so foreign to our ears. She never grew impatient, but repeated the sounds with us until we got it right. Once we could string together letters into simple words and phrases, we sang songs and recited nursery rhymes. Everyone clapped when one of us succeeded, and we got to choose prizes of candy, a shiny medal on a red ribbon, new pencils and a notebook, or a chapter book to take home. That was how I came to own my first books.

As the weeks passed, I began to catch more words and sentences watching television at home or in Mrs. Wilson's class. I strained and struggled to understand. It was exhausting, but the knot in my middle slowly eased.

"Put away your workbooks and take out your readers," Mrs. Wilson directed. The room filled with whispers and the flutter of books and papers scraping in and out of desks.

I glanced over and noticed Blia had finished only half the addition problems and answered three incorrectly. Numbers did not come easily to me, but unlike Blia, I worked hard and managed to do well. I had offered to help her, but she turned away defiantly. She caught me looking and slammed her workbook shut, tossing it carelessly into the desk drawer and rummaging through the jumble of scrunched up papers and broken pencils to find her reader. My desk was obsessively neat. In Thailand the school had so little, only one textbook for each class and no history, science, art, or music lessons. Father had to buy my pencils and paper as money allowed. Now, I treasured the wealth bestowed upon me— lovely yellow pencils that I sharpened every morning, a thick pink eraser, my own box of crayons in twelve colors, crisp sheets of lined paper, and books with glossy colored pictures, hard covers, and a line on the inside page that said, *This book belongs to*, where I got to print my name in pencil. Mrs. Wilson had decorated the walls with a huge map of the world, posters of Native American tribes, and our art work and writing projects. Mobiles of the planets, stars, sun, and moon dangled from the ceiling and danced in the breeze from the heating vent. In the back of the classroom three easels held pads of paper, wide brushes, and jars of red, blue, yellow, green, and purple paint. Mrs. Wilson kept baskets of colored pencils, chalk, and more crayons on the back counter, which we could use with her permission. On Friday afternoons she played the piano and we sang songs. The two best behaved students of the week got to accompany her with the tambourine and a shiny triangle. What I liked best were the books on a shelf that ran the length of the wall under the windows. Mrs. Wilson let us borrow them during silent reading time. And on Tuesdays we went to the library to explore the endless stacks of picture books, chapter books on science and geography and people and animals, more subjects than I had ever imagined. I got to pick two to take home for the week. At first I could only look at the pictures, but soon I was able to read them out loud to my little sisters.

As with most of the world I had encountered since our arrival in Minneapolis, my new school both thrilled and intimidated me. The old brick building had been constructed in the 1930s, and scuffs and stains marked the brown linoleum floors and faded tan walls. Dank, musty smells of rusted pipes, cleaning fluids, wheat paste, dust, and sweat, accumulated over fifty years, permeated the crowded rooms. Over seven hundred students ages five to twelve years old, in every shape and size and color, speaking a multitude of languages, attended the school. The older kids loomed like fierce warriors, crowding the halls, pushing and yelling. At first I did not understand the slurs and taunts that flowed from their mouths. That would come later.

The bell rang, and I breathed freely at last. Mrs. Wilson walked us single file to the auditorium for lunch. Blia and I raced to meet Tou and Mee, and the four of us stood in the cafeteria line. Along with close to half the children in the school, we received free lunches because our parents were poor. I was unaware of this distinction at first. The school lunches presented me with a vast array of culinary delights: American cheese sandwiches, grilled and buttery, hot dogs, and peanut butter with grape jelly on airy white bread. On Fridays there were cupcakes with pink icing or brownies or oatmeal cookies. I even liked the meatloaf with greasy brown gravy and stringy pork chops with mushy peas. After the years of deprivation in Ban Vinai, I could not satisfy my hunger. On this day, they had my favorite: spaghetti and meatballs and applesauce.

We carried our trays to one of the long tables, crowding in next to a group of girls. Shouting, laughter, and occasional shrieks bounced off the walls and high ceiling. May sunshine streamed through the windows. If we hurried, we could play outside. Tou shoveled food into his mouth anxious to join the other boys in a game of dodge ball. Blia, Mee, and I liked to swing from the bars on the jungle gym with the Cambodian twins and two Hmong girls in third grade.

"We're adding and subtracting six-digit numbers," Tou said through a mouthful of spaghetti. He excelled in math.

Blia shrugged. "Math is stupid."

Tou swallowed and took a drink of milk. "I heard my teacher talking to Mrs. Martin and she says your class is for slow learners. You don't do any of the same work we do."

Slow. The word hit me like a slap across the cheek. But I was not slow. Father would never have let them put me in a slow class. Maybe I had misunderstood. I waited for Mee to refute

Tou's allegation, but she just stared at her plate, running her spoon through the applesauce.

"You're a liar," Blia said at last. She stood up and grabbed her tray, carrying it to the return window. She sat back down, crossed her arms over her middle, and glared at Tou.

Mee looked up quickly. "My dad said he'll take us to the zoo Sunday." Blia's face brightened slightly as she turned her attention on Mee.

My cousins had told me about the zoo with bears and lions and dozens of other animals, many of which I had only recently learned about at school. I thought it odd that tigers and elephants, like those roaming the hills of Laos, had been captured and placed in cages for people to watch. But America was full of strange and wonderful diversions.

That winter my cousins and I had reveled in the icy snow, throwing snowballs and building fat snowmen with rocks and cigarette butts for eyes and noses. After big storms we piled fresh powder into a small hill and slid down on a cardboard box. Once spring arrived we spent Sunday afternoons at nearby parks. I discovered the delicious joy of running barefoot through green grass as soft as goose feathers. I flew through the air on the swings, pumping my legs to get higher and higher, and slipped down corkscrew slides. Once the whole family went to a beautiful lake, the deepest blue I had ever seen. The sun sparkled off the glassy surface as we wiggled our toes in icy cold waves lapping onto the muddy shore.

The miracle of pictures appearing on our tiny television screen and voices traveling through telephone wires still baffled me. The first time I rode an elevator I believed it was magic. Nothing else could explain walking into this tiny box from one room and when the doors opened again, emerging into another.

On my second Sunday in Minneapolis, Uncle Shoua took us ice skating. Blia had been on a school field trip the year before and had begged him to take her ever since. Uncle decided my arrival offered an appropriate occasion for such extravagance. We rode a bus across town and got off in front of a great domed hall. Uncle Soua helped us lace up the rented skates. I couldn't stop giggling as I tried to walk on the narrow blades, stumbling and grasping at Mee's arm. We stepped onto the frozen rink, and I immediately fell on my bottom. Mee giggled and put out a hand to pull me up, but unsteady as she was, we both fell down. We laughed and laughed, a deep, side-aching laugh, slipping and sliding. Blia and Tou slid past us into the center, holding on to each other, repeatedly falling and getting back up. Mee and I managed to crawl over and pull ourselves up on the railing. I edged my way around the rink, my ankles wobbling and periodically collapsing. Uncle Soua laughed and waved from his seat in the gallery.

Music blared from huge speakers and echoed through the vast space, pulsing in even rhythms. Skaters crowded out onto the rink and glided over the ice with graceful, sweeping strides. A man skated backwards, his feet weaving in and out, while another made figure eights on one foot, lifting his other leg out behind him. A young woman in a pale pink leotard and tights and bright pink muffler spun in circles as her short black skirt flared out like an umbrella. All I wanted in life was to skate like this. I watched and studied until at last I found my balance and took a few awkward steps, scraping at the ice. The tempo of the music alternated fast and slow, waltzes and rumbas, disco beats and slow love songs. I skated round the rink gaining confidence. The room grew dark, and a mirrored ball, hanging from the ceiling, splashed pulsating silver lights across the ice and walls. Skaters turned into slow motion robots.

We stayed the full ninety-minute session, stopping only once to rest. I tasted my first cup of sweet, hot chocolate. By the end I was keeping up with Tou and Blia. My movements became smoother, less cautious as I learned to swing my arms with each stride. Faster and faster. I closed my eyes and tried to memorize the sensations of cool air rushing over my cheeks, the syncopated tempo of the music pulsing in my ears, the thrill of soaring over the ice oblivious to time and space. This was the feel of freedom.

At the end of June when I was ten, two sisters, seven and eight years old, drowned in Lake Harriet. The girls' mother left for five minutes to buy sodas. They were floating on plastic rafts, drifting out onto the lake, and their mother called to them to paddle back to shore before she walked away. Neither girl could swim. Five other adults were sitting on the shore, watching their own children play at the edge of the water. No one noticed. One woman remembered yelling and splashing, but she thought the girls were teasing. The story led on the front page of the morning paper and ran on the local evening news for several days.

I remembered the special afternoon when our family had taken the bus to Cedar Lake, how my cousins and I had waded knee deep in the shallow waters, splashing and playing. I studied the smiling faces staring back from the television screen; the girls sat on a chair, arms around each other. Their features were so alike they could have been twins. I did not know them. Yet the thought of their lifeless bodies sinking to the bottom of the lake triggered an ache deep inside me. I imagined them on the rafts, giggling, bobbing in the light breeze that sent gentle ripples skipping across the water's surface. Maybe one slipped off by accident, or her sister, teasing, pushed her, not meaning to send her into the water, then desperately tried to save her and disappeared into the cold depths as well.

The next week, the nightmares came. I was falling into a lake, thrashing and grabbing for a raft that drifted just out of reach. My limbs grew heavy and useless as the water dragged me under and sucked the air from my lungs. I woke up crying, my body cold and damp. Father or Mother would hold me close until at last I slept again. The dream came back to me in unexpected flashes as I washed the dishes or gave Moa and Houa a bath.

After the story of the two drowned girls, Auntie Kia signed my cousins up for swimming lessons at the YMCA. But I did not go. Father said it wasn't a good time. Mother needed me at home. It was only one more disappointment in a string of small injustices. Father would not allow me to go to the Sunday school classes at St. Paul's with my cousins. He was very clear that we would not become Catholics. I had to stay home while my cousins played at the park or went to the occasional movie. I chafed when they prattled on about the soccer game they had watched or the ice cream Uncle Soua had bought them on the way home. Blia and Mee spent afternoons that summer making art projects at St. Paul's community center while Tou played softball with a group of boys from the church.

It felt as if my cousins embellished their fun to make me jealous of their good fortune. Blia couldn't wait to show me her new yellow swimsuit and goggles. I tried to act as if I didn't care. In time I came to blame them more than my father for what I was missing. Our relationships had grown precarious and complicated with shifting circumstances at school and home. When third grade had begun the previous fall, I was placed in the advanced class with Mee and Tou. Blia would not speak to me for a week, as if I had betrayed her. But I knew my success in America depended on speaking English well and getting good grades. Father had drilled this into me night after night. When I no longer qualified to take Mrs. Swenson's English class, she volunteered to tutor me once a week at lunch. With her help and encouragement I flourished, and in January the principal moved me to a fourth grade class. My cousins reacted as if I had challenged them to a competition. It was one that none of us would ever win.

I passed the long, hot days of summer doing chores and caring for my siblings. Mother had given birth to my sister Boa our first July in Minneapolis and my brother Tong the following May, right before school ended. Between his work and English classes, Father spent little time at home. The demands of four small children seemed to overwhelm Mother. My aunties helped out when they could, but they had families of their own. Auntie Yer watched little John and baby Adam while Kia went to work and volunteered at the church. And so I carried the burden. Since Ban Vinai Mother had relied on me for many household tasks, but life in Minneapolis added another dimension to her dependence. She had no time or inclination to learn English. I became her translator and ambassador to the outside world, escorting her on errands and counting out money at the grocery store. It fell to me to call the social worker and explain why Mother hadn't taken Boa to the free clinic for her immunizations.

Father's insistence on my presence at home drew from a darker need, one we never really acknowledged. The depression and grief that had pulled Mother from us in the refugee camps returned. On bad days, Father would say she had a headache. It was a small lie we both accepted. Better not to speak the truth. Some days she never left her bed, crying and whispering to the corners of the room. She would not eat or dress and barely heard me when I handed her Tong to nurse. I held her hand and tried to pull her back to us with idle chatter, but greater forces worked against me.

My only compensation for being home all summer was the new color television Father had bought and a trip to the library every two weeks. Father took me on his Thursday afternoons off to the big branch downtown. I looked forward to our outings. No one else was invited. We spent several hours, each in our respective sections—children's books and magazines for me, history and geography for Father—perusing up and down the aisles, pulling out books and feeling the weight of sturdy covers, leafing through lovely crisp pages. I had my own library card. Each time I selected five books to take home, always taking one picture book to read to Houa and Moa. On our outings Father and I spoke English so he could practice. Sometimes, with a great deal of trepidation, I corrected his pronunciation. He nodded and tried again.

That summer I saw with uncomfortable clarity the intolerance that undermined our tenuous hold on happiness in this place we called home. At school, older kids taunted my cousins and me, along with other Hmong, Cambodians, and Vietnamese who gathered in small groups at lunch: *chinks, gooks, slant-eyes, ching-chongs.* They hurled slurs across the playground the way they threw French fries in a cafeteria food fight. It was a sport, a game.

Other, more subtle messages made me feel inadequate. While my teachers were kind, I shrank from their probing questions. *Did you eat breakfast this morning, Nou? You're such a tiny thing. Is there anyone at home who speaks English to help with your schoolwork? Do you have any other clothes to wear? I can get you some clothes from the PTA. How many people did you say are in your family? Would you like to tell the class about your New Year's celebration?* I could see into their hearts and read their thoughts; poor little Nou, such an odd family. Such strange customs. All those children.

One morning in early August, Mother and I set out to shop. She was having a good day, up at dawn to fix breakfast before Father left for work, bustling around the apartment cleaning. We would take the bus to the supermarket--not Auntie Kia's market but a closer one. Every few weeks we went to buy staples like rice, cooking oil, toilet paper, and bags of fresh vegetables, where the prices were cheaper.

As we left the apartment, Mrs. Johnson, the elderly black woman who lived three doors away, came down the hall carrying a grocery bag. She was always friendly and sometimes gave my little sisters and me cookies or slices of apple when we played in the hall. She stopped to fuss over Tong, who was tied to Mother's back in an embroidered cloth baby carrier.

"Look at this boy. He is getting so big," she cooed. I had Boa in my arms, and Mrs. Johnson patted her tangle of dark hair. "My goodness, how does your mother keep up with all these little ones?" I smiled. "Well, God bless you. You have a lovely family." Mother smiled and nodded, and Mrs. Johnson shuffled to her door.

In the lobby, the Russian lady, whose name I could never pronounce, was standing by the mailboxes visiting with Mrs. Lopez, our next door neighbor. I heard them whispering as we passed. *Another baby already? She's pregnant all the time, poor thing. He's never home. The relatives are popping out babies too. They'll take over the country soon.* And they laughed and shook their heads. I kept my eyes cast down, my cheeks growing warm, wondering if they knew I understood their words.

We left my sisters with Auntie Yer and hurried to the bus stop. The sun sent heat waves rippling off the streets and sidewalks even though it was only ten o'clock. The stifling damp air settled like dew on my arms and pressed on my lungs. The weather report predicted 101 degrees by mid-afternoon.

As we reached the bus stop, a hulking man with dark chocolate skin stumbled down the street and halted in front of us. He leaned over and put his face, beaded with sweat, near Mother's. He reeked of alcohol. "What are you gooks doing in my neighborhood?" Mother grasped my arm and tried to step around him, but his hand flew out and grabbed her shoulder. "You're taking all the damn jobs. That's what you're doing. Why don't you go back to the jungle where you came from?" He threw his head back and spat on Mother's face, then staggered away.

I could not bear her expression as she wiped away the spittle on a piece of paper from her pocket. Tears formed in her eyes and trickled down her cheeks. I wanted to protect her, to run after the evil man and scream at him. But I was too afraid. I could only hang my head in shame. Our day was ruined. Mother's happy mood vanished. We completed our shopping trip in silence.

Mother said not to tell Father, that it would upset him too much. We must forget about the bad people. But that evening my hurt and bewilderment would not give me peace. Father came home for dinner before leaving for his night job. When Mother left the room, I told him what had happened.

He was sitting in a chair, watching television and eating a bowl of noodles. He put the bowl down, looking very weary. His eyes wandered for a moment to the television screen and a report of a bank robbery near downtown on the local news. At last he turned to me. "Many people hate anything that reminds them of the Vietnam War. A lot of American soldiers died there. They blame us for the tragedy even though we fought on their side. You must ignore these things. You are so young, it is hard to understand. Things will get better."

Another lie we both accepted.

Chapter 11
PAO

Shone and I bought a truck one Saturday in late October 1984. Our new pride and joy was a faded green 1970 Ford pickup, a sorry conglomeration of dents, scraped paint, broken tail lights, and bald tires. As we drove home the engine rattled and shook, spewing a gray stream out the tailpipe. We paid $745 in cash to a young white man in Bloomington who had used it for his construction job. Splinters of wood, rusty nails, and splotches of yellow and white paint littered the truck bed.

Shone pulled front first into a parking spot across the street from his apartment building, easing the truck in, then backing up and forward three times until at last it was parallel to the curb. He had only had his license a week—the first in our family to attempt such a feat—although he had driven a forklift for his job at the paper warehouse. His truck driving involved a lot of checking the rear view mirrors, pumping his foot on and off the gas pedal, and slamming on the brakes. He had laughed when two different drivers yelled at him and flashed obscene gestures as they zoomed around us.

Tou opened the passenger door, which produced a loud creak, and ran to get the family. Shone and I waited on the sidewalk with silly grins smeared across our faces, like little boys with their first bow and arrow. An icy wind swirled scarlet and gold leaves over the lawn and into the gutter. I zipped my cotton jacket up to my neck. The whole family emerged and circled around our wonderful prize.

Soua gaped and smiled, running a hand over the rim of the truck bed. "Very good. Very solid," he said.

"The seats are torn and the filling is coming out," Kia said as she inspected the cab.

Shone shrugged. "No problem."

Kia clucked her tongue, her hands on her hips. "I'll make a cover for them."

Nou and her cousins climbed up the bumper and into the back, giddy with excitement. Houa wanted me to lift her up, and then Moa asked as well. When I told Moa she was too little, she threw herself on the grass and sobbed. I relented and plopped her into the back. Yer stood back, holding Tong in her arms and looking askance. She still needed convincing of the soundness of our plan.

It was Shone's idea. He had met a Mexican man in an ESL class who made a good living with his own gardening business. Shone proposed the idea to Soua first, but Soua preferred to stay at the paper company where he'd been made a supervisor. When I arrived in Minneapolis, Shone laid out his plan with such enthusiasm and hope that I could not say no. All we had to do was save a little money to get started. We calculated the cost of equipment, and we decided to put aside three months income as a cushion until the business took off. For almost three years Shone and I scrimped and saved each month for our business. It took a long time as we were also saving to bring the rest of our family from Thailand. We watched the want ads for used lawn mowers and blowers. Several Sundays we took the bus to yard sales in the suburbs and picked up clippers, shovels, trowels, and hoes. Finally, we were ready to get our truck.

"Come on, Soua. I'll take you for a ride," Shone said, dangling his keys. "Who wants to go after that?"

"Can we ride in back?" Tou asked.

"Only if you sit down and hold on to the sides," Shone said.

I worried, but at the speed Shone drove not too much could go wrong. I sat with the children to make sure they were safe, clutching Moa in my lap. We took four trips around a three-block circuit, first with Soua, then Kia, then cousin Yer, and finally my wife. By the last round the sun was dipping down over the city and my ears and hands turned numb.

Such a celebration we had that night. Our wives prepared a great feast with pork, chicken, spinach, rice, and green papaya salad. Kia brought out beer, sodas, a big bag of potato chips, and a package of Oreo cookies that she had bought at her store. We listened to a new music tape from Thailand. Since I rarely had evenings off, I relished this time with family to laugh and remember, to look forward to better days.

As we settled back in our chairs to smoke our cigarettes, I pulled a paper from my pocket and unfolded it. "Here is the flyer." I handed it to Shone. I had made an advertisement for our services on the computer at work and paid for a hundred copies. The next day we would drive the truck to the suburbs with nice houses and big yards to pass out our flyer. Then we would wait for calls. Shone had quit his job at the paper company, and I had given notice at the restaurant. As soon as we had enough customers, I would quit my night job too.

"Very good." Shone scanned the sheet. "I like this, *many years experience in cultivation.*"

I smiled. "How different can growing grass and flowers be from corn and rice?"

Soua brought out a bottle of whiskey. He handed out glasses and lifted his in a toast. "To your new business. Much success and good fortune."

"To freedom," Shone said. "Not quite our own land to farm, but it is a start."

"No more bosses telling us what to do," I said, hoping Soua did not take this badly since he would still be working at the paper company. He smiled and tipped his glass back.

"Pao, can I see the letter again?" Soua asked.

I had received a letter from Chor the day before. Gia, now nineteen, had married a girl named Ia. Everyone was happy for them, but otherwise life was grim. Conditions in Ban Vinai had become even more intolerable. Thousands of people were hungry and sick, and the officials grew more abusive every day. The Thai had started forcing families to go back to Laos where the communist government imposed severe punishments. Our family was now desperate to come to America, but immigration had become trickier.

Soua scanned the letter and shook his head. "I'll call the immigration people on Monday. We must get the paper work completed as quickly as possible."

"Chor says his wife's family is trying as well. They have done quite well farming in California. Perhaps they will have more luck," I said.

Soua frowned. "I hope they will come to Minneapolis."

"Of course. But the first step is to get them to America," Shone said. "Then we can work out a way to be together."

I glanced at Yer chatting with Kia and her cousin in the living room. She seemed so happy in this moment with Tong asleep in her arms and Boa curled beside her. If only it could always be like this. I struggled every day to understand what afflicted her. My prayers to our ancestors to restore the balance to her souls brought little relief. I talked to her, cajoled her, but I was met with a wall of indifference. Of course it was difficult for her caring for the children. My dear Nou, we could not have managed without her. She never complained. At times I grew angry and frustrated with my wife, at what I sacrificed laboring day and night at menial jobs to support my family.

At my first job in Minneapolis, I loaded towels and sheets into washing machines and dryers in the basement of the big hotel downtown from five in the afternoon until three in the morning. The smell of detergent and bleach saturated the hot, steamy air. A woman from Mexico helped with the laundering while two others from Puerto Rico ironed and folded the linens. They talked to each other in Spanish all night. Their chatter, like birds chirping in a tree, blended with the whirling and chugging of the machines.

I registered in ESL classes at the adult school, and no matter how tired I was, I went to class. I studied the lessons while I waited for loads of laundry to finish. At home I listened carefully to the television and practiced with Nou when time allowed. After eight months, I made an appointment with Mr. Bryant, the hotel manager, and in my rudimentary English I asked him to consider me for other positions. He brushed me off. But I went back every week for a month until at last he said he'd give me a try as a busboy in the coffee shop. The pay was the same, but I got a small share of the tips. For six months I worked the early shift, pouring coffee and water, clearing dishes, and stacking plates in the buffet line. Once more I made my case to Mr. Bryant. I moved to security for $1.50 an hour more. All night I walked the property with my two-way radio and flashlight in snow and rain or the heat of summer.

Six months after we arrived, social services canceled our food stamps. Mrs. Robinson said that now I was earning a steady income, we no longer qualified. But my salary barely paid the rent. In the want ads I found a second job washing dishes at the Thai Palace restaurant, not too far from the hotel. The owner, Mr. Tongkao, had come from Thailand ten years before. He understood the difficulties of starting a new life in America. When my hours at the hotel shifted, he made accommodations for me. I moved up to busboy and then waiter.

Every day I showed up at my jobs and did the tasks asked of me, even though they were women's work, things I would never have done in Laos. I was an educated man doing laundry and washing dishes, but I overlooked the humiliation and never complained.

Yer laughed at something Kia said and glanced my way. Her eyes were warm and inviting. I sighed. Nothing was easy for any of us. We all floundered to find our feet on this unstable land. I dedicated myself to work hard and promised myself it would get better. And for a long time I believed this.

Chapter 12
NOU

Tou slammed down the door of the truck bed and glared at me as he lifted the leaf blower onto his back. At the end of the first week of summer vacation he was not happy to be edging lawns and blowing leaves. He had planned on playing water polo at the YMCA and softball with the church team. But Uncle Shone had tripped over a hose and broken his knee cap and lay in bed with a full leg cast. For the past three years Uncle and Father had been driving to the suburbs six days a week, shoveling snow in winter and tending gardens the rest of the year for ten hours a day. Father had his driver's license now, but with sixty-two weekly customers, he could not handle the work alone. Tou and I, twelve and thirteen now, were recruited to fill in until Uncle Shone healed. Blia and Mee had been excused as they were taking summer school classes. I was just as happy not to have them. They would only ignore me like they always did, and Blia would have complained about doing the slightest bit of work.

I was free to help out because Mother had improved. Her headaches came less frequently since she had given birth to my brother Nao a few months before. Auntie Yer kept her company almost every day. She brought along Auntie Kia's boys John and

Adam and took it upon herself to keep Mother from slipping away. Mornings they went on outings to the park or market with Nao tied to Mother's back and the six other children marching down the sidewalk in order of height, holding hands, looking like a flock of baby ducks. On Tuesday and Thursday afternoons Mother and Auntie joined the Hmong sewing group at St. Paul's parish hall to stitch and gossip. Two teenage girls kept the young children busy while the women made quilts and purses to sell at crafts fairs or new clothes for the New Year's celebrations.

Working with Father was a welcome treat, an escape from my chores at home. As we drove back and forth to jobs and ate lunch under a tree, I had time to talk with him, to share the books I was reading and the things I had learned at school. I loved being outdoors all day in the haven of spacious homes and gardens along clean, tree-lined streets.

The first few years in Minneapolis my family and I had watched television, mesmerized by images of beautiful homes and happy families. These families had smiling white faces and ate barbecued dinners on their patios. They played board games and laughed around dining room tables. They drove expensive new cars to the beach or camping in the mountains or to a wondrous place called Disneyland where cartoons came to life. Nothing about my life remotely resembled this world, not our cramped apartment in a crowded, dirty building, the multi-colored faces of our neighbors, or the fear that pervaded the rough, noisy streets. I wanted to know where this television world was, if these people and places really existed in America. The day Uncle Shone and Father took my cousins and me in our new truck to hand out flyers for their business, I discovered this other world. It was only a twenty minute drive away. This was the life I wanted.

On this Friday, we worked in a neighborhood I had not seen before. The homes were grander than any of the others all week. Our second stop was an enormous two-story Dutch colonial painted white with dark green shutters and lush gardens of brilliant green lawn, banks of flowering azaleas, and beds awash in a profusion of pinks and purple and white. Father gave me instructions to start on the flower bed that wrapped around a maple tree in the middle of the front yard. I sat down on the soft, damp grass and worked my trowel into the dirt, pulling up weeds and snapping off faded blooms from snap dragons and pansies. The air was still and quiet.

Across the street a woman in a blue suit, carrying a brown leather briefcase and a beige purse over her shoulder, walked down the driveway, her high heels clicking on the cement. She climbed into a sleek silver sedan and drove away. Next door the garage door opened, and a man driving a two-seater convertible backed out. The car was squat and rounded on the ends. I thought it looked like a shiny red beetle.

Tou, standing nearby fiddling with the blower, let out a low whistle. His eyes followed the car as the driver revved the engine and roared down the street. He was obsessed with cars, checking out every book he could find from the school library. For his birthday, he had begged his parents to pay for a subscription to Car and Driver magazine.

Tou and I had little in common as we stretched into adolescence. He'd become moody and distant and was embarrassed to be seen with his sister or Blia and me. He spent his time with a group of boys from the church youth program, shooting baskets at the park or taking the bus downtown to wander the streets. He liked to swear a lot around his friends, as if it made him seem older. Auntie Kia and Uncle Shone let him do whatever he wanted.

Tou turned on the blower and swept leaves and fallen blossoms from between the bushes and across the lawn, shattering the peace. I finished with the flower bed and found Father in back mowing the lawn. The rear of the house had two sets of sliding doors that opened onto the patio from the big modern kitchen with a counter and stools that divided it from a family room with a fireplace, sofa, chairs, and a huge television. The patio, dotted with chaise lounges, a barbecue, and table and chairs, spread around the rectangular swimming pool. The aqua blue water shimmered in the early morning light. A tricycle and a small bicycle with training wheels sat in the corner of the patio, and in the back corner of the lawn was a sandbox and set of swings.

A wave of envy washed over me. This family had everything I could ever dream of. I tried to picture my family living in this house, my little sisters and brothers riding the bikes, playing in the sandbox, all of us swimming in the pool. Mother would surely plant the yard with vegetables. But the image didn't fit. We didn't belong here.

Father gave me his clippers. I attempted to trim the box hedge along the right side of the yard, but the clippers were heavy and awkward to use. Two girls about my age, still in their flowered cotton pajamas, stepped outside through the sliding glass doors. One had short brown hair, the other a blond ponytail, and both were pink cheeked and pretty. The blond grabbed a book off the patio table. They looked at me and giggled, then hurried inside. The sliding door shut with a loud bang, and the lock snapped into place. A hot flush crept up my neck and cheeks. I wanted to hide under the hedge so they wouldn't see me in my worn, faded shorts and t-shirt. I tried to focus on the clippers, but I couldn't keep myself from looking over. They sat on the stools at the kitchen counter with bowls and a box of cereal, huddled together over the book, sharing secrets and laughing. I wanted to know what they were reading, what they were saying, how they thought and felt with nothing before them but a lazy summer day by the pool. The dark haired girl glanced up and our eyes met. She lifted her hand with a self-conscious, awkward wave and smiled.

I wanted so badly to be these girls. Every year I became more embarrassed of my Hmong heritage and our family's shabby life, but then ashamed of myself for these feelings. If only I could start again somewhere else. Become another person.

The school bus stopped and three white girls got on. I recognized the two with long, bleached blond hair from my gym class. The third girl was tall and heavyset and had dyed the top of her spiky hair purple. She wore purple lipstick to match. I had seen them at lunch hanging out with a group of black guys from the south side gang. These girls wore tight, revealing clothes and oozed a sexuality that made me blush. Their eyelids sparkled with emerald green and teal blue eye shadow layered over lashes caked in mascara. I stared out the window, avoiding their eyes as they came down the aisle. I had learned never to invite trouble. The girls plopped down on seats several rows behind me. Their voices carried through the half-full bus as they gossiped about a friend who thought she was pregnant but didn't know who the father was.

I had to ride the bus alone to the high school. My cousins had another year at the junior high. At least the bus was better than walking twelve blocks through the worst part of town where drunks slept in the doorways of boarded-up businesses next to porn shops and bars. Groups of kids, headed for school, strutted down the street with their boom boxes blasting, pushing and shoving, looking for a fight.

I pulled *The Outsiders* from my backpack. We were reading it for freshman English class, although I had already read it twice the summer before. I cried every time Johnny died. The book had prompted heated discussions in class with kids who normally didn't read the assignments and sank into their chairs, hoping to remain anonymous. Even though the story was set in another era and place, it resonated with us all. Our school was rife with gangs, vying for turf and terrorizing everyone else who lived in their wake. I learned the finer distinctions by listening to girls bragging in the bathrooms about boyfriends and brothers. The gangs divided up by race-- blacks, Polish, Mexicans, Vietnamese, and Puerto Ricans--depending on neighborhoods and family alliances. Even a handful of Hmong boys had formed a gang. The school district had hired two security guards to patrol the halls and break up fights that erupted without warning. The vice-principal conducted random locker searches each week, unearthing drugs, knives, and guns. The second week of school, a girl had been knifed in the bathroom for going out with another girl's boyfriend.

I dreaded each day, afraid and lonely as I walked through a field laden with bombs waiting for one to go off. I kept my eyes down and avoided large groups that gathered in the halls or lunch room. I had met a Hmong girl named Ma in my French class. Sixteen years old, she had come to the states the year before and spoke very little English. I felt sorry for her. We gravitated together like inmates in a prison, eating lunch in the back corner of the courtyard. But all she talked about was her life in the refugee camp as if she might be returning soon. There had been a boy she wanted to marry, but now she might never see him again. My memories of Ban Vinai had faded, and my only reality lay in how to survive the present. When the weather turned cold, I escaped to the library and the familiar comfort of books.

Behind me, one of the girls said her boyfriend had been arrested for selling dope and would probably get sent back to youth detention. Without thinking, I turned to see who was speaking.

The purple hair stared at me, holding my gaze and making my breath catch in my throat. "What are you lookin at?"

One of the blonds curled her lip in a sneer. "She's one of those gooks." She raked her bangs with fingernails painted blue and sparkling with little gold stars. "Mind your own business."

I spun around, my heart beating. Big puffy flakes of snow drifted down, sticking to the window in tiny crystal patterns, coating the sidewalks and cars with a fine white silt, covering over the poverty and desperation. But it could not cover my despair at the thought of suffering through four years at this high school. Green and red Christmas lights blinked on and off in the window of a pawn shop, the glass painted with a Santa Claus and the words, *Get Cash for Christmas.*

In August Uncle Boua and the rest of our family had finally arrived in America. The brother of Chor's wife Lia had succeeded in processing paperwork for their immigration. They were living temporarily with Lia's brother in a place called Sacramento, California. Phone calls buzzed back and forth every week. Then Father and my uncles would huddle together discussing possibilities. At first the plan was to bring them to Minneapolis as soon as another apartment was available. But one evening in October, Father told me there was a chance, just a chance, we might move to Sacramento. The money saved for our family's immigration could be used now to lease farmland. It all depended on whether they could get the right price. Uncle Boua said the land was very fertile. And it didn't snow in Sacramento.

Ever since I had been lighting incense and leaving offerings on the altar in our apartment as I prayed to my ancestors. For good measure, I stopped in St. Paul's several afternoons to light candles on the altar where a statue of a beautiful woman gazed down with a kind and sympathetic smile. I needed a miracle. Just the word California sent me dreaming. I knew what it was like from watching the shows on television. California was Disneyland and golden beaches, big homes, palm trees, and brilliant blue skies. Beautiful blond men and women ran through the waves along the shore. Everyone had a swimming pool and convertible car.

Through classes and homework, as I washed the dishes and tried to go to sleep, the allure of a new life dangled before me. My mind filled with improbable fantasies of transformations, schemes to reinvent myself. At fourteen, my optimism knew no bounds. Then, the idea came to me: I would take an American name. I would say goodbye to Nou, the timid, lonely Hmong girl who struggled to survive in Minneapolis.

I searched my favorite books and wrote out lists of names in my notebook, trying them on, listening to the rhythm as I said them out loud. I could be anyone I wanted. No one in California would know the difference.

Chapter 13
PAO

The first week of March 1988, we left Minneapolis for Sacramento. Uncle Boua and Chor had finally negotiated a deal to lease thirty acres of farmland, and we needed to arrive in time for the spring planting. The excitement and promise of a new life in California rippled through the family. I saw it in Yer when she sang to little Nao and in the way she laughed at Boa and Tong bouncing up and down on our bed. Nou showered me with questions. Where would we live? Where would she go to school? How big was Sacramento? How far away was the ocean?

We left behind little of consequence, only a small group of friends from the Hmong community center. Kia regretted leaving her job and friends at work. We sold the old pick up and bought a used van that seated nine. In a rented U-Haul truck we packed all our worldly belongings: two color TVs, a stereo and tape player, Uncle Boua's shaman tools, two wood tables, eight chairs, a sofa, three armchairs, five mattresses, a crib, two dressers, four boxes of pots and dishes, and ten garbage bags full of towels, blankets, and clothes. Kia, Tou, John, and Adam rode in the truck cab with Shone. I drove everyone else in the van. The younger children sat on laps and straddled two coolers full of food.

I gazed back at our apartment building one last time and pulled the van out into the street. If there were good memories to carry with me, they seemed too faint to remember. A seedy looking man in a torn jacket darted out from between two parked cars in the middle of the block. I had to throw on the brakes to avoid hitting him. He flipped me the finger. Goodbye Minneapolis.

Shone followed us down the freeway in the truck. A light veil of snow made the pavement icy and slowed our progress. The drive stretched through the flat, forested landscape of Minnesota and into South Dakota. Nou perched in the seat behind me and traced our progress on the map I had bought at the bookstore downtown, counting off the miles. We pulled off at rest stops to eat the food we had packed and to take short naps. The sun came out the second day as we reached Wyoming. That night we shared two rooms at a Motel 6 outside Jackson, sleeping on the beds and floors.

We had to put chains on the tires through part of Idaho and again as we crossed the Sierras. My hands gripped the wheel, shoulders hunched over, as the van swerved, the chains clicking and slapping against the icy asphalt. I had never driven in the mountains. The tension gathered in my neck until I had a wrenching headache. When we crossed the border from Nevada into California, we all cheered.

Somehow we made it without an accident or flat tire or breakdown. Late Thursday afternoon we arrived in Sacramento, coming out of the foothills onto the valley floor. The area was larger than I had expected with houses, shopping malls, and gas stations spreading in all directions. A gray drizzle spread from dark, tangled clouds to the glistening pavement. The windshield wipers beat a steady rhythm. We were almost there.

I pulled off at the exit and turned down the first street that ran parallel to the freeway. A group of rental storage sheds and a Budget Hotel lined the right side of the street. A gas station and convenience store sat on the left corner next to a vacant lot overgrown with weeds and garbage. Beyond this an electrical substation sprouted a string of transmission lines that headed off into the distance. Midway down the road we found our new home, the sole residence on the block, a two-story, rectangular structure made of crumbling plaster and concrete painted the color of dead leaves. Lia's brother had found the apartment building for us. It was a stroke of luck, Chor had said, and the rent very cheap. There were six units, all vacant, so the whole family could live together. Now I could see why the building had been empty. We piled out of the van and were hit by the roar of the freeway rising from behind the building. I wondered how we would ever sleep.

A door on the ground floor flew open. Chor, Lia, Uncle Boua, and Auntie Khou spilled out. We melted into a mass of hugs and tears, children racing in and out of the circle, tugging at our legs. We met Gia's new wife Ia and four little ones born since we had left Ban Vinai. We could hardly think of what to say, how to start after the years of separation. Words stuck in my throat with the strength of my emotions. Such joy. After six long years, our entire family was finally together and safe. Free. In California.

We picked our apartments and began unloading the truck, the children creating chaos as they raced up and down the stairs. Yer got busy scrubbing counters and wiping out cabinets in the kitchen as Auntie Khou unwrapped our box of dishes and pans.

We were clearing out coolers and trash from the van when Nou turned to Uncle Boua.

"Where is the ocean, Uncle?" she asked.

He looked surprised and shrugged. "It is far from here."

"But can I take the bus there?" Nou said, her forehead gathering in a frown.

"It would take several hours, I believe," Uncle said.

Her face fell as she let out a long sigh.

I smiled and put a hand on her shoulder. "One day soon, Nou, I will take you to see the ocean." My intentions were true. Someday. When we had time.

Chapter 14
NOU

The first week I watched and waited, observing the pace of my new school, the nuances of crowds that formed at lunch and after school. I recognized three Hmong boys immediately. They eyed me from the far side of the cafeteria where they huddled together on a bench, talking to a white boy with a crew cut and bad acne and a tall, skinny Hispanic kid. Would they give me away? I had no idea if the other Asian kids could recognize my features as distinctly Hmong. What amazed me was the way kids of different races mixed together. As if they didn't see the differences.

In this new life I wanted American friends, to sit with the popular girls at the lunchroom table, gossiping and giggling as the boys walked by. I spotted them right away, the chosen group, girls with long golden and auburn hair and pretty faces; girls with names like Emily and Molly who wore pressed jeans and gold hoop earrings. In the bathroom mirror at home, I could imitate them perfectly, smiling nonchalantly, tossing my hair over one shoulder, peeking out provocatively from slightly lowered eyes.

My experiences in Minneapolis had convinced me these girls would never accept someone with a past as troubled and different as mine, from a culture so foreign to their own. I created the story of my new life from the made-for-television movies my family and I had watched as we tried to absorb the American dream. I would use an American name and tell them I was from Minneapolis, my family Chinese-American. I convinced myself these were only half-lies that held elements of truth. After all, our Hmong ancestors had migrated from China to Laos two hundred years ago.

I needed an entrée, someone hovering on the periphery of the inner circle, welcomed some days and excluded others, depending on the leader's whim. It must be a girl who needed a friend as well. The redhead from my French and geometry classes sat with the popular crowd for four days, tentatively joining in the banter, laughing too easily at their jokes. On Friday, she arrived to find the table filled. She stood a few minutes, tall and gangly, shifting from one foot to the other, clutching her lunch. One of the girls glanced up with a thin smile and shrugged an unconvincing sorry.

I followed the redhead as she stomped through the noisy room and escaped outside, flopping down on the wooden bench that ran the length of the cafeteria, her endless legs folding like limp springs. Gray skies threatened rain. I pulled my denim jacket closer against the damp air, took a deep breath, and slipped quietly onto the bench a few feet away.

She pulled an apple from her brown paper bag and bit down sharply. After a minute, she turned to me with her clear blue eyes. "You're new."

My heart skipped a beat. "No." How could she know my real name? Then I realized. "I mean yes. I moved from Minneapolis."

"Oh." She tossed her half-eaten apple into the garbage can and searched her sack.

"California's okay. At least it's not snowing." I tried to sound friendly, but not desperate.

"It's not exactly sunny." She opened a bag of corn chips and stuffed three in her mouth.

"You should try Minneapolis in January."

I studied her heart-shaped face and tiny nose almost lost under the mass of freckles spreading like dirty rice across her cheeks. The bench burned hard and cold through my cotton pants, sending a shiver down my back. Her ski jacket looked warm.

I searched for something to say. "You're in French class."

"Yeah." She ran a hand through the wild tangle of red waves floating around her face and down her shoulders. "Oh my God, I'm completely lost in that class. Can you understand anything Mrs. Green says?"

I smiled. "Can you believe she wears that stupid beret like she's French or something?"

She let out a hearty laugh that drew stares from two boys walking by. Everything about her seemed untamed and slightly out of proportion. "You know anybody here?"

"Not exactly."

She scrunched her mouth to one side. "My best friend since second grade moved to Texas this summer. It's been a really shitty year." She crushed her lunch bag against the bench and slammed it into the trash can.

"I've seen you with friends."

"I wouldn't exactly call them friends. The girls here are total bitches, always talking behind your back."

I flinched. I never said words like shitty or bitches. "I know. It's like they think they're so much better, but they're really *stupid*."

She smiled and held out her bag of chips. "Want one?"

"Thanks."

"I have to go to my locker." She stood up, and my heart sank. "Wanna come?"

"Sure. I'm Laura." I offered the name with only the slightest hesitation.

Chapter 15
YER

Kinder spirits inhabited this new place. They brought good luck. Happier dreams returned. Our second year in Minneapolis, I started to dream of my boys again. But frightening, terrible dreams. I chased them through the forest. They ran ahead, always just out of reach, disappearing into the sounds of gunfire. Other times they were wounded, blood dripping down their bodies. I could not wake from this horror. But here in California, the boys came to me happy and well. We walked together in peaceful fields. I stood straight and strong. Young again.

Sacramento, California. The words grated harsh on my ears like all English words. I tried to form the sounds. But my tongue and lips could not find the tones. The children giggled at my efforts and slowly repeated the words. It was no use. I would never speak this strange language.

So wonderful was our new apartment. Even though it creaked and sagged with peeling paint and faded carpet the color of a soldier's uniform. It did not matter. Our apartment had two bedrooms so the children could be more comfortable. Our six families filled the complex like a small village. I spent every day with my sister-in-law and cousins, sharing the shopping and caring for little ones. A yard behind the building gave the children a safe place to play near where we kept chickens. No Americans lived near us. No one cast disapproving eyes or called us ugly names when we performed ceremonies and offered sacrifices to the other world.

My heart sang at the sight of my children preparing for school each morning, chattering nonsense and bouncing around like the little monkeys that played in the trees of Laos. Fear and worry left their faces, replaced by smiles. Every Saturday morning my daughter Houa, seven years old, babbled on. *When can I go back to school, Mother? I read another book and played jump rope yesterday. My teacher says I'm smart.*

And Nou, my oldest, finally could be young. Lightness lifted her step. A blush touched her cheeks. No mother should admit this, but she occupied a special corner of my heart for the suffering and burdens she had endured in her short life. Perfection came naturally to her–obedience and respect for elders, helpfulness with chores and caring for the younger children. What more could a mother ask for? No one would deny her beauty, the fair, smooth skin like the porcelain doll I had once seen on a Chinese trader's cart, and her delicate nose and chin, which came from my father. Her long black hair streamed down her back like a powerful waterfall. When my eyes gazed upon her, I felt a rush of pride and happiness. But I dared not speak these thoughts out loud and risk making the evil spirits jealous.

Her world opened wider every day. As we prepared the evening meals, words tumbled out. *You should see the school library, Mother. There are more books than you can imagine, and I want to read them all. Mrs. Lincoln, the librarian, is really nice and helped me find a book for my report on Greece. Today at school we had a pep rally. It's a kind of party to get kids excited about the basketball game. The band played and everyone cheered. It was fun. I have a new friend, Mary.*

I nodded and smiled as she spoke. But what could I answer? I had no knowledge of school and learning. I was not an educated woman. None of this made sense to me–her life at school, the friend she called on the phone each night. I could only say, *yes, Nou, I am glad.* Pao said our children needed school to be successful. But sometimes, a small edge caught in my chest. I did not know where this path would lead her.

The first morning I went to our land, I woke before first light. My heart raced, and my mind filled with all that must be done. I prepared a special soup with bitter melon and onions for breakfast and picked up the house. The younger children had to be dressed for school. Ia and cousin Yer took the babies that day.

Seven of us crowded into the van and drove fifteen minutes south. The air was cool, but the sun shone. Kia chatted with Auntie Khou about the big market that was opening at the shopping center across the freeway. Maybe she would try to get a job there. I listened and watched out the window. Hundreds of new houses, some still being built, spread out from the highway. Soon these gave way to open land. We passed over a muddy river that meandered slowly to the west. Ducks with shiny brown feathers swam through the reeds along the banks. Everything was green. Tall grass, dotted with yellow and pink wildflowers, grew among groves of giant oak trees and cottonwoods. Wisps of early morning fog drifted across the land and curled around trees. A man on a tractor was turning his field into long, even rows.

Shone turned the van onto a narrow road. After five minutes he pulled over. Here was our land, unkempt and abandoned, calling out for care. Beautiful land. Birds sang from the oleander bushes and willows that lined the borders, welcoming us. I walked into the rutted, overgrown field and crouched down, feeling almost shy, as if greeting an old friend I had not seen in many years. I dug my hands deep into the ground, grasping clumps of dirt. The soil crumpled into fine strands and ran through my fingers like silk caressing my skin. The loamy scent of earth and peppery weeds filled my nostrils until I could taste them on the back of my tongue. Tears welled in my eyes. At last, a place where I belonged.

I passed the day hoeing and weeding, pulling rocks and old roots from the dirt, careful not to hurt the squirming brown worms that tunneled in the soil. I hummed to myself, enjoying my solitude, relishing the warming sun and the ache in my back that grew each hour. The earth called to my soul and radiated life into my body. The loosened dirt was ready to receive tiny sprouts of squash, spinach, and beans, ready to breathe life into roots, to nourish and support healthy plants that would bear rich harvests. I would water and keep the weeds away. Shoo the bugs off and tie the vines to stakes. And in time I would pick the bounty of our labor. Once more I was useful.

PART III

Chapter 16
LAURA

The air in the courtroom grows heavier with each passing minute, warm with the vapor of sighs. Yet I shiver as Mrs. Hernandez stands up to address the judge. Her chair makes a small squeak of protest as it scrapes along the floor. Father does not turn to look. His shoulders hunch over once more, and I can feel his shame across the stretch of linoleum marking our division. Now the entire story will be repeated, splattered across the room for strangers to hear. I regret this public display. The years of suffering and sacrifice, the poverty and insults, have left each of us worn down. I am thankful my mother cannot understand and will only catch the few phrases that Uncle Boua deems worthy of translating. She sits in stony silence, her tears spent now, looking frail and vulnerable. Her obvious pain gives me greater pause than anything else.

Mrs. Hernandez is a plump, middle-aged Hispanic woman with soft brown eyes and curly auburn hair streaked with red highlights. From the beginning she has been kind and fair. She listened to my story and asked dozens of questions, trying to understand the sequence of events. I was impressed with her knowledge of the Hmong people and culture, her understanding of our history as refugees coming to

America from the war in Laos and struggling to adapt. She knew that many Hmong girls marry young and was familiar with the practice of kidnapping brides. It did not surprise her that my father and other men in the family would exert their will. Many conflicts from our community had come to her office in the past. She remained open in the meetings with Father and Uncle Boua as they raised their voices, attentive to their arguments, deflecting angry words, patiently explaining California's laws, until finally their intransigence brought her to her feet, and she declared the meetings over.

She puts on her reading glasses, narrow black frames that sit on the end of her nose, opens a manila file, and pulls out a single sheet of paper. After clearing her throat, she begins. "Your honor, I am Carmen Hernandez, the assigned social worker from Sacramento County Child Protective Services. Two weeks ago Laura Lee, seventeen years old, called our office and asked us to intervene on her behalf."

I glance back at Mary and her parents sitting in the row of chairs behind me. Mr. Shannon appears stiff and uncomfortable, his arms crossed over his middle. He gives me an almost imperceptible nod. This family has been my source of strength, my protection. He has been careful in his remarks to me, but I overheard discussions with Mary's mother where he raised his voice in outrage. Just like my father.

Mary has wrapped her arm through her mother's, resting her head on her shoulder. Her faced is pinched. Mrs. Shannon is the most composed among them. She has been handing me tissues and patting my arm with each new spate of tears.

I cannot get through this ordeal without them. It is because of this family that I found the courage to stand up for myself, to expect more of my life. I cannot help but wonder how things might have turned out differently if Mary had not become my best friend. If I had not chosen to take a separate path. Was this preordained? Would Father explain it as my fate written on my life passport? Or is it the consequence of my many, many lies, the ones I came to believe in?

My story continues. I cannot predict where it will take me, only that whatever happens, it will be of my choosing.

Chapter 17
LAURA

Rain dampened the promise of spring. Intermittent sunshine and occasional showers, breezy, almost warm April days, had succumbed to a week of gray skies and relentless downpours. I didn't mind. It meant Mother was not working in the fields and I didn't have to rush home from school to care for my five siblings.

Mary's mother drove us to their home, and we immediately retreated upstairs. Mary plopped down on the double bed in her room and hugged one of the rose colored throw pillows. Pajamas, a pair of jeans, a t-shirt, underpants, and a jacket lay strewn across the floor. A faint odor of sweaty socks mingled with the rose-scented cologne she always wore. She complained about her room with its flounced sheer curtains and wicker furniture. It's a little girl's room, she would say, wrinkling her nose.

But I adored the swirl of pink and lilac peonies fanning out across her comforter and the alternating smooth and rough textures of painted wicker under my fingertips. I longed for a bedroom like this, a place of my own, instead of sleeping on our living room floor on a lumpy mattress with my three sisters. Our tiny bathroom provided the only refuge where I could be alone, and invariably someone was banging on the door demanding to get in.

"Do you have lots of homework?" Mary asked.

"Only geometry. Want to do it?"

She made a face. "I hate geometry. Mr. Hopkins picks on me because he knows I don't get it."

"Maybe he's trying to help," I suggested. I wanted to tell her she would do better if she paid attention instead of daydreaming out the window. She was smart, but lacked the motivation to work hard. My father expected me to do well if I wanted to stay in school. I didn't have the luxury of being lazy or mediocre.

It still surprised me how naturally our friendship had evolved, how easily we slipped into each other's company. I loved her buoyant, guileless personality, her dramatic gestures and long rants on the injustices of life. I couldn't help but shed my shyness with her endless flow of chatter and the way she welcomed me unconditionally into her life. What surprised me most was how she accepted my explanations about my life and the many inconsistencies in my stories. She settled for simple answers, vague on details. If she asked where I lived, I waved in the general direction and said it wasn't as nice an area as hers. If she asked what I had done over the weekend, I answered with flippant remarks—*it was so boring, you don't even want to know*—and shifted the conversation back to her. I never really told big lies, only omitted certain facts or stretched the truth to let her draw her own conclusions. Surely she sensed my hesitation as I played with the ends of my hair and avoided her eyes.

Everything in Sacramento was different, more approachable. Unlike Minneapolis, kids at school mixed without attention to color or background. I could not identify the presence of gangs, and only occasional scuffles or rivalries broke out. Mary and I managed to drift among the group of girls who set the social pulse. If Mary demanded few details from me, these girls asked even less.

I leaned back into the rocking chair and glanced out the window. Rain poured off the eaves and flowed in tiny rivulets down the divided panes. A row of two-story houses, each slightly different in style, stretched down the quiet street, bordered by manicured lawns, azalea bushes dripping white and red blossoms, and flowers beds bursting into bloom. The neighborhood was not anywhere as grand as North Oaks near Minneapolis, but the homes were spacious and well tended, comfortable in a way that was not as intimidating.

The Shannons' house had airy rooms painted off-white and pale pastels, the luxury of four bedrooms and three baths, a family room and kitchen larger than our entire apartment. I marveled at the formal living room and dining room, spaces they only occasionally used. It was not stuffy or pretentious, but inviting, with hardwood floors and plush carpets, polished cherry and walnut furniture, shelves of books, a vase of fresh flowers on the entryway table, and photos of Mary and her brother on birthdays. Framed prints decorated the walls and mementos were scattered on end tables and shelves. A pile of magazines and half read books sat next to the leather recliner. A collection of music was piled on top of the baby grand piano. Our apartment had never had any of these things.

Mary put the pillow under her arm and propped herself up. "I forgot to tell you I saw Pete and Kevin in P.E." She raised her eyebrows up and down.

I smiled and shook my head. She obsessed over these boys, talking for hours about them, analyzing what they did or said, creating scenarios where one day they might discover us and fall madly in love. Her enthusiasm poured out unchecked by reality. They were the frivolous thoughts of a teenage girl who had everything she needed with no worries in the world. All I could do was laugh and play along, pretending to share her fantasies. But I fostered no illusions. There could never be a boy like Pete or Kevin in my life even if my parents allowed me to date, which they wouldn't. And certainly not someone who was not Hmong.

"I'm so excited about Jenny's party. Pete and Kevin are coming."

I lowered my eyes to the arm of the rocking chair and played with a loose piece of wicker. I dreaded telling her. The night before, I had finally gathered the nerve to talk with Father about the party. When he asked if there would be boys attending, I had answered truthfully. He shook his head. His decision was final. I had been foolish to hope his answer would be anything different.

"What're you going to wear?" Mary jumped up and opened her closet door, pulling out a new top.

I surveyed the overflowing rack of clothes and shoes. I had nothing to wear to a party anyway. There were some aspects of my life I could not finesse. My entire wardrobe consisted of a pair of jeans, one pair of black pants, three faded t-shirts, a red blouse, a white pullover sweater, a denim jacket, and a pair of black tennis shoes, fraying at the toes, all purchased from thrift stores. Surely Mary and the other girls had noticed. I asked Father for money to buy more clothes, but he had nothing to spare. He said I should worry about my studies instead.

"I'll have to ask my parents," I said softly, "but I don't think I can go."

Her mouth fell open. "Why not?"

"It's Tommy's sixth birthday. We're having a family party." When I spoke to Mary about my siblings, I gave them American names.

"I thought your brothers were one and two."

I forced a laugh; a sick feeling spread through my middle. "I have three brothers. I guess I didn't count the baby because, well, he's just a baby."

Over the weeks my convoluted stories had mounted one upon another like a tower of wooden blocks. I felt I might topple at any moment from the weight of my secrets, trying to keep straight the lies I had spoken to Mary and my family. I had not told my parents that I was using the name Laura at school. Lots of Hmong children had American names, even my younger cousins. But Father could be old fashioned, and I did not want to risk his displeasure. I had larger offenses to hide. My parents had no idea that I spent afternoons and sometimes Saturdays with Mary. I pretended to be at the library studying, the only excuse that got me out of chores at home or working in the fields.

I lay on my mattress at night, listening to the roar of trucks and cars speeding down the freeway, as I agonized over how to disassemble the complicated puzzle I had constructed. What frightened me most was the possibility that Mary might discover the truth about me before I could find a way to tell her. I had never had a friend like this, someone outside my family and the tightly woven Hmong community, someone who trusted me with her every thought. Together we navigated the slippery path of high school. She bolstered my flagging confidence. I couldn't survive without her.

"Maybe you can come to the party a little late," Mary said, hanging the top back in the closet. "I could wait and go with you."

"I doubt it. But I'll ask."

Her eleven-year-old brother Justin stuck his head in the door. "Mom says to tell you she has cookies." A wicked grin spread across his face. "You left this in the bathroom." He pulled one of Mary's bras from behind his back and dangled it in her direction.

"Give me that, you little shit."

"I'm telling Mom what you said." He threw the bra across the room and slammed the door shut.

Mary threw a pillow. "I hate him!"

It shocked me the way Mary and Justin fought, the language she used with him. I still carried the guilt of the angry, hateful words I had blurted out to my cousin Ger many years ago, the words I could never take back before he died. And while my brothers and sisters were noisy and underfoot, a constant drain on my time as I tried to do chores or study or sleep, I loved them. My family was precious to me. Perhaps if Mary understood what it was like to lose a brother or cousin, she would act differently.

Mary grabbed a clip and pulled her hair back. "Come on. Let's go downstairs."

Mary's mother, Nancy, stood in the kitchen transferring a batch of chocolate chip cookies from the pan onto a rack. She wore jeans and a sweatshirt. Her light brown hair, streaked with blond highlights, was pulled into a ponytail. She was always friendly and cheerful with us, so young and vibrant compared to my mother.

Mary and I settled on stools at the breakfast bar that divided the kitchen and family room. The sweet fragrance of chocolate made my mouth water in anticipation. I had never tasted freshly baked cookies until I came to this house. Sweets like this were not part of our Hmong cooking. The parents at my schools in Minneapolis were too busy surviving on welfare checks or eking out a living from minimum wage jobs to bake cookies for our classrooms. If anyone bothered to bring holiday treats, it was a package of Oreos or Animal Crackers.

Nancy smiled. "How did school go?"

"Same old boring stuff," Mary said.

"And math?"

"Terrible."

"Dad can help you after dinner." Nancy took a plate from the cupboard, filled it with cookies, and placed it on the counter. "Heaven knows I'm hopeless with geometry."

"My point exactly," Mary said. "How can you expect me to do it?"

Nancy laughed as she placed glasses of milk before us. She came around and took the stool next to Mary.

"I had three referrals from County Services and they all need help immediately." Nancy explained to me that sometimes she took cases from the county in her private practice as a family counselor.

"Tell them you're too busy," Mary said.

"They have serious problems, honey. I want to help. But I want to be home after school too."

"Oh, Mom, Justin and I are old enough to take care of ourselves." Mary made a face of exasperation. "You treat us like babies."

Nancy put an arm around Mary's shoulders and kissed her cheek. "Before we turn around, you'll be going to college. And Justin's not far behind."

The warmth between Mary and her mother created a yearning inside me. Such intimacy with my mother seemed impossible. On television families hugged and kissed, fought, and talked about their feeling. This was not the Hmong way. My parents had not demonstrated any affection since I was a small child. It was understood they loved me. My mother and I had never spoken of that night crossing the Mekong River or the loss of my brothers. We never acknowledged her dark moods. We never shared our sorrow. At times she seemed grateful for my presence and the care I gave her, but it was as if she had erected a barrier that I could never breach. Over the years the distance grew. I didn't understand why she could not stop for a few minutes from whatever task filled her attention and listen, really hear what I had to say, and ask questions, be interested, or at least offer words of encouragement. Instead she glanced at me with a face clouded with doubts. The only things we shared each day were the details of cooking, cleaning, and caring for my sisters and brothers.

"The cookies are great. Thank you." I licked a stray morsel of chocolate from my finger.

Nancy went to the sink and rinsed her glass. She peered out the window at the rain. "It's really coming down. I can take you home, Laura, when you are ready."

"That's okay. I'll take the bus. My mother's expecting me soon."

"I don't want you standing in this rain."

"You could drop me at the library."

Mary looked puzzled. "I thought you had to go home."

"I do, but I need a book for my history report," I said quickly.

Nancy walked over and patted my arm. "Whatever you want."

Rain pounded on the roof, echoing my lies.

It was Father's birthday. I stood at the sink washing the left over breakfast dishes, slowly wiping a soapy rag over bowls, plates, and spoons. The sounds of idle chatter filled our kitchen as we crowded together in the tiny space, barely able to move. Mother chopped and sliced peppers, lemon grass, cilantro, and mustard greens with practiced and precise strokes. Water boiled in a pot as Auntie Khou cut pork into cubes and her daughter-in-law, Ia, prepared rice in the electric steamer. We would celebrate with a family dinner.

I glanced at Father relaxing in the living room, watching television on the sofa he had purchased the week before at the used furniture store. A musty smell came from the scratchy plaid fabric covering the sagging cushions. I thought of the sectional couch in Mary's family room upholstered in plush velour the color of the sky at dusk. I loved to run my fingers over the soft, pliant nap and watch the blue turn from light to dark and back. Everything about our living room was different, from the mattresses stacked in the far corner to the wood altar mounted on the wall with its bowl of incense where we left offerings and prayed to our ancestors. The floor of our apartment shook when we walked across the room, and the paper-thin walls carried voices from next door. Strips of ancient yellow paint lay exposed underneath a coat of muddy beige.

The conversation in the kitchen turned to the cotton material Auntie Yer had bought on a discount table at the fabric store. I half listened as I thought about the homework I still needed to complete. I would ask Father to help me with my French.

My uncles came in, freshly showered after work, and joined my father in the living room with bottles of beer. Mother turned to me. "Nou, get the children." We would eat in shifts, the men first and then the children and women.

As I turned to leave, Ia took a deep breath and sank onto one of the plastic chairs around our table. "I can't stand any longer," she sighed, wiping sweat from her forehead and stretching out her legs. Her enormous belly, her third pregnancy, engulfed her tiny frame. Her ankles were swollen double, and her sweet face lined with dark circles under her eyes, making her appear much older than her eighteen years. We all worried. She had lost her last baby at five months.

I stopped to fill a glass with cold water and handed it to her. She had only been sixteen when she married Gia and first became pregnant, not unusual in the refugee camp in Thailand or in Laos. But here, now, I could not imagine myself married and pregnant within a year. I wondered if she was content, if she did not see more in her future beyond family and household tasks.

From the balcony that ran the length of the second floor, I leaned on the metal railing and gazed down the street. The late afternoon sun cast shadows off the electrical towers onto our parking lot. My cousins Blia and Mee came out of the Fast Stop half a block away, strolling down the street as they gnawed on long ropes of red licorice. Auntie Yer always gave Blia money for treats, and she grew heavier every year. In contrast, Mee looked like a tiny sparrow with skinny legs, a narrow face, and intense dark eyes that darted nervously around, taking everything in.

An old Cadillac with a dark blue hood and rusty burgundy body waited at the curb to pull out of the gas station onto the street. The engine rattled and strained to stay alive, as black smoke puffed out the tailpipe. The car started up and a series of explosions burst through the air. The terror was instant and visceral. Flashes of dark, tangled jungles filled my mind with the echoes of machine guns and bullets, popping and whizzing past my ears. I found myself crouching down on the porch, my arms over my head, my heart pounding. After a few moments I stood, shaking, and felt my way down the stairs.

"Man, did you hear that?" Mee said, as they raced up.

I tried to reconcile the logical cause of the noise with my violent reaction. "It was that car." I pointed in the direction of the Cadillac, now speeding round the corner at the end of the street.

"I thought the Fast Stop was being held up again," Blia said, lifting her hair off the back of her neck, her moon-shaped face relaxing. "Where're you going?"

"To get the kids for dinner."

Blia made a face. "I forgot, we have to come to your place tonight. It's so boring. Same old talk and nothing to do."

I shrugged. She was right, but my father deserved a celebration for his birthday.

Blia turned to Mee. "We can sneak out after dinner and go down to my place to listen to some music." As usual, the invitation didn't include me.

I walked around to the small yard, separated from the freeway by a high cement block wall where the incessant whine of wheels on asphalt poured over the top. I smiled at the site of my sisters and brothers playing with their cousins, a noisy, unruly brood. The older boys were kicking a soccer ball across the sparse patch of lawn. The girls were jumping rope, chanting rhymes in sync with the twirling rope, giggling when they missed the beat and tripped. The younger children had turned on the hose to mold mud into small patties. I found my brother Nao at the center of this group, his chubby little fingers covered in muck. I envied them such simple pleasures.

149

"Come to dinner," I called out, squatting down next to Nao. He pointed with great delight to his efforts. "Good work, Nao," I said. He beamed as I lifted him, his weight pulling at my shoulders.

It took two more reminders before everyone clambered up the stairs. I followed with Noa, laughing as he patted his nose with his muddy fingers.

The men finished their dinner and continued drinking as the women ate. The apartment filled with boisterous exchanges of jokes and laughter and birthday wishes for father. The younger children played and pushed and shoved until they were sent out back again. The women retreated to the kitchen to wash dishes and gossip. When my cousins abandoned me to listen to music at Blia's, I pulled out my homework.

Father and the other men talked about crop prices and markets, nothing to catch my attention. But I looked up from my math book when Chia said he had had a call from a clan leader. They wanted more contributions to send additional arms and supplies to the faltering resistance in Laos. The fighters' numbers had been reduced to almost nothing, and they remained trapped deep in the forests. Father sighed and said nothing would change, that it would be better to get them out of the country and stop their slow starvation and slaughter by government troops. Everyone grew quiet. Only Uncle Boua still spoke occasionally of returning to Laos. For the others that dream had faded long ago. Uncle Soua cleared his throat and reminded everyone that we had many blessings in our new life. We could not abandon those left behind no matter how hopeless the cause. Uncle Shone agreed and offered to take care of the matter.

The evening ended after ten o'clock with sleeping children hauled to their beds and tipsy men weaving down the hall and stairs to their apartments. I asked Father if he was too tired to help me with my French translation.

He shook his head, "I am fine."

We sat at the dining room table, and I opened the book. Father smelled of beer and cigarette smoke as he leaned over and studied the pages. His face was relaxed, his eyes drooped. I wondered if he was too drunk to decipher the words. Once his lids closed, and I thought he was asleep, but then he sat up and smiled.

"I was thinking of how difficult learning French seemed when I started at school in Vientiane. I was not such a hard worker like you. I have almost forgotten those days." He slowly nodded his head as if lost in another place. "Everything seemed possible then." He looked at me. "You are doing well, Nou."

It was the first direct complement my father had ever given me, and I blushed with pleasure, staring down at the paper. When we finished, I placed my homework carefully in my notebook. "Happy birthday," I said, embarrassed at the inadequacy of my words to express my love and gratitude for all that he did every day in good times and bad.

He stood up unsteadily. His voice grew thick. "Laos is only a memory. You are our future, Nou." He walked behind me, running his hand gently down my hair, the only way he knew to tell me that he loved me.

Once again, I felt ashamed of my lies. Would he be as proud of me if he knew I used a different name at school and pretended to be someone else other than his daughter?

Chapter 18
PAO

We looked like a line of ants, marching to the truck at the end of the field with our bulging bags, depositing our loads and trotting back to start again. Almost the entire family angled down the rows, furiously picking red tomatoes and shiny green and yellow peppers from vines that spilled and strained over the supports. Ears of corn with yellow silk peeked out from the top of pale green husks. A distributor had ordered twenty-five boxes of each to be delivered to the warehouse at the end of the day. The younger children packed and stacked the boxes while the rest of us gathered the vegetables. Any extra would be sold from the back of our truck the next day at the farmer's market downtown.

I could not help but admire the bounty of our crops, the delicious bouquet of lush ripe tomatoes and pungent leaves, the snap of crisp stems between my fingers. We had been up at five and in the fields as a spray of pink and gold light painted the horizon. Now the July sun beat down, searing the edges of leaves yellow and sucking water from the damp soil, turning it into clots under my shoes. It was only ten in the morning and already close to 90 degrees. No cooling breezes drifted up the delta sloughs. My shirt clung to my back drenched with sweat. Dried out grasses, dandelions, thistle, and mustard sagged in the untended field beyond ours, and in the fenced pasture next to this a dozen cows huddled in the shade of two oak trees, twitching their tails, sending swarms of flies into the air. A brown hawk, dappled with white spots and a black tail, circled lazily overhead. A chorus of songbirds, fluttering between shady branches, stirred the leaves of the cottonwoods to the south. I could hear only a faint hum from the freeway a mile away.

That first season we learned the ways of farming the rich soil of the Sacramento Valley, so different from our steep mountainsides in Laos. We had struggled to survive there as our crops leached nutrients from the land and monsoon rains eroded the thin layer of dirt. Every five or seven years we were forced to move our village to till fresh fields. But here we did not have these problems and could replant year after year. Other Hmong at the Community Center shared their experience and told us about advisors at the Farm Bureau and university agricultural services. Many resources were available to help us find success. We soon discovered where to rent machines that turned the earth into neat even rows in a fraction of the time it took us to do it by hand. We got recommendations on plant varieties that thrived in the valley soil and climate and learned how to irrigate and fertilize. Not everyone in the family embraced these new ways. We still did many tasks by hand, pulling weeds, picking off insects and leaves mottled with mold or disease. Yet, we were all happy to be working the land again.

Shortly after we arrived in Sacramento I had been lucky to find a position translating at the Hmong Community Center that paid more than I had earned in Minneapolis. Chor, Gia, and I worked full time to keep the family fed as we waited to harvest our crops. After work and weekends I joined the others in the fields until the light began to fade. Our labor had begun to pay off. We would plant a second round of crops in the fall for winter harvest.

Yer headed down the row next to me with her empty bag, humming to herself and smiling. A new contentment had settled over her since we had arrived in Sacramento. She talked of nothing but working in the fields and the progress of the plants she tended, as if they too were her children. At times her mind drifted, distracted by something unseen, but she remained with us. And I was grateful.

A sassy blue jay with shimmering, long tail feathers swooped down, squawking at us as if we were intruding in his home. Yer looked up, mumbling something in response.

I spied Nou gathering peppers on the other side of the field, her shoulders stooped, her face hidden under a straw hat. All morning she had kept apart, her discontent hovering about her like the swarms of fruit flies rising up from overripe tomatoes. It still startled me when I turned to her expecting an awkward, quiet child with gangly legs, one who delighted in telling me about the latest book she had read, the paper she had written for school, or a funny thing her little sister had said. I remembered the daughter who had wanted nothing more than to spend an afternoon at the public library with her father and had patiently corrected his English, always careful not to offend. Instead, now I found Nou transformed into a beautiful young woman on the brink of her own life. It seemed to happen overnight.

She had adapted well to the new school and remained dedicated to her studies, spending hours at the library. I was proud of her diligence and good grades. Yet since the move to California, she had grown guarded and aloof, no longer sharing her thoughts. She still turned to me for help with school work and in this purpose we shared a bond. But there were other changes I did not care for, as if she were imitating the other teenagers here. She monopolized the bathroom each morning, fussing with her hair and clothes. Once, Yer caught her putting on makeup after I had forbidden it. She asked me several times for money to buy new clothes, her disappointment and even resentment apparent when I explained our limited income could not be stretched any further. I worried she would forget to honor our culture and past. Sometimes she replied sharply to her mother's requests for help around the house and protested about working in the fields every weekend and during the long summer days. These things would never have happened in Laos.

When she acted badly, I tried to temper my anger. She shouldered many responsibilities on top of school from an early age. She had never failed me when Yer abandoned us to her darkness, taking over without a word. Everything was a balancing act in America, a struggle of hard work and changing expectations. We were all drawn to the constant promise of more. I told myself this teenage behavior would pass without harm. I focused on the hope for my children to complete their education, not be denied this chance as I had been. Even though the girls would marry and leave us, their education would lead to a better life. Nou was bright, a special girl. She set an example for the others. But as the weeks and months passed, my worries over Nou worked at the back of my mind with an unease I could not shake, like a shadow growing longer in the late afternoon. Sometimes an image of her tumbling into the waters of the Mekong River, all those years ago, sprang up without warning. Once again I felt her slipping from my grasp.

A week later I returned from visiting with Uncle Boua in the early evening and found Yer at the dining room table sewing a story-cloth of village life in Laos to sell at a store that marketed Hmong crafts. The apartment was unusually quiet and calm. Our young ones were engrossed in some television show.

"Where are the girls?" I asked.

"Moua and Houa are in the bedroom drawing, and Nou has gone to her friend's house."

I sat down opposite Yer and lit a cigarette, glad for a moment of peace with my wife.

Yer looked up, her brows knitting together. "Nou is with these friends too much. Four nights this past week. They are pulling her away from her family."

"Sometimes I feel this too, but she is a good girl. She does well in school."

Yer shook her head. "The girls she meets, they cannot be good. You have heard the way she talks to me. This is not the Hmong way."

Yer echoed my own concerns. Young girls in Laos remained obedient and respectful of their elders. They did not talk back. I let out a long sigh. "I will speak to her. But it is hard for all of us. Things are different here."

Yer's eyes narrowed. I had touched a raw spot. She had never wanted things to be different, to adapt to an American life, to learn English. Many of the older Hmong refugees I met through the community center shared this attitude. To accept the present, to change their ways, meant relinquishing all hope of returning to Laos. No matter how far they traveled, despite the terrible memories, all they desired was that simple existence they had once known. I understood that, but we could not live in the past forever. I suspected that Yer's refusal to give up her dream of Laos was tied to the loss of our boys. I thought she believed they were waiting for her there, alive and happy. I could never be sure what confused thoughts wandered through her mind in the lost hours of her sickness. Many times I had asked Uncle Boua to use his shaman powers to help balance her souls again. But his efforts brought only temporary relief. Always I remained careful in how I spoke to her and the subjects I brought up, not wanting to risk setting her off again.

Yer's voice softened. "It is time to think about a husband for Nou."

My breath caught in my throat at the suggestion. "She is too young."

Yer gave me a sly smile. "Only a year younger than when I married you."

"That was Laos. Here she must have an education first. Maybe in a few years, when she is finished with high school."

"Your heart is too soft when it comes to Nou," she scoffed. "If we do not marry her soon, it will be too late. Boys do not want a girl who is too smart. And she is getting too many big ideas of her own."

"It will be fine." I took a long draw on my cigarette and flicked the ashes into a bowl. But in my heart, I worried she would go astray.

"You are busy with work and the farm accounts. You must take time to ask more questions. Find out where she is going, what she is doing. She does not listen to me anymore." Yer put down her sewing and leaned close. "Maybe she doesn't always tell the truth."

I frowned and stubbed out my cigarette. Surely Nou would not lie, but a seed of doubt had already taken root in my mind. I must remind Nou of the importance of family and traditions. She would listen to her father and understand. She was my pride, my dear child. I could not let her fall away from us.

Chapter 19
LAURA

 I sat at the dining room table with Mother and my sisters. Our one air conditioner, mounted in the living room window, droned incessantly in a vain attempt to cool the suffocating air. Sweat dampened my shorts and t-shirt and formed beads on the plastic chair where my thighs rested. That second day of September, the temperature had soared to over one hundred degrees, and the evening brought little relief.

We were sewing new outfits for the New Year's celebration in late November. For me it represented endless hours of tedious effort completing intricate designs on jackets, skirts, blouses, sashes, vests, aprons, and trousers. Mother did the majority of the work. It was her favorite task, her labor of love for her family. She cherished this rite of passage between generations, the opportunity to teach us her secrets. I admired her fine stitches and artful combinations of patterns and colors, but I had no talent or interest in following her craft. After picking tomatoes and eggplant all day, my fingers felt stiff and unnatural grasping the needle.

I had nowhere else to go. My parents had grounded me for the last two weeks of summer vacation because I had come home over an hour late one night. Even the phone was off limits.

"It's too hot," I said, putting down my needlework and wiping my hands on my shorts. I spread out my blue and green sash on the table for Mother to see. I had used reverse appliqué and embroidery in a traditional snail-shell pattern to show connections to family, my feeble attempt to appease her.

She inspected the stitches and frowned. "Maybe add a yellow loop around the side."

Moa held out her neat stitching, much cleaner than mine, for Mother to critique. "Do you like the mustard flowers?" she asked, wanting nothing more than to please Mother, to do it perfectly.

"Yes." Mother smiled. "Maybe a little smaller here, like this." She demonstrated by running several tiny, perfectly even stitches through Moa's cloth.

I picked through Mother's basket of threads. "Do you think I should use this thread or the brighter one?" I asked, sounding like Moa, begging for reassurance. Mother simply shrugged in response.

Her indifference hurt me. Over the summer we had been increasingly at odds. She criticized everything I did and demanded I help her more at home. Some days my frustration flew out of my mouth before I could stop the words. In quiet moments I burned full of despair, trapped in the narrow circle of my family and our Hmong customs. Across the freeway my friends lived tantalizing lives of plenty that seemed a million miles away, and then again, just out of my reach. Once more, disturbing dreams plagued me as they had in the refugee camp and later in Minneapolis after the two girls had drowned. I found myself alone on a bamboo raft, drifting into the current of a vast gray river. My father stood on a barren, rocky shore, waving for me to come back for him. Sometimes my brothers stood next to him, at other times the drowned girls appeared. Always, they were slipping farther from my view.

"Yer says Blia and Mee are excited to start high school," Mother said without looking up from her work. "It is nice you will have your cousins at school."

I kept my eyes on my sewing. "When Blia and Mee are together they don't even talk to me." My sisters sat very still, taking in my words.

Mother cleared her throat. "You must try harder. Maybe you should spend less time reading all those books and be nicer to your cousins. Go visit them more."

The heat rose in my cheeks. I didn't understand why Mother begrudged my reading. Once a week I retreated to the local library, a cool quiet haven, to bring home another stack of books. At the end of the year, Mrs. Wong had given our English class a recommended list of literature for summer reading. If we wrote short reviews for five books, we could get extra credit. Most students had groaned and thrown the list away in a fleet of paper airplanes floating into the wastebasket. But I wanted to read every book. Late into the night I worked my way through Jane Austin, Pearl S. Buck, Charles Dickens and Ernest Hemmingway, discovering amazing new worlds of dreams and possibilities, the secrets to how others chose a future, found love, defined happiness. Our culture seemed narrow in contrast to these vast other worlds. My Hmong life drew tighter around me like the tiny stitches looping over and under my cloth.

I dreaded the thought of my cousins at school. They could undo all that I had created for myself. I would have to confess to them about calling myself Laura and beg them not to mention it at home. The last thing I needed was for my parents to discover my secrets.

Mother gazed at me with a faraway look that so often came into her eyes. I wondered once more where she traveled to, what she felt. Did she wish it had been me--not her precious sons--lost that night in the Mekong River?

Despite my fears, the school year progressed without a problem. Blia and Mee showed little interest in intruding on my life. Neither of them cared enough to cause me trouble at school or home. I introduced them to Mary once when we met in the hall, but they said nothing to give me away. For now, my secrets were safe.

A month into the first quarter my English teacher, Mrs. Wong, asked me to stay after class as the lunch bell rang and students filed out of the room. She was my favorite teacher, even though I found her brusque and a bit intimidating. No one in class dared to challenge her. She had a talent for making Shakespeare relevant to our adolescent lives and drawing students into animated discussions. Her high expectations inspired me to work harder and think critically about what we learned. I could not imagine why she wanted to speak with me.

She moved one of the neat stacks of papers from the corner of her desk to the center and leaned on the vacant space. She wore sleek black pants that fell straight over her narrow hips and a jade green silk blouse with one button open at the top. The composite of her features—high cheekbones, a small, flat nose with wide nostrils, full lips, and black hair that hit just below her chin—made her attractive if not pretty. I could not guess her age. She appeared neither young nor old with smooth skin and only the slightest insinuation of wrinkles around her eyes. While only standing a few inches taller than me, her air of self-assurance made her seem taller. I wanted to be like this, confident, capable.

She crossed her arms over her middle, wasting no time on the niceties of small talk. "Laura, would you be interested in working on the school newspaper? You're a good writer and we need another staff member." She waited a moment and added, "You'll earn extra credit."

I fell into the seat next to me. Mrs. Wong thought I was good enough to write for the paper. "How much time would it take?"

"It's usually about two to three hours a week, depending on your assignments."

"I'll have to ask my parents." I wondered if Father would find it a worthy use of my time.

"Tell them it will strengthen your writing skills and look good on college applications."

I focused on the ink stain on the floor beside of the desk, avoiding her probing gaze. I knew the limitations of my future, the culture I could not escape. My parents most likely expected me to marry by the time I finished high school if not sooner. Then my life would belong to my husband. "I don't think I'll be able to go to college," I said at last.

Mrs. Wong frowned and slipped behind the desk next to me. "I've talked with your other teachers and we're all impressed. Is it financial?"

I nodded. That and so much more, but how could I begin to explain.

"There are lots of options, scholarships and student loans. You could start at a junior college and transfer to university after two years."

I ran a finger over the inside of my hand, still rough with calluses from my summer working in the fields. "I'm not sure my parents will think I need to go to college. Maybe only my brothers."

She leaned forward, hesitating a moment. "Because you're Hmong."

I looked up, alarmed and uncertain. "I've never told anyone that."

"I won't say anything." She smiled a small, weary smile. "I understand your situation better than you might think. My parents emigrated from China right after I was born." She explained how hard it had been growing up with parents who didn't speak English well. They had scraped by to save enough for her older brother's college education. He had always been their priority. "My parents didn't have money for me to go to college, but I was determined. I got scholarships and worked part time. It took me an extra year to finish, but it can be done."

Suddenly, I saw her toughness and demanding standards in a new light. She too had struggled and knew the mark of being from somewhere else, of having parents from a different culture. She understood.

"I shouldn't make assumptions. Do you want to go to college?"

A spark of hope formed in my mind, and I knew I wanted this more than anything. "Very much."

"Have you talked to your counselor about it? Are you taking all the college prep classes?" she asked.

I shrugged. "I'm not sure what I need."

She moved quickly to her desk, grabbed a scratchpad, and began to write. "You have Mrs. Martin right? I'll make sure she explains the university requirements and helps you plan your classes. I'll try to sit in on the meeting."

"Thank you."

"If you have questions, come to me. I'll help however I can."

I sat very still, too awed and overwhelmed to speak. I wanted to believe her. I wanted to succeed.

"Talk to your parents and let me know about the newspaper." She turned and smiled. "Set your goals high and you'll accomplish them, Laura."

All afternoon I vacillated between the elation of hope and my nervousness about talking with Father. To my surprise, he seemed pleased that Mrs. Wong had asked me to work on the paper. He said as long as I completed my chores it would be fine. Another choice had appeared before me, and my life took on new purpose. Mrs. Wong became my mentor, prodding me to try other activities like student council and French club to improve my chances for getting into college. With her encouragement, anything seemed possible.

Chapter 20
YER

 In January the familiar nausea plagued me once more. I craved sleep. I told myself it was the endless tasks at home that drained my body. But I knew. Another baby. The thought of caring for another infant as Chou remained strapped to my back and little Nao ran in every direction, overwhelmed me. Pao worked long hours. Even with my cousins and aunties to help, some days the demands seemed too much. I might become sick or too tired to carry on. I could not bear the thought of giving up my time in the fields. Only when turning the earth and tending our plants, feeling the sun on my back, listening to the cheerful chatter of birds, did I find peace. Only under the open sky with the wind brushing my cheeks could I feel the reassuring presence of Fue and Fong.

One night in bed I whispered the news to Pao. He reacted with little enthusiasm. In Laos when we first married, all we wanted was the blessing of many children to share our lives and honor us after we joined our ancestors in the other world. Throughout the war and long years of hardships each child seemed a precious gift. But the joy of new life had been slowly pushed aside by our struggles and disappointments.

As my middle grew large, I gathered my four girls together when they returned from school one afternoon. "You will have another brother or sister by summer," I told them. "I need all of you to help me."

Moa and Houa jumped up and down and clapped their hands. They promised to do whatever was needed. Boa ran over to hug my legs. She put her ear to my stomach, eyes wide with wonder. Then I caught the frown on Nou's face, the long sigh that rippled over her lips. I could not imagine why this news troubled her. I remembered her delight when Moa and Houa were born in the refugee camp. She had hovered over me and tenderly cared for the babies. I had called her my little mother. Now when I asked for help, it fell on her as a heavy burden.

What did my Nou want in life? I hoped she would marry and have children of her own before too long. If she found the right man, surely it would settle her discontent. But these days all she wanted was to be off with her friends. Every request I made turned her hard. Against me.

I sent the other girls out back to look after their little brothers. "Nou, help me fold this laundry."

She drew her lips tight and dumped the large basket of clothes and towels onto the table. I watched her work for a moment. It always pained me to think of her young years in the aftermath of war. She was forced to sacrifice much of her childhood to care for me and the rest of the family. If only she understood that all I wanted was her happiness. My exquisite Nou, her dark eyes flecked with flashes of gold. She could have any boy she wanted. If only she felt for someone what I had felt for Pao. If only she understood the joy the right match could bring.

"You are getting older. Maybe you will meet someone special soon. Perhaps someone to marry."

Her head jerked up. "I want to finish high school. Maybe go to college."

"Why would you need to do that?" I took a deep breath to wash away the impatience from my voice. "Still, you'll want a family of your own. Don't wait too long."

166

She held out her arms to encompass our small rooms as angry words spewed out. "I want more than cooking and taking care of children. We hardly have enough to get by and now another baby?" Her voice rose into the high pitched call of a Mynah bird.

The shirt I was folding dropped to the floor. My hands trembled. I could not believe the evil flying from my own daughter's mouth. She had never spoken to me with such disrespect. Fury overcame me. I raised my hand to slap her face, then stopped, my hand frozen midair. We stared at each other in silence. She turned and slammed out the front door.

I collapsed on the chair. I should have remained calm, not let the anger overcome me. When I became a parent, I promised myself never to be harsh and unforgiving like my own mother. I had never hit any of my children. I tried to be a good and patient parent. At times I failed, when the darkness carried me away. All her young life, Nou had never complained. Surely she understood how much her devotion meant to me. Now everything had changed. She had grown as distant as the moon and stars.

I longed to share my life and traditions with her. Yet her eyes held only contempt for my cooking and sewing and hard work. I could see the embarrassment in her expression for a mother who did not speak English or understand about the world around us. Maybe Nou wanted a smart American mother. Not me. My mother had warned me not to tempt the spirits by pretending to be something more than a simple woman. After all, she said, I was bad luck from the beginning.

The day my mother's labor began the wind shifted. The fires burning in newly cleared fields sent smoke billowing across the hills and into our house. Our village of ten families had moved higher into the mountains seeking virgin soil and refuge from the growing troubles below. The Viet Minh were creeping into Laos, trying to recruit farmers and take their land.

"So many hours passed before your birth," Mother told me one day when she came to visit after I had given birth to Fong, "even though you were the third child."

I was the disappointing third girl, not the son Mother so desperately wanted to give my father. They named me Yer, meaning youngest girl, in hopes that the next child would be a boy.

"You should have fallen into my hands before sunset. But the night passed and smoke burned my lungs and eyes. I grew very weak." As she told the story, she stirred a pot of soup and stared into the fire with a distant look that often consumed her face. "You tried to come out feet-first, ready to run away and cause trouble. The midwife had to turn you around in my womb. You were bad luck."

Mother blamed me for all the hardships that followed. No more children came to her. When I turned four years old my father died. Every evening as they finished in the fields, Father would stop in the forest to find a papaya for his "little Yer". It was my favorite food. But one evening a giant hooded cobra, coiled beneath a bush caught him by surprise. He died before anyone found him.

Youngest uncle took Mother as his second wife, as custom required if we were to remain with Father's family. It was a marriage of convenience. My Grandfather, aunts, and uncles were kind people who cared for my sisters and me. I knew laughter and love from this family. But Mother withdrew into her own private world.

After Father died, streaks of white peppered her hair. Her face might have been pretty, but I only remembered the downward pull of sour words. On the rare occasions that she turned her attention to me, nothing seemed to please her. No matter how hard I tried. I didn't pull weeds fast enough or dig holes deep enough to plant the seeds. My sewing was too messy, my cooking too spicy. For such a tiny woman, she nourished a vast and unrelenting bitterness. She expressed her displeasure with me by a quick slap or a beating with a bamboo switch.

When I married, my mother said she was pleased I had made a good match. I knew she was glad for me to leave home. To be rid of such bad luck.

In early February, I woke in the middle of the night with terrible cramping. I found myself in a pool of blood. Pao helped me wash and made an herb drink to slow the bleeding. He held me until at last I fell asleep. But in the morning the bleeding grew heavy again. He insisted I must go to the hospital. I felt very afraid, thinking of my poor cousin Yer. What if I too would never have another child? The doctor said our baby was lost.

I blamed myself. I had not held good thoughts, not appreciated the blessing bestowed upon me.

Soon, I drifted among the hills of Laos looking for my boys. They had disappeared into the forest. From the top of the mountain, I called to them. I heard the roar of engines. Giant green birds filled the heavens and opened their bloated bellies, dropping a stream of death. Bombs whistled through the air until it felt like my ears would explode. The sun glinted off shiny metal objects that spun and twisted, opening high above the ground and scattering hundreds of yellow balls. The earth burst into great plumes of brilliant red and orange. The grounded trembled and jarred my bones. Louder and louder. Deafening noise reverberated in my head. Mothers grabbed their children, raced up the hills, and hid among the trees. I had to find my boys. A hand touched my shoulder. I woke as I turned to find Nou standing behind me. Only her face was a blur.

Chapter 21

LAURA

My morning started at five o'clock when Chou threw up. I got everyone ready for school and fixed breakfast. Moa spilled apple juice everywhere. Noa threw a tantrum. Boa couldn't find her left tennis shoe. Finally, Father took my older siblings to school.

As I prepared to leave, I stopped in the hallway and slowly opened my parents' door. Mother lay in the bed on her side, turned toward the back wall. Her arm moved through the air as if she were beckoning to someone. She mumbled words I could not hear and let out a small cry. I called softly to her, but she remained somewhere else, a place I could not reach.

I dropped Chou and Noa with Ia on my way out. It was well past the final bell when I arrived at school and stopped in the office for a pass. I explained why I was late to the attendance monitor. She was a pudgy woman with frizzy, faded blond hair. "Save the excuses, I've heard it all," she said not even looking up as she wrote a late slip. "This is the second time this month. One more and you get detention."

I slipped into biology class and handed the pass to Mr. Charles. Opening my backpack, I discovered the bottom of my homework was soggy with apple juice and the ink on the last two answers blurred. Mr. Charles took my pages and raised his eyebrows but didn't comment. The cover of my book was damp and sticky. I wanted to crawl under my desk and stay there the rest of the day.

I slogged through the morning unable to concentrate on the lessons as I worried about responsibilities at home. As always, my mother's affliction gnawed at me like a worm wriggling deeper and deeper into my consciousness until it consumed all other thoughts. Ever since the miscarriage two months ago she had disappeared into her private world for days at a time, becoming nothing more than a faded outline on the bed, a ghost without substance. Unexpectedly, she would emerge one morning, quiet, but cooking breakfast and leaving in the van to work in the fields. Perhaps it was the unpredictability of her lapses that wore on us most. I watched the growing strain on Father's face, his sagging shoulders, and sharp responses to my siblings and me. He hardly ate and weight fell from his already spare frame. Yet our shared burden remained unacknowledged. Unspoken.

I feared that our argument the day Mother told me about her pregnancy had contributed to the miscarriage. All my frustrations had escaped that day in a way I could not excuse. If only she had not pushed me about finding a boy and thinking of marriage. We had barely spoken for three days, until at last I apologized and told her I was happy about the baby. She had nodded as tears formed in her eyes. And we had carried on cooking the dinner.

The lunch bell rang. I met Mary at her locker and joined the usual group in the cafeteria amid the din of voices, jostling of lunch trays, and smells of pizza and hamburgers. The sunshine pouring through the high windows did nothing to relieve my gloom. I sat quietly next to Mary, my arms around my middle, wallowing in misery and listening to the inane gossip. As the hour slipped by, I had less and less patience for these girls' complaints about homework, a bad grade on a biology test, a fight with a boyfriend, a volleyball coach who was too demanding, the expensive outfit someone's mother wouldn't buy her. Their problems sounded trivial and ridiculous.

A mocking, angry voice whispered in my head that I didn't belong. I was a phony, a fool to pretend to be part of this circle.

They knew nothing of hardship and sacrifice while my every free moment was filled with chores and responsibilities to family and a culture completely foreign to their own. Each morning I left the confines of our tiny apartment from a life ruled by ancient traditions and indisputable rules, speaking a native language of sliding tones and words with multiple meanings. I stepped out the door as if stepping out of a tiny village in the mountains of Laos and crossed the freeway to another world. Instead of my preordained Hmong fate, I found a place of learning that promised other possibilities. I smiled and giggled and gossiped, speaking English interspersed with the latest teenage slang, with girls oblivious to the abundance and freedom that was their birthright but not mine. I smoothed the gaps and transitions with my lies, all the time struggling to remember who I was supposed to be.

Mary glanced over with a puzzled frown. She was the only person I could truly call a friend. I longed to confide in her, to be honest and true. Instead, I betrayed her with my secrets. The guilt wore me down, kept me unbalanced. At that moment I regretted every story I had ever told to her and my parents. And for what? To fit in with a group of silly, empty-headed girls.

Across the room, Blia and Mee sat at a table with the three Hmong boys, Chia, Leng, and Blong. They were talking and laughing with a Hispanic boy from my history class. As I watched them, a lump formed in my throat. I didn't belong with them either. I didn't belong anywhere.

Mary came to my locker after school. "Want to get a coke?"

"My mom needs me at home. My brother's sick."

"Can't you be a tiny bit late?"

My sisters and Tong would be waiting for help with homework then permission to go out to play. A pile of laundry had to be washed, and stacks of clothes folded and ironed. Chou would be sick and fussy, and Nao, who had been particularly wild and difficult lately, would vie for attention. I needed to organize and cook dinner and supervise baths. Father was teaching English class until late. My homework and the newspaper article I still had to write would patiently wait until at last I was free. And once again I would fall asleep over my books at the dining room table.

I looked at Mary's hopeful face. "Just for a little while."

We walked four blocks to Jerry's Ice Cream Parlor in the shopping center next to Safeway. Scattered clouds flitted across the blue April sky. Kids from school milled about outside at tables and on wooden benches beneath liquid amber trees coming into bud.

Mary punched me with her elbow and nodded her head toward Pete and Kevin. They were sitting with Jerome from the basketball team. She bought us both cokes as I didn't have any money. We headed to an empty bench. She patted her hand over her heart and whispered Kevin's name.

I laughed and sipped my coke, glancing back at Pete. I loved the way his white blond hair curled down his forehead and neck and his blue eyes crinkled into tiny slits when he laughed. He sat next to me in math class, pulling my hair and whispering jokes to me when our teacher turned away. I was not immune to his charms. When he flashed his big grin in my direction, my stomach danced and a warm flush rose to my cheeks.

"I should call to say I'll be late," I said, knowing Houa and Moa would be watching for me.

"There's a phone in the pizza place."

We walked into the restaurant that smelled of rising dough, spicy tomato sauce, and melting cheese. My stomach growled, and I wished I had the money to take home pizza for dinner.

"Aren't those your cousins?" Mary asked, nodding toward a booth.

Blia and Mee were sitting with the Chia and Blong from school. Another boy with long shaggy hair and an acne-covered face was next to Blia, his arm resting over her shoulders as he whispered in her ear. She saw me and started, pulling away from him. Her parents would not approve of this behavior. These were Hmong boys who knew better. If they wanted to see my cousins outside of school, they should show respect to their parents and ask permission to visit. But then, these were only our parents' rules.

"Come on," I said and bolted for the back of the room. I called Moa and told her I would be home soon, something had come up at school. When Mary and I walked back out, the cozy group had vanished. We settled on a bench outside protected from the wind.

Mary put her head to one side. "How come you don't talk to your cousins?"

"We don't get along."

"Do you know those guys they hang out with?"

"Not really."

Mary hesitated a moment. "Sherry told me they're from Vietnam or something."

Hidden in the tone of her voice, the inflection of the words "or something" I heard a question, perhaps a suspicion. This was my opening, a chance to finally tell the truth. I sat very still, staring down at the brown plastic buttons on my jacket. One had a small chip. My mind whirled with what I could say, how to begin to create a bridge to my past and present. A car parked in the space in front of us. The door opened. The driver got out and slammed it shut again. The silence stretched out. Words stuck in my throat, and I lost my nerve. The moment passed.

Chapter 22
LAURA

Mother languished once more. Over the long, hot summer and early fall she had been happy working in the fields harvesting crops. The sun had cast a healing glow and the delta breezes soothed her. It had been a welcome relief for us all. But as the weather grew colder and the days shorter, something shifted. I had no idea what triggered the relapse or why she receded into her darkened bedroom and the familiar pattern of her illness. The first three days she was unreachable. Whenever Father was home, he sat by her side and pleaded with her to eat. He lighted candles and incense and prayed. Uncle Boua conducted yet another *hu plig*, bargaining with the spirits to bring her back, but nothing helped.

The only bright moments in my days came at school when I did well on an exam or had an extra hour to spend with Mary. Mrs. Wong watched over me, providing guidance and advice. When the school newspaper editor contracted mononucleosis and was forced to stay home for six weeks, I was asked to take over. I refused to let the drain of my problems at home hold me back.

Into the muddle of my existence another complication developed. It started with an innocent request. Pete Williams trailed behind me out of calculus one day and called my name. I turned around as kids knocked into my arms, noisily merging into the crowds rushing between classes. He put his hand on my elbow and ushered me aside, leaning over me, his face close to mine. I noticed a small blue stain on his white t-shirt in the middle of his chest and the faint scent of lemon verbena like we grew in our garden behind the apartment.

"We have that test next Wednesday," he said. "Could we study together? I'm really having trouble with this stuff."

He caught me off guard. I glanced up into the face that always unsettled me. "I don't know."

"We could go to the library after school." He gave me one of his most disarming smiles, humble and pleading.

This was the Pete who teased me for my neatly printed notes and perfect quiz scores. I struggled to think of clever comebacks, but only mumbled inane responses like a silly child. As our teacher went over formulas, I secretly studied the details of Pete's profile, the curve of his fingers around his pencil, the way he ran his fingers through the side of his hair when he didn't know an answer. Every girl in the school had a crush on him. He was a track and basketball star, quick with a joke, friendly with everyone. And yet he seemed remarkably unaware of the adoration of others, the way people tried to edge into the circle of his universe. As he tilted back in his chair at ease and unaware, I wondered what it would be like to have everything you ever wanted in life. How would such perfection feel? If only I could wear it for a day.

He waited for my answer. I could say no and be done with it. Something deep inside me knew it was a mistake. But a little wrinkle in his forehead made me waver. It was only one afternoon.

"Okay. Monday."

"Perfect." He shifted his backpack on his shoulder. "Thanks."

I watched him head down the hall and my knees shook.

On the Monday following the mid-term, Mrs. Garner handed back tests. She smiled at Pete. "You must have studied."

"You bet." Pete grinned and held up his paper to show me the *B*1, *Good Job* scrawled across the top of the page in red ink. "Not bad, huh?"

I smiled with a rush of pleasure. Our hour studying together had been strictly business. Pete had abandoned his usual jokes and listened intently as I explained the problems.

He grabbed my test that was turned face down on my desk, grinning and shaking his head. "I knew it. You only missed one."

As we started out of class, he cocked his head to one side. "Will you keep helping me? Any afternoon." He leaned in and whispered, "I promised my mom I'd get a good grade. It's really important to her."

I couldn't afford the time or temptation, but my resolve melted in his anxious gaze, the sweetness and lack of bravado with which he spoke of his mother. "Maybe Wednesday at four o'clock? We can meet in the library."

He blinked a few times as if surprised by my answer. "Great! I'll think of some way to repay you."

I headed to Mary's locker, confused and needing to talk to her. But she raced to my side, panting and in another world. Kevin had asked her out for Friday night. Her contagious excitement rippled through me, yet in the middle of my chest a small ache settled. I wasn't sure if it was jealousy or simply sadness that I could never experience such a moment. I longed to be like any other girl, able to go on a date with someone special, to share the anticipation and hopes, the giddy exhilaration. What magic floating across the skies could I conjure up to make Pete ask me out? How could I change the positions of the stars to make it possible to say yes?

Every other Wednesday Pete and I settled into the wooden chairs at the library and spread out books, notepads, and calculators. He would tease me or tell a silly joke before we focused on formulas and axioms. We lost track of time as one hour slipped into two, and I completely forgot about the responsibilities waiting for me at home.

He remained polite and appreciative during our sessions, never straying beyond the boundaries of the tutoring relationship. I told myself this was best. It couldn't be any other way. But no matter how hard I tried to guard against the inevitable, my attraction to him intensified. My eyes traced the curve of his ear lobe and the patterns of freckles down his nose and cheeks. I longed to brush my face against the pale lashes that fluttered as he squeezed his eyes tight with concentration. When he bent close over the math book, I inhaled the scent of his skin and hair, tangy with lemon and sweat. I felt his warm breath tickle my arm until my brain slipped into a trance and my body grew warm with a strange yearning. When he lifted his head and gazed into my eyes, his lips only a heartbeat from mine, I couldn't hear or breathe.

The Wednesday before Thanksgiving break, Pete turned to me as I inserted papers into my notebook and got ready to go home. "Is there any way you could do this every week?" He ruffled the hair on the side of his head. "I'm getting A's in all my other classes, and I really need one in math. My mom wants me to go to Stanford where she went."

In my mind, I argued back and forth with myself. I knew the best thing would be to end our sessions. But then again, he had asked nothing more of me than help with the math. The end of the semester was only a month away.

"Sure. The review helps me too."

"Great." He smiled and touched my arm, sending an electric wave through my body. "How about going over to Jerry's for ice cream? My treat."

"My mom's expecting me, but thanks."

He shrugged and gathered his things. "Are you going anywhere for Thanksgiving?"

"No." I put my backpack on my shoulder as we headed for the front of school in silence. Rain spilled out of the gutters and off the roof into great waterfalls that splashed onto the cement and sprinkled my legs. "What about you?"

"My family is coming to our house." Pete hunched his shoulders. "My mom's been sick."

"I hope she's better."

The muscles in his jaw rippled. "It's cancer," he said at last in a faint, hoarse voice. "But she's going to be okay."

I stopped, stunned by his revelation, unable to think of anything to say except I was sorry. His perfect life was marred by a tragic defect. Cancer. The word conjured up fear and dread, the probability of death. Now I understood his urgency to do well in math and please his mother. It touched me deep in my core. Like me, he staggered under the weight of a seriously ill mother and the anguish and uncertainty that clouded the future. I knew how it felt to hurt for a person you loved, the hopelessness of not being able to help. I wanted to support him through whatever might come. How could I possibly do less?

Chapter 23
YER

 In November, I woke one morning yearning to be in the fields, longing for the fragrance of wet soil, the touch of fresh green leaves and sturdy stalks. I could hardly remember the weeks before. Visions of terrifying monsters had hung from the ceiling. Fue and Fong, injured and begging for help, lurked in the corners of the bedroom. I was desperate to help them. My mind clouded until I could not see or hear anything else. My arms and legs stuck, my body sinking into a deep mud. I needed to return to the one place that calmed my dark thoughts and drove away the demons, hoping for a sign from my boys.

The family carefully eased around me, speaking softly, as if I were a fragile piece of glass that could shatter with one harsh word. Perhaps I was. Days of harvesting tightly-budded broccoli and great white rounds of cauliflower gave me a purpose. The dirt yielded beneath my feet, pliant and forgiving, and crumbled through my fingers full of the sustenance of life. I grew stronger. Clouds swirled across the sky like a swarm of gray doves and dropped raindrops that tickled my nose and cheeks. One morning the wind embraced me and the faintest echo of my boys' voices reached my ears like the distant chants of monks in a Buddhist temple calling out prayers of peace, the gentle harmonies rising and falling. I could feel their spirits in the cool damp air. My heart filled with relief and happiness like water pouring into a jar. They were safe.

As the days passed my boys continued to comfort me as I wound up and down the rows, pulling stubborn weeds from the wet earth. I allowed my thoughts to wander to happier events. The New Year was almost upon us. I focused on the pleasure of familiar rituals and festivities, the laughter, games, and music. The thought of being among so many of our people once more stretched my spirits higher. I could not help but catch the contagious excitement of my young ones who grew wilder as the days approached. At last my husband would have a few days to relax and enjoy the companionship of other Hmong men. I knew the toll my lost hours and days took on him. And as I turned the soil, I nourished another hope. Perhaps Nou might meet someone special and at least begin to think of her future.

On the second day of the Thanksgiving weekend we drove to the fairgrounds dressed in our new clothes. Midday skies threatened rain, but the weather had not discouraged anyone. Thousands of Hmong congregated wearing their new clothes in a parade of brilliant colors and intricate patterns. People mixed in a chorus of greetings and good wishes that made my heart glad.

Pao headed immediately for the pavilion where the older men assembled. They drank beer and reminisced about Laos, recounting old war stories and tracing clan and village connections.

Mee and Nou slipped away among the dozens of booths displaying the latest tapes and videos from Thailand. Music blared from a hundred speakers and left me covering my ears from so much noise. Kia, Yer, and I, with the young children trailing behind, circled the stands displaying Hmong instruments, *paj nuab* embroidery, jewelry, healing herbs, imported fabrics, and steaming bowls of hot food.

"Where Is Blia?" I asked cousin Yer.

A distressed expression crossed her face. "Her stomach hurt. She stayed home."

"Too bad to miss the fun and all the young men," I said.

184

Kia, standing behind Yer, raised a hand to warn me not to say more. I wondered what had happened. I had seen a skinny boy visiting Blia once or twice. Yer did not say much about him, but it was clear she did not like this boy.

I dropped the subject. We bought bowls of noodle soup and wandered over to the groups of girls and boys playing *pob pov*, tossing tennis balls back and forth. The banter and flirting brought happy memories of a New Year's celebration in Xieng Khouang many years ago. I was only fifteen at the time and shy and uncertain. I had wrapped my black cloth tight and smooth into a perfect round ball so it might travel directly to the object of my yearning. Then I saw Pao, standing across from me, young and handsome, a man of wealth and education. My pulse quickened to that of a frightened bird. Butterflies fluttered in my stomach. He looked at me, a slight smile on his lips, and stepped forward. I knew he was my fate. I tossed my ball, my heart soaring through the air, into his waiting hands. It landed as gently as a mother bird swooping into her nest, home at last.

Nou stood apart from the crowd, watching Mee toss a ball with a noisy boy who teased her and made her laugh. My cousin Yer rushed over, chiding and pushing my reluctant daughter into the line. A tall boy with a nice smile stood opposite Nou. He tossed a ball her way. They spent the rest of the day together.

Over the next few weeks, Dang came to visit Nou at our home. I found him pleasing and polite. Finally, she had found a suitor, an honorable young man, who stared at her with sparkling eyes. Auntie Khou made inquiries about the family and found they were honest, hard-working people from Savannakhet in southern Laos. Not as good as being from Xieng Khouang, but still good. Nou laughed at his jokes and talked comfortably with him. True, she did not gaze into his eyes with the deep yearning I had felt for Pao. But a friendship was a start.

This turn of events did not surprise me. Around this time Fong and Fue visited me in another dream. They were older this time, young men. We sat quietly together on the top of the mountain above our village, the one we had lived in right after the war ended.

Dawn turned the sky the pink of frangipani and pale lilac of orchids, then berry red and the orange of glowing coals. A rainbow streaked across the sky until a brilliant ball of gold appeared and filled the day with light.

The boys were eating langons, competing to see who could spit the shiny, black seeds the farthest. From our perch we viewed the land below in all directions--deep green forests weeping pale gray mists and distant houses in neighboring villages where life was stirring. The air filled with the crisp cool smell of pine needles and a hint of smoke from the cooking fires. Our family appeared in the valley below ready to work in the golden brown corn fields. My children were all there, even little Chou who was tied to Houa's back. We called to them. But they could not hear us. The young ones chased each other through the stalks of corn.

Nou sat to one side with a faint smile on her lips, her image fading in and out of view like an apparition. I blinked my eyes trying to keep her in focus. I told my boys how I worried about the children, especially Nou. If we could have stayed in Laos, everything would be fine. And the boys smiled. Fong took my hand, his palm and fingers smooth and cool and comforting. Do not worry, he told me, it will turn out well, my sisters and brothers will find their right place. Fue nodded. Our ancestors will watch over them, he promised, and so will we.

After this dream I felt sure that Dang was an omen of good things to come. I could trust in our ancestors to keep my Nou safe.

Chapter 24

LAURA

At the New Year's celebration, Dang Moua caught me by surprise. When he positioned himself across from me and tossed a ball into my hands, I thought he was simply another Hmong boy, cocky and sure of himself. I expected to thoroughly dislike him. But somehow the message got lost in the shy dark eyes searching mine for a reaction. A soft smile and voice soothed away my inclination to flee as we began a halting conversation. *Where do you go to school? Where is your family from? How old were you when you left Laos? Which refugee camp were you in? When did you leave Ban Vinai? Where did you settle? How long have you lived here?* Soon the awkward exchanges ebbed and flowed into a comfortable rhythm. I lowered my guard with the relief of speaking openly, discovering our shared history and journey. For once, I did not have to lie.

He was a senior at St. Ignacio, a friend of my cousin Tou. He wore a traditional Hmong shirt, vest, and sash over blue jeans with black Nike running shoes. This compromise of old and new pleased me for some reason. He was tall by Hmong standards and athletic. Shaggy hair framed an angular, handsome face. I liked his generous smile that revealed a slight gap between the top front teeth.

During the afternoon events, he stayed unobtrusively at my side, reading my wariness and matching it with patient determination. He said he had seen me the previous year and had hoped to meet me this time. I looked into his eyes, cautious of encouraging him. But after listening to Mary talk endlessly about Kevin, I too wanted someone special to care about me, a break from the drudgery and demands of my life.

Rain began to fall in the late afternoon as my family gathered to head home. My cousin Tou punched Dang in the arm and pushed him toward me.

"I was wondering, maybe," he said, clearing his throat, "if maybe I could visit you this week,"

"I'm hardly ever home." I concentrated on smoothing my sash with its pattern of brilliant mustard flowers and a border of protective tiger's teeth to fend off evil spirits. "I'm so busy at school."

"I study with Tou sometimes." He hesitated and licked his lips. "Maybe there will be a day when you're home." Splotches of red emerged on his cheeks.

In this way Dang slowly seeped into my life. He came to Tou's apartment that week on the pretense of studying and waited until I arrived home. He came the following week and the next, and four days during the Christmas vacation. We sat in the living room and talked, sometimes with Tou. My sisters and brothers milled around curious about him as Mother watched from the kitchen wearing a satisfied smile. I told myself I would keep it light, merely a friendship. It didn't have to be anything more.

I was chopping squash and onions for dinner, glancing out the window at the January sky that threatened another storm. Mother had gone to visit Auntie Khou and returned wearing an odd smile.

"Have you heard?" she said. "Blia is getting married. The negotiators meet tomorrow." The knife slipped from my fingers and fell into the sink. Over the summer and fall months Mee had confided in me that she was worried about Blia's reckless behavior. She had been sneaking off to meet Bee--the boy I had seen her with at the pizza parlor--even though she knew it was forbidden by our

Hmong culture. I had tried to talk to her once, but she laughed and told me she could take care of herself.

Chou screamed with outstretched arms, and Mother lifted him from the floor. "Auntie Khou told me everything."

My stomach felt queasy. I ran cold water and splashed it on my face. Oh Blia, I thought, what have you done to yourself?

"The school called yesterday. Blia did not go to class. She didn't come home. Soua and Yer were crazy with worry. Mee finally told them she was with Bee.

"Blia came sneaking in at two in the morning," she continued, becoming more animated. "A terrible fight. Soua found out where the boy's family lives. Uncle Boua went this morning to demand payment for their daughter's dishonor." She wagged her head.

Chou wailed and grabbed at Mother's hair. She turned to him distracted, pulling his sticky little hand away and handing him a cup of water. "Bee's family said he must marry her. They have to pay the money anyway. Auntie Khou thinks they will give a big bride payment." Mother crowed as if she were completing the negotiations herself.

Her enthusiasm appalled me. I thought nothing would make her happier than to marry me off in some triumphant coup that brought great honor for the family. She didn't care about my dreams for the future. But who would pick up the pieces when she disappeared for days in her bedroom?

"Blia is an idiot. She'll end up pregnant and dropping out of school. She'll be nothing but Bee's wife." My body felt unnaturally heavy. Our Hmong culture taught me to honor and respect my parents, but I no longer understood anything my mother valued.

Mother's mouth trembled as she took a deep breath. "Go get some lemon grass from the garden and check on the children." She walked into her bedroom and slammed the door. Chou began to shriek.

The wedding celebration for Blia and Bee fell as flat as the notes my sister Boa tried to play on Father's bamboo flute. Auntie Yer and Uncle Soua strained with the effort of smiling as they greeted family and friends. A pale sun shined in the clear sky, but inside a dark mood pervaded as everyone pretended pleasure over the occasion. They brought gifts and money for the newlyweds and wished them a long and prosperous life together. No one believed it. Least of all me.

I sat on the living room sofa observing the farce. Mother glanced over at me and smiled, undoubtedly nourishing delusions that I might be next. It was hard to imagine my cousin, only fifteen years old, married to this scrawny, ugly boy of seventeen who from that day forward would dictate the shape her life. Mee had confirmed my worst fears. Blia was almost five months pregnant. Now I understood the protruding roundness of her belly beneath the layers of her clothes. She would have to drop out of school before the year ended and plunge herself into a world of babies and tending house for her in-laws. It was not a legal wedding. But in the eyes of the Hmong community this ceremony would bind her to Bee more tightly than any paper from the government. It seemed wrong and out of kilter when so many other opportunities awaited us.

Blia and Bee stood beneath a black umbrella draped with the embroidered ribbon removed from Blia's black turban, which had indicated her single status. The best man and maid of honor, negotiators, family, and friends surrounded the couple. Elders from both families lit candles and incense and sang blessings as they tied a string on the wrist of the bride to the wrist of the groom, uniting their spirits. Relatives and friends sang toasts to love and honor and family connections. Others offered jokes and laughter and more toasts. Bee had begun to sway unsteadily from the rounds of whiskey and beer. His demeanor appeared as that of a man sentenced to a life of hard labor. Blia whispered in his ear several times before he finally knelt on the floor before Auntie Yer and Uncle Soua to show his respect. When he read the list of his in-laws' ancestors, he stumbled over the names, slurring his words together.

Blia stood by watching. Her skin had turned pasty and her face puffy, making it look too broad and square, her nose too flat. But she reveled in the extravagant clothes her mother had sewn over the past few years in anticipation of this moment. She wore a densely pleated white skirt made with fabric brought from Thailand. The sleeves of her deep blue, silk jacket and the black apron and sash showcased beautiful designs fashioned with reverse appliqué and delicate embroidery in forest green, bright yellow, red and pink, trimmed with colored beads and silver coins, which jangled when she moved. Auntie Yer had used the beauty of nature in the vegetable blossom and eye of the peacock, and then the snail pattern for family connections and the wandering maze of the love design. Tiger teeth provided a border to keep Blia safe from evil spirits. I wondered if any of it would be enough to help this marriage.

Around Blia's neck was her parents' most prized possession, a silver necklace carried out of Laos and across the ocean, from Minneapolis to Sacramento. Back in another lifetime, in a far away village, Uncle Soua had fashioned the solid ring of silver that supported tier upon tier of silver mesh and filigree, adorned with coins and squares of pounded silver. In the refugee camp, links had been removed and sold to provide needed cash, but were replaced when fortunes improved. No matter what my aunt and uncle thought of Bee or the marriage, they were sending their daughter into her new life with the best they had to offer. It was a matter of family honor.

The afternoon passed as guests feasted on roasted pig and two chickens, which had been sacrificed to honor family spirits, enjoying the luxury of ample meat to mark the special occasion. Bottles of vodka and whiskey continued to flow, and Bee grew more obnoxious until he no longer seemed conscious of his actions. At last the best man and the maid of honor prepared to escort the couple home. There had to be an even number of people to maintain balance. By now Blia's expression was pinched with strain and worry. Was this how she had expected it to end? Had she really wanted to marry and give up her life? Watching her, I vowed not to allow myself to fall into the same trap.

Chapter 25
LAURA

 I arrived home at six thirty one evening in late February and found Dang sitting on the stairs. He showed up every Tuesday, but I had been so busy at school that day I'd forgotten.

"I thought you were never coming." He stood and smiled. "I'm happy to see you."

I shivered in the cold wind.

"Can I come up?"

"I have so much homework." A ring of irritation crept into my voice. I didn't have time to entertain him.

"We can study together."

I wanted to say no, but kept silent. Over time, Dang had revealed himself to be full of contradictions. Beneath the pleasant smiles and agreeable words, the patient, placid face, he harbored an unbending will. He might ask my opinion about something or what I wanted to do on the weekend, but invariably I found myself manipulated into acquiescing to his wishes. Perhaps he could not help the imperious edge in his tone that reminded me he was the man and therefore inherently right. My upbringing had taught me to be a nice Hmong girl, polite and accommodating to men. But anger welled inside me at allowing myself to yield so easily.

He took my backpack and followed me up the stairs and into the apartment. When he saw Mother in the kitchen, he greeted her with his usual faultless manners. She immediately invited him to stay for dinner and brought out chips and cokes, special treats she never bought except for Dang's visits. I hated the way she doted on him and threw knowing glances my way, as if we shared in a conspiracy. However, I had reaped the benefits of her pleasure with his presence. Suddenly, I was the dutiful daughter again, graced with her favors. She took over some of my chores, leaving me more free time, presumably for Dang. All I had to do was play the game.

Father arrived home from work and nodded as Dang stood up to say hello. During dinner, he asked him about school and his plans for college the following year. Father remained polite with Dang, but I could not read his thoughts. Did he like him? Did he favor me pursuing courtship and marriage?

After dinner, I shooed my sisters and brothers off the sofa so we could spread out with our homework.

"Everybody is going to the St. Ignacias game Saturday. Can you come?" Dang asked.

"Probably."

I had spent the last three Saturday nights out with Dang, my cousins, and their friends. While our parents would not allow us to go on dates alone with a boy, we could go out in a group, at least with a Hmong group. We had been to two basketball games and a dance put on by the Hmong Community Center, where a deejay played American rock interspersed with the latest hit tunes from Thailand. On the slow songs Dang had held me, his arms loose and awkward around my waist. I felt his heart pound and listened to his breath catch in his throat as he nuzzled his head against mine. But I did not feel the same.

Dang and I studied for two hours while the TV played an endless stream of game shows and sitcoms. We talked intermittently about a math problem or something that had happened at school, speaking half in English and half in Hmong, laughing at our mixed up sentences.

When I finally got to bed that night, my mind wandered through the labyrinth of competing emotions that too often kept me awake. I desperately wanted to confide in Mary and seek her advice, but how could I explain about Dang and what his attentions might mean. Where would I start when she still knew nothing of the truth about my life? These days we had little time to talk anyway. I was busy with school work, activities, and demands at home, while her world revolved around Kevin. Only my cousin Mee shared an interest in Dang. She would corner me with giggles and questions. *What did Dang say yesterday? Did you have fun with him at the dance? Did I tell you Tou says he really likes you and talks about you all the time? What if he wants to marry you, what will you do?* Her words infused me with dread.

Yet I could not help but like Dang, even if at times he annoyed me. He was Hmong, part of all things familiar and comfortable, the essence of my splintered past and present. We shared a common heritage and journey, the experiences of war and exile from our homeland and the hardships that followed. He made me laugh and feel special. I didn't have to pretend to be anyone but Nou. Like me, he balanced family obligations and loyalties with the demands of school. He didn't scoff at my dreams for college, but then he was always agreeable about anything I said. He planned a career in engineering, a job that would bring a good income to support a family, he said. When hope and longing flashed across his face, the desire for more than I could give, guilt settled in my stomach like rancid oil. I asked myself how I could be so cold. My heart was not made of ice. It was simply full of another.

My feelings for Pete grew stronger each day, no matter how hopeless the situation. Perhaps it was fate or the trick of impish spirits wanting to cause trouble, but he was the one who made my insides quiver and my heart race with an attraction that could not be reasoned away. We came from opposite poles of the earth, north and south, foreign worlds never meant to meet. With my dark Asian features and his fair Nordic coloring, our incongruous histories and families, we could not have been more unalike. Yet some bond I could not deny connected us. In his presence all thoughts of Dang faded away like a vague, unsettling dream.

As the weeks passed, Pete started showing up unexpectedly at my locker, slipping unobtrusively onto the cafeteria bench beside me at lunch, appearing oddly nervous and unsure. I waited impatiently for our Wednesday afternoons, wishing they would never end. After the Christmas holiday our sessions at the library ran longer as math review gave way to whispered conversations about friends or upcoming basketball games. We both knew he didn't need my help any longer. When he repeatedly asked me to go with him for ice cream, I had to explain that my parents wouldn't allow me to go places alone with boys. He reacted with surprise and disappointment, but he did not press me. My thoughts raced between the insanity of taking another step outside the boundaries of my parents' rules and how to get away with it. When I offered a solution, it was Pete who hesitated, worried that I might get into trouble.

The Sea Treasure became our secret haven, an out of the way place where no one would see us. Soon we skipped the library and went directly to the tiny fast food outlet that smelled of deep-fried fish and potatoes. Hours raced by as we sat undisturbed and anonymous, staring at each other across the sticky plastic table.

At school Pete maintained his easy banter. Only Kevin, Mary, and I knew about his mother's illness. He said he didn't want to face the pity of others or uncomfortable pauses in the conversation. But with me he dropped his defenses, revealing small glimpses of the growing chaos at home as his mother's life slipped away. He spoke of nurses coming and going and well-meaning relatives trying to help but creating more stress in a situation already at the breaking point. I listened and tried to reassure him it would get better. We both knew it wouldn't.

On a Wednesday in late March, Pete seemed particularly low as we lingered longer than usual over a basket of fries. I should have started for home, but I couldn't bear to leave him. The sky had disintegrated into clouds of slate and charcoal gray. We sat in silence listening to rain pound the pavement outside like fingers drumming impatiently on a table. Car lights flashed through the windows and disappeared, creating a slow-motion strobe that intermittently cast Pete's face from light into shadows.

I hesitated a moment, afraid to ask. "How is your mom?"

"She's really sick from the chemo. But she'll be better when it's over." He looked out the window again and ran his fingers through his hair. It was not the words he uttered that pulled at my heart, but the plaintive tone of his voice that begged me to promise him his mother would be whole again.

"It's just…I'm really scared."

I swallowed the lump forming in my throat and focused on my clasped hands. "I understand." Quietly, in halting phrases, I revealed a sliver of my own tattered life, describing the depression that had plagued my mother over the years, the way it turned my world upside down, and the fear gripping me that one day she might slip away forever. "It's not the same, but I know how it hurts."

Pete put a hand gently over mine. "You should have told me before."

"I've never told anyone, not even Mary." I looked into his sad eyes. The relief of finally sharing this secret washed over me. And I wanted to be free of pretending, to tell him the entire truth about my life. But the moment was not right.

His hand remained on mine, and the knot in my middle relaxed until I felt safe and protected, as if this was where I belonged.

"I'm glad you trusted me." He squeezed my hand tighter. We sat several minutes without needing to speak.

"It's weird the way we got together, like we're meant to help each other." He gave a short, harsh laugh. "Except it's all been you helping me."

"Not true."

He glanced up, almost whispering, "You're the only person who keeps me sane. I think about you all the time." He straightened and let out a long sigh. "Is there any way we could spend more time together? I mean, besides here."

His words filled me with joy and longing. I struggled with how to answer. *Why not? Why should my parents keep me from this boy I cared for so deeply? How could this possibly be wrong?*

"I don't want to get you in trouble, but if only we could go to a movie or out to dinner. I need to be around you."

"They let me go out with a group of kids, just not alone with boys."

He leaned forward again, his face brightening. "Really? Our team has a home game Saturday. Maybe you could come with Mary, and we could go out after with her and Kevin." He smiled his first genuine smile of the day. "That's a group!"

"I'll talk to Mary." I would find a way. Adrenalin, laced with fear, rushed through my body in a surge of reckless happiness.

In the midst of my euphoria, I remembered Dang. I would have to tell him something had come up, that I couldn't go to the movies with the group on Saturday after all. There was no question in my mind where I wanted to be.

Mary and I sat at opposite ends of her bed, each a bit tentative at first. We had spent less and less time together since she had started dating Kevin and my life had been complicated by the presence of Dang and Pete. As my secrets multiplied, I had pulled away from her. We rarely talked on the phone and only had time for quick exchanges at our lockers or at lunch with the group. A disconcerting distance had grown between us that left me sad and lonely. I missed her.

When we had arrived at her house, Nancy met us at the front door and gave me a welcoming hug. It felt good to be back in what had become my second home.

We settled in Mary's room with a bag of chips and glasses of lemonade. Mary prattled on about Kevin and what they had done the previous weekend. Slowly, the awkwardness between us began to melt away, and we found the easy pace of our friendship.

I took a deep breath and pulled my shoulders up tight. "I have so much to tell. I don't know where to begin."

Mary leaned forward, her eyebrows lifted. "What?"

"It's Pete. We're going out with you and Kevin on Saturday."

Mary clapped her hands. "I knew it! Didn't I tell you he'd ask you out?" She paused a moment. "And your dad is letting you go?"

"Sort of. All he knows is I'm going with you to the basketball game."

Father had agreed to my request with only a moment of hesitation, trusting that I was telling the truth. And I had pushed away the guilt as I had pushed it away time after time. I wanted so much to be honest, to talk freely with him and have him understand my life. I missed the special relationship we had once shared, a closeness that had disappeared with all my lies.

"I'm so excited," Mary said, pulling me back and closing off my doubts. "Tell me everything. Every detail."

I explained about my afternoons with Pete, the way our feelings had deepened. For once I could be like any other girl, completely besotted by my first crush, reveling in the possibilities of romance. I told her how my pulse raced when he leaned close, and how beautiful I found his eyes. Mary interrupted with countless questions. We discussed what we would each wear on Saturday, and she made me promise to get ready at her house. The guilt over my parents and Dang faded into the background in the giddiness of sharing my good fortune with my best friend.

Out of the blue she said, "I forgot to tell you. I think I saw your cousin Blia the other day at the gas station down on Florin." She paused. "I'm not sure, because this girl was really pregnant."

It stopped me short. My elation drained away. I ran a finger over the flowered pattern of the comforter. I felt sick over Blia's unhappy situation. She was miserable with Bee and his family and had no way to escape. "She is pregnant," I said at last, "and married."

Mary's mouth flew open. "When did this happen?"

"Do you remember the guy in the pizza parlor last spring?" Mary nodded. "They got married a few months ago."

"But she's only fifteen. I didn't even think that was legal."

"It's complicated."

Mary stared at me, clearly concerned, waiting for the rational explanation I couldn't provide. I was weary of trying to keep up with the explanations and pretenses, always afraid I might say the wrong thing and give away the divisions of home and school. My competing worlds had stretched me until I could no longer meld one with the other into a whole. I thought of how relieved I felt telling Pete about my mother's illness. Something inside me shifted. A thread worked loose, a silkworm cocoon unraveling layer by layer, miles of lies falling away and collapsing in a pile at my feet. I couldn't do it any longer. Tears pooled in my eyes and dribbled down my cheeks.

Mary drew close and put a hand on my arm. "Laura, what's wrong?"

I looked at her unable to continue with anything but the truth, whatever the consequences. "My name is Nou." A small sob escaped like the yelp of an injured dog. "There's so much you don't know. My family is Hmong. From Laos. There was a war. We had to leave."

A flicker of confusion passed over her face. "But you're from Minneapolis."

"That's where we lived when we first came to America." Through a shower of tears, I began my family's story until the words poured out, my voice rising and falling through the years. Distant, vague memories suddenly became vivid and real as I relived my fear of the communist soldiers who occupied our village in Laos and the long trek out that had taken the lives of so many family members and friends. I told her of my brothers who had drowned in the river that fatal night, how we didn't have any pictures of them and I couldn't even remember their faces now. I recounted the years in the refugee camp with all its hunger and hardships until finally the opportunity to come to America arrived.

She shook her head, tears spotting her face. "It's so awful." She hugged me close. "Why didn't you ever tell me?"

"It was so hard in Minneapolis. Kids made fun of my cousins and me because we didn't speak English. They called us terrible names and said we looked funny and had strange names. I could tell you so many stories." Mary offered me tissue from the box on her nightstand, and I blew my nose. "When I came here I decided it was safer to be American, to call myself Laura. I wanted to start over and fit in."

"I don't understand." She sat back, crossing her arms around her middle. "You're my best friend, and for two years you didn't say anything?"

"If I had told you when we first met, would you have become my friend?"

Her voice grew indignant. "I can't believe you'd even ask me that. I don't care where you're from."

I swallowed hard and met her gaze. "But how could I have known? My life is completely opposite from yours. My family hardly has any money. We live in an ugly apartment on the other side of the freeway. My clothes are from thrift stores. I'm not anything like the other kids at school."

Mary sighed. "I pretty much figured that out already."

"Our Hmong culture is so …" I searched for a word, but couldn't find one. "People don't understand our customs. They think they're weird."

"You think I'm like that?"

"No. You and your family have been wonderful. I was miserable not telling you. But the longer I waited, the harder it got."

"Why now?"

"I can't do it anymore. I want to share everything, be completely honest. I don't like the person I've become." I felt desperate to make her understand, to be forgiven.

We sat a long time not speaking. Mary stared out the window, biting her lower lip. I silently prayed to whatever spirits or powers might exist that she would forgive me.

"Are you mad?" I asked at last.

"A little. I hate that you didn't trust me." Her voice broke as tears trickled down once more.

"I've never had a best friend before." I began crying.

She threw her arms around me. "I'll get over it."

"Just be my friend."

"Always." She pulled wads of tissue from the box and dabbed at her nose. "So what else haven't you told me?"

We talked for hours, before and after dinner. Mary peppered me with questions about my family and culture. I told her about the humiliating incidents in Minneapolis that had made me wary and untrusting. At times she grew testy with flashes of anger that I had kept so much from her. We talked of Blia's unhappy marriage and the expectations for Hmong girls to marry young and start a new life with the husband's family. I confided to her about Dang and how it worried me that he might envision a similar future with me. She agreed. I should tell him I couldn't see him any longer.

It might take time to navigate the change in our friendship, but we would be fine. And I would tell my story to Pete. I didn't want to pretend anymore.

On Saturday night, Mary and I reached the gym with only minutes to the start of the game. My excitement floated in the hot, steamy air. The floor vibrated beneath us as the opposing teams thumped a dozen basketballs up and down the court practicing setups and shots. Throngs of fans stood in the aisles and milled along the front of the stands. The pep band played the school song with pounding drums and blaring horns. Three hundred people sang and swayed as we climbed up the bleachers to find seats. My heart beat wildly as I searched the blue and gold jerseys. Pete turned and flashed me a smile.

The few basketball games I had attended had proved remarkably boring and mysterious to me. But tonight it didn't matter as long as I could watch Pete careening down the court and tossing the ball through the hoop. I strained to keep track of his long limbs in the jumble of bodies. After two overtimes, our team won the game eighty-two to seventy-eight.

Mary and I waited in the courtyard outside the locker room. Pete and Kevin emerged in high spirits.

"Are we the greatest or what?" Kevin whooped, throwing his arm around Mary and kissing her hard on the lips.

"You picked the right game," Pete said, gently slapping my palm in a high five. His fingers lingered for a moment. "Kevin has his car."

It was already after ten. "I have to be home by eleven thirty." I shrugged. "I'm sorry." I had argued with Father, but he had been insistent.

"It's okay. Shall we get something to eat? I'm starving."

We drove to a McDonalds where Pete and Kevin inhaled hamburgers while Mary and I sipped cokes and nibbled fries. It seemed like only minutes before it was time to go home. Pete and I sat in the back seat of Kevin's Honda. He took my hand, his palm warm, and it didn't matter that the night was over. It was already perfect.

I directed Kevin to my street, wondering what they all must think of the deserted, run down area. "You can drop me off on the corner," I said as we came up on the Short Stop. "I don't want my dad to see me." I didn't mention my cousins or Dang.

Kevin pulled over, and Pete got out with me. "Can I walk you part way?" I nodded. We walked across the street, staying in the shadows away from the street lights.

"I'm glad you came," he said softly. "Maybe we can try again next week."

"It was a great game." I shivered in the icy wind. "Thanks."

He bent over, put his arm around my shoulder, and gently kissed my lips. We both giggled at our awkwardness. He kissed me again, longer and deeper. And in that moment, nothing else mattered.

He stepped back, grinning. "I'll stay here until you walk the rest of the way."

I covered the half-block to my apartment and turned to find Pete standing where I left him. He waved one last time. When the sound of Kevin's car had died away, I climbed the metal stairs to our apartment.

I was surprised to find my father sitting at the dining room table pouring over the farm accounts. Usually he was in bed early, but he must have stayed up to check on me. For a moment, I worried he might have seen me with Pete, that somehow he knew I had not told him the truth.

He looked up and gave me a rare smile. "You're home on time." He stretched his arms over his head. "Did you have a good time? Who won the game?"

I sat down, suddenly excited to share the details of the game as I used to share books and things I had learned in school. The young girl still existed inside me, the part of me that adored her father and longed to bridge the gap to connect once more. As I began to tell him about the game, we were interrupted by the sound of feet pounding up the stairs. The door to our apartment flew open. Uncle Soua stood in the entrance, his face ashen.

"Pao, help me."

My father jumped to his feet. "What's happened?"

Soua looked at us dazed. "Blia's been shot. Bee is dead."

Uncle Soua's words—shot, dead--lingered in the air, but I could not connect them with any reality I knew. It was not possible to comprehend this image of violence here in America, where we had come to be safe. I read the same disbelief in Father's eyes as he looked about wildly. A cold chill of fear raced through my body.

Chapter 26
PAO

Two Saturdays after the shooting, the family worked in the fields preparing for the new crops. We were still stunned by the terrible events. I tried not to give in to the feeling of hopelessness pressing on me, even though it seemed that violence followed our people wherever we went. We could not escape. But in a few weeks sunlight would penetrate the soil sufficiently to welcome tender new plants of tomatoes, corn, peppers, cucumber, squash, and beans, sown and nurtured in our greenhouse. I told myself to concentrate on the resurgence of life. I should enjoy the luxury of quiet hours and uncomplicated labor where my mind could wander.

Uncle Boua turned to me from the next row where he knelt, clearing spent onions and weeds. "Is Soua coming this afternoon?" he asked

"Yes. They should be back from visiting Blia soon." I glanced at the far end of the field where my wife and others were removing the last of the Chinese broccoli and beets. The shock of Bee's death hung about us like the haze rising from the ground in the early morning hours. It was a sad and shameful thing for Soua and Yer to bear, and we all mourned for them.

Blia and Bee had been with a friend in a liquor store parking lot, sitting on the hood of their car. Another car drove through the lot, fired three shots, and tore off into the traffic. The bullet that burst through Bee's chest, killing him in seconds, had continued on, slashing Blia's neck as she tried to duck. She had lost a great deal of blood and two days later went into early labor. Now she and the baby were recovering.

"Did you hear they arrested two boys last night?" I asked.

He stopped his digging for a moment. "Ia said they're Vietnamese, fourteen and fifteen years old. How is it possible they had a car and guns? Where are their parents?"

"They stole the car. Who knows how they could get hold of guns. Bee's friend was in a fight with one boy's brother last week. I don't know if Bee was involved or not. They're from a rival gang."

"Such a waste of young lives." He sighed as we inched our way up the row.

I methodically turned the soil and pulled bunches of weeds from the clods of dirt, thinking how out of place the cheerful, yellow dandelions seemed. "After the funeral tomorrow, I will go with Soua to negotiate with Bee's family. Blia and her child must come home."

Uncle paused again. "Will they agree?"

"It has been unhappy from the beginning."

He shook his head slowly. "These gangs are destroying our young men. This makes four deaths in recent months."

My chest grew tight as I thought of the evils besetting our people each day, heaping more tragedies upon us. In Laos we knew our enemy, the face of communism. But the enemy here was amorphous, a creeping fungus, slowly choking us to death.

"I don't know what to think," I said. "Parents who come to the community center are lost, unable to control their children. Sometimes their kids speak so little Hmong, they can hardly talk to them." I waved my trowel in the air, cutting at my frustration. "I interpreted for a family last week. The boy, only fifteen, goes to this Kennedy High, where Bee went. He told me they need the gangs for protection. If they don't join, they'll be beat up and hurt. His mother cried and begged him to stop, to be a good son again. The boy said he couldn't get out, even if he wanted to. The father sat in silence, ashamed." I hit the ground hard with my trowel. "The boy spewed so much anger." I thought of his words and how they had struck a chord within me. He told me he couldn't talk to his parents. They didn't understand him. Their ideas came from the past as if they still lived in Laos. It frightened me. I could not help but wonder if there were things I did not know about my own children. Did Nou feel this estrangement from her mother and me? Did this cause the distance between us?

Uncle straightened to stretch his back. "Our children no longer respect their elders. They have no appreciation for our past and what we have sacrificed. How many of them really understand what it's like to have your life and land threatened by enemies carrying guns and false faces, to be without food or shelter?"

I nodded, full of the same thoughts. Most of our children had not experienced life in Laos and the horrors of the war. They were little children when we left, or were born in the refugee camps or America.

Uncle stood and carried his basket of weeds to the wheelbarrow at the end of the row. He returned with heavy steps. "What do these gangs think they can accomplish but more violence and death?"

"They see all the wealth around them, flashy cars, nice clothes, big houses. They want to have these things too. They prove how tough they are by selling drugs and robbing stores. I asked one boy, why he wanted to get in trouble and maybe go to jail or die. I told him to work hard in school and get a good job, respect his parents. He just laughed in my face, said I didn't get it. Said he was never going to belong here." I shook my head.

Uncle's eyes flashed. "We can't give up. Our children must succeed. First they learn English, and some will go to college. They will have good jobs. It takes time. Someday Americans will understand what the Hmong are made of and respect us."

I sighed, hoping he was right. I could not allow myself to give up. I only hoped to keep my own children safe.

That night I lay in bed with Yer. I reached out for her and she did not stiffen or pull away. The conversation with Uncle Boua had stripped away the protective layers of logic, and my fears lay exposed to the night air. I wanted to explain how I needed the comfort of her warm body to heal the cold eating at my heart. I wanted to tell her how much I loved her still, how dear she was to me, how hard it was when she slipped away from me. But I did not know how to form these words with my lips, so I simply stroked her long silky hair, hoping she understood.

She turned on her side to face me and put an arm lightly across my stomach. "I'm glad Blia and the baby will come home to live. Her mother has been so lonely."

"It is better for everyone."

"Bee's parents are not good people, yet I feel sad for them. It is terrible to lose their only son."

The words floated around us with the ever-present memory of our own boys. I did not want Yer to start again on this path.

Yer snuggled closer. "We are lucky our children are doing well and not getting into trouble."

"They are in good schools, free of gangs."

"I can picture Nou's future now. I'm sure Dang's people will come soon to arrange a marriage. I see the way he looks at her."

"Are you sure Nou is ready to marry? I would like her to finish high school. She wants to go to college if we can find the money."

"All that talk. What does school have to do with being a good wife or mother? As soon as Dang wants to marry, her big ideas will fly away. He is a smart boy. He will get a good job. Nou doesn't need to worry."

"Nou is stubborn. If we push her too hard, she might resist."

"You'll see," Yer assured me.

So many worries swirled in my head. I could not say why I did not leap at the thought of marrying Nou to a good boy from a respectable family who had a bright future. He was the husband every father would want for their daughter. But I did not believe Nou would be that quick to jump at an offer for marriage. She wanted to continue her education. I was proud of her intellect and ambition.

Marriage and children could easily deny or postpone those dreams. I did not want her to suffer the same disappointment I had felt all my life. Yet every day I saw her traveling in a different direction from her Hmong upbringing. I felt saddened by the way she addressed me at times, the flat, insincere tone of her voice, and the words, the truth, she seemed to hold back. I was never sure how she spent her time at school and with her friends. Soon the gulf between us might be too great. If a marriage to Dang kept her safe and saved the honor of the family, perhaps it was best.

Chapter 27
LAURA

I abandoned all sense of caution falling in love. Nothing else mattered. I spent every possible moment with Pete during and after school, meeting at Mary's house or the Sea Treasure, driving around town in the back seat of Kevin's car, sitting close, holding hands, stealing tender kisses, content just to be in one another's presence. I felt happier and freer with him than I had ever felt in my life, sharing my secrets, wanting him to know my family's story and the confines of my Hmong upbringing. I explained the complicated situation with Dang, reassuring him that Dang was nothing more than a friend. Pete leaned on me as his mother slowly faded from this world.

I convinced myself our relationship could remain secret without consequences, even as I constantly looked over my shoulder. We didn't tell anyone at school we were together for fear my cousin Mee might find out. Of course it must have been obvious from our gazes and smiles as we walked through the halls, the way we casually brushed shoulders and touched hands.

My behavior at home became more erratic and volatile. I grew agitated trying to come up with ever more improbable excuses to be off with Pete. My appetite disappeared, sleep eluded me, and

I found it hard to concentrate on my studies. At times I escaped into blissful daydreams, absentmindedly folding the dirty laundry, knocking over a glass of water at dinner, or forgetting to bathe my little brothers before bed. Mother chided me, asking where I had left my head. You must be thinking about Dang, she would say. My vehement denials only reinforced her beliefs.

I had tried for weeks to gently break things off with Dang, claiming I was too busy when he called or came by to visit, making excuses why I couldn't go with the group on the weekend. Surely he would see it was hopeless and give up. I couldn't tell him there was someone else, someone my parents would never accept, or that I could no longer bear his attentions and expectations. Yet the more I avoided him, the more impatient and cold I became, the more he persisted. He loomed in the background like the specter of Blia's ill-fated marriage.

Blia and her baby daughter had returned home to live with her parents much to the delight of her mother and mine. They doted and cooed over the newest addition to the family, a chubby, demanding infant with robust lungs and a shock of black hair that stood straight up like needles on a frightened porcupine. Mother lauded the joys of motherhood and prattled on about how wonderful it would be to have a grandchild of her own one day. But all I observed were the physical and emotional scars left by Blia's unhappy union and her obvious distress at the prospect of raising a child when she was still no more than a child herself.

One evening in the middle of April, Father sat down after dinner to open the mail. I was doing homework on the sofa in the living room with my siblings scattered around me in front of the TV. Father called my name, and I looked up. He held two pieces of paper in his hand. His expression filled with confusion.

"This is from a Mrs. Martin. About something called the SAT test."

"That's my counselor. Remember? I told you I need to take the test to apply for college."

He nodded slowly. "She says the school has funding to help pay the fee if I fill out this form." He glanced at the pages again and frowned. "She refers to you as my daughter Laura."

My stomach lurched.

"Why would she call you that?"

The absurdity of keeping this from my parents all this time, letting months and years slip by suddenly struck me. I licked my lips. "I meant to tell you. I decided to use an American name at school."

"Since when?"

"For a while."

Father narrowed his eyes. "How long?"

I paused and took a deep breath. "Since we moved here."

Disbelief flickered across his face as he jerked his head back. "And only now I find out?"

Words tumbled out, "I didn't know what you would say. If I use Nou, then I have to explain I'm Hmong and from Laos. No one even knows where that is."

Mother emerged from the kitchen, where she had been listening to the exchange, and stood next to Father. She shook her head. "What is wrong with being Hmong?"

I met her gaze. "You know how kids treated me in Minneapolis, all the teasing and name calling. I didn't want to be different."

Mother threw her hands up and returned to washing dishes in the kitchen.

Father took off his reading glasses and rubbed the bridge of his nose. At last he turned to me again. "You could have told us. Hmong people are always honest."

I folded my hands in my lap, staring at the worn, dirty carpet beneath my bare feet. I dreaded his anger, but all I heard was disappointment.

"What kind of life is it if you have to pretend to be someone else?" He let out a long, weary sigh. "How can I know if there is more you are not telling us?"

"I'm sorry." The guilt and lies and subterfuge gathered in a burning lump in my middle. I loved my father. I wanted him to be proud of me. This disappointment with me might pass, but I had damaged our relationship and his opinion in ways I couldn't repair. A deeper truth kept us at odds, for I would never be able to reconcile his rules and expectations with the reality of my dreams. At some point, I would have to choose.

Chapter 28
PAO

Everything changed overnight. Like a sack of rice split open, the grains raining onto the ground, becoming dirty and spoiled. The days took on a confusion that refused to end. I could not distinguish the sequence of events or reconcile the pain in my heart. I had not felt as lost and full of despair since our fateful journey out of Laos across the Mekong River.

It started in late April when the weather turned hot and our fields sprouted healthy young plants. Everything seemed deceptively as it should be. Then Nou became sick to her stomach and ran a mild fever. That Monday we insisted she stay home from school. Yer prepared an herb drink for the fever and massaged her body with mint to relax the muscles. When this did not help, I rubbed her back with a silver coin wedged in the middle of a hard-boiled egg to draw the illness from her body. But these cures provided only temporary relief. I gave her aspirin, but this upset her stomach more. Still the fever persisted. She could not keep any nourishment down. Her cheeks became pale, her eyes dull.

Dang and Mary called every day, but she was too weak to talk to them. Mee reported Dang was very worried about her. Yer reminded

Nou how lucky she was to have such a good and caring young man. Nou only groaned, holding her middle and turning away.

On the third evening Nou burned with a high fever again, drifting into fitful sleep. When Mary called, I told her Nou was sleeping and not to disturb her again. Perhaps my voice sounded too sharp out of worry. But I did not appreciate the interference of an outsider.

I asked Uncle Boua to perform a *khov kuam* to determine what was wrong. He took his split buffalo horns from his altar and prayed to the spirits to tell him the source of Nou's illness. Five times he threw the horns on the floor before the answer came. It was as I feared. Three of her souls had fled her body, and evil spirits held them in the other realm. He continued throwing the horns for twenty minutes, questioning what we must do to appease the spirits and allow her souls to return. After much negotiation, an agreement was reached. If she became better within three days, we would hold a *hu plig*, a soul calling, and sacrifice a pig.

When Nou woke again, I asked her if she could think of any event that might have caused her souls to become upset and run off. Was she burdened by a problem that she had not told me about? She offered no answers, but grew agitated and withdrawn when I persisted. The only explanation I could think of was her decision to change her name. Perhaps the weight of this secret, the disrespect of denying her Hmong heritage and ancestors, had offended her souls. This could explain why I felt her slipping away from her family, becoming more remote, already departed on another path.

That night Yer and I took turns watching over Nou, placing cool rags on her hot, damp forehead, trying to get her to sip a few drops of water. When I finally succumbed to exhaustion, frightening dreams woke me. Strangers called to me from across a vast, swift river with important secrets about Nou, but I could not catch the meaning of their words. I woke in a sweat, full of dread.

By morning Nou's fever had subsided, and she was able to keep down a cup of vegetable broth. Her breathing ebbed and flowed without effort. The spirits were keeping their part of the bargain, and I would keep mine. Yer informed the family we would hold a *hu plig* Saturday morning. She told Mee to invite Dang, saying this would help Nou feel better.

Auntie Khou and Kia arrived early that morning to help. Yer showed them the collection of fresh mangos, bananas, papayas, and flowers she had purchased the day before, which now decorated the dining room table. They bustled about the kitchen readying pots of water on the stove, chopping mounds of pork and vegetables and filling the rice cooker. I selected two chickens, a male and female from our coop, to help Uncle Boua in reaching the spirits. I had purchased a three-year-old sow to offer its soul in exchange for the safe return of Nou's souls.

Nou, listless and silent, watched from her mattress as the family completed the preparations. Uncle Boua brought his shaman's bench, the horse he would ride into the other realm, and set it in front of our altar. Yer placed a bowl of rice with a raw egg on a small table by the door to welcome the spirits and her returning souls. Houa and Moa punched out patterns on special gold paper to make a stack of spirit money. Boa cut lengths of cotton string for each member of the family to tie around Nou's wrist, which would keep her newly returned souls safe with her body.

As I watched the girls work, I thought of all the soul callings performed for our family over the years—each New Year, during illnesses, and before we embarked on major journeys from Thailand to the U.S. and Minneapolis to Sacramento. The first time I tied a string around Nou's wrist, she was only a tiny baby, three-days old. It was a moment of great joy as we held the naming ceremony. Yer and I had selected Nou, meaning sun, for our precious child. She had brought the light back into our lives after the dark chaos of the war finally ended.

A shiver snaked down my back thinking of how close I had come to losing her that night in the Mekong River, her hand slipping from mine. It had taken all my strength to pull her back.

Uncle wore his black shaman's pants and silk jacket tied with a bright red sash. He placed his hood on the bench. He smoothed the patterned paper covering the altar, arranged his tools, candles, and incense, along with three cups of holy water and bundles of spirit money. Everything was in place.

The family began to assemble. Gia, Soua, and I would assist Uncle. Dang arrived with Mee and Tou and rushed to Nou's side. Nou frowned, hardly looking at him, as if his presence sapped what little energy she had left. The phone rang, distracting me as we were set to begin. Once again it was Mary inquiring about Nou, insisting she must talk to her for a moment. I explained it was not a good time and hung up, impatient with her intrusion at this critical moment.

Uncle sat Nou on a chair in the center of the room, wearing her t-shirt, pajama bottoms, and best Hmong jacket made of black silk with indigo sleeves. She seemed weak and woozy, uncomfortable with all eyes focused on her. He lighted candles and incense to provide light in the realm of the unseen and put on his finger cymbals tied with pieces of red cloth, representing helping spirits. He banged the gong to alert the family to get ready to begin.

I took over the gong, beating a slow steady rhythm as Uncle sang the familiar chants calling to the spirits. He placed a stack of spirit money on Nou's shoulders, a payment for the renewal of her life passport. The gods had issued this paper before she was born, determining her luck in life and the date of her death. He must insure that date was not due for a long time.

Gia brought the chickens in from their cage on the front porch and held them one at a time over a plate, quickly slitting their necks. The animals' souls would help Uncle negotiate with spirits in the other world. Yer took the chickens to clean and boil. Later we would examine the chickens' skulls, tongues, beaks, and feet for signs that Nou's wayward souls had been returned. The two feet must match exactly and the tongue remain uncurled.

Shone and Gia carried the pig, tied and wrapped in a sheet, upstairs from the pen beside the apartment. It squealed and struggled, its chest heaving up and down, as they laid it on the plastic sheeting covering the rug. The pig gazed up, eyes full of distress, straining to be free. Uncle ran a string around the pig's upper body and wrapped the other end twice around Nou's middle, walking back and forth between them and shaking his rattle to make contact with Nou's souls.

He called to his *neng*, his familiar spirit. On the second throw of his buffalo horns the pieces landed flat side down--his *neng* had heard him. He placed spirit money next to the pig and thanked it for offering its soul in exchange. The pig accepted with the first throw of the horns.

Gia swiftly slit the pig's neck. Blood gushed into a wide shallow bowl, sending the smell of hot metal floating through the air. Uncle dipped spirit money into the blood and placed it on Nou' shoulders, and in exchange, took the spirit money already on Nou's shoulders and placed it on the pig. He dipped his finger-bells in the red liquid to mark several lines on Nou's back to keep her safe from any harm by evil spirits.

He was ready to embark upon a trip to the heavens. Uncle slipped the black hood over his head to blind him to the outside world. Accompanied by his rings and finger-cymbals, he sat on his horse, ready for his *neng* to assist him on the long journey. The trip might take four or five hours, and afterward he would have no recollection of the tongues in which he spoke, the many places he passed, or his negotiations with the spirits. I continued the steady beat of the gong as he relaxed into a dreamy state and freed his mind of the present world. Soua and Shone watched to make sure Uncle did not fall as he stood on the bench bouncing up and down, shaking his rattle, traveling farther and farther away.

Then a strange commotion erupted from the front porch. The front door flew open and slammed into the wall. A rush of air poured over me like the cool breath of a ghost. Kia gasped. I turned, temporarily blinded by the sun streaming through the open door.

Mary stood in the doorway, a halo of light behind her. Her enormous eyes darted from the string tied around Nou's middle and red streaks down her back to the slaughtered pig on the floor, the sheet covered in globs of blood, now turning a rusty brown. She let out a short, piercing scream.

Uncle collapsed on the bench and pulled his hood from his head. Then footsteps pounded up the stairs. A young man, tall and blond, dressed in blue jeans and a white t-shirt, pushed past Mary. He looked around and rushed to Nou's side. He threw his arm around her shoulders. "Are you hurt? What are they doing to you?"

Nou shook her head. "I'm fine. It's okay."

Dang, standing against the wall, lunged forward, his eyes wild. "Don't touch her." He pulled the stranger's arm away and pushed him hard. They began shoving and yelling at one another to back off.

Yer grabbed my arm. "Pao, do something."

"Stop! Stop! Please stop!" Nou came out of her chair.

I tried to step between the boys, but an elbow flew out and hit me hard in the head. I reeled back. Everyone was shouting. Shone, Gia and Soua crowded in, dragging the boys apart, holding them by the arms.

Mary edged toward Nou. "Laura, I'm, I'm so sorry. We thought something bad had happened to you."

"Everyone calm down," I said, finding my voice at last. "Nou, what is going on?"

Nou turned to me with tears streaming down her cheeks, her face as panicked and distressed as the pig's had been before we took his soul to the other world.

"Who is this person?" I asked. In the pit of my stomach I knew I did not want the answer.

The boy twisted free of Gia's grip and offered me his hand, which I did not take. "I'm Pete Williams, Nou's friend."

He pulled his hand back, surveying the pig and pool of blood, the lighted candles and incense, the shocked faces of our family. He appeared baffled and lost.

Anger welled inside me. "What are you doing intruding on our family? What right do you have?"

He stood there haplessly, staring at Nou.

"Who is this guy?" Dang demanded of Nou. He stepped toward Pete again. "She's my girlfriend. You'd better get out of here."

"You don't own her," Pete said softly. "She can choose who she wants."

220

Nou sank onto her chair, sobbing. She looked up at Pete. "It's best if you go."

Pete glanced at me and turned to Nou. "I can't leave you alone like this."

"I'm fine. Just go. Please," Nou begged.

Silence fell over the room as Pete and Mary reluctantly departed. Family members quietly slipped out. Only Uncle Boua remained.

I felt sick to my stomach. Clearly my daughter had been seeing this boy, hiding the relationship from us, lying about where she was going. She had done this knowing he would never be acceptable to her family. And here, in front of everyone, Nou's dishonesty had been revealed. Her reputation would be ruined, our family disgraced. All the years I had cherished my perfect, dutiful daughter, believed in her intelligence and purpose, supported her dreams. This is how she repaid me.

I asked Dang to leave us to sort things out. Nou, stripped of all defenses, offered a tearful confession. She loved Pete with all her heart, she said. It could not be wrong to care for someone so deeply, someone who needed her and felt the same. This was America, she said, everything was different. Why couldn't we understand?

Yer was beside herself, full of angry recriminations. I was too upset to ask anything but the most basic of questions. I had no idea how to fix this, to stop the situation from ruining all our lives. There was the honor of the family and clan to think of. I forbid her to see Pete again and hoped she would see the error of her choice. But this would not fix the damage she had done.

Much later, as I reflected on the dark and bitter weeks that followed, I thought about the *hu plig*. Uncle had never completed his travels to the other realm and retrieved Nou's missing souls. She had recovered her physical health, but she was lost to her family forever.

Chapter 29
LAURA

The judge concentrates on every word Mrs. Hernandez says, as if hoping to glean additional information beyond what is in the report he has read. Mrs. Hernandez stops to take a sip of water. The court reporter coughs and shifts in her seat. Mary leans forward and squeezes my arm. My heart begins to beat an irregular rhythm. My fingers feel tingly.

Mrs. Hernandez speaks in a calm and noncommittal voice as if she is describing the temperature outside. "Your honor, as you see in my report, the difficulty began when Laura's parents found out she was seeing a young man outside their culture."

I want to speak up and add that my family took a chance coming to America, with its promise of freedom. Yet they cling to ancient customs and rigid ideas, which contradict everything we have strived for. Yes, I lied and kept secrets, trying to survive in a strange place. But I am a good daughter. How could it surprise them that I want the right to choose my future?

"Her family is insisting she marry another young man, Dang Moua. Laura does not want to marry him. She is only seventeen, and has another year of high school. While many Hmong girls

223

marry young, obviously, it is not acceptable for her family to force or coerce her into marrying against her wishes."

Dang and his father returned to our apartment that night with the marriage proposal. I pleaded with Father not to ask me to do this. I did not love Dang. I begged him to let me finish school. I promised never to see Pete again, even if it broke my heart. But Father was blinded by disappointment and anger. He said I had forfeited all rights with my lies and unacceptable behavior. He could never trust me again. The family's honor was at stake.

My parents would exile me to another family with a husband I hardly understood and did not love. How could I trust that Dang might behave differently in this life in America. I feared that as a Hmong husband, the head of the household, his expectations would remain rooted in the old ways. My dreams for college and a career could disappear before I ever had a chance to start.

I lay in bed all that night, struggling to understand what was happening to me. Distress turned to panic like a vise closing in and choking the air from my lungs.

As the first hint of dawn turned the sky from ebony to sapphire and stars faded into nothingness, I slipped from my bed and crept out the door. My hand lingered on the doorknob a few seconds. I understood the consequences. There would be no turning back.

The metal stairs under my bare feet sent cold chills up my spine. In the parking lot, I put on my shoes and began to run. Still sick and weak, my legs felt weighted down. My lungs strained for air. But I ran and ran, down the street in the shadows of the streetlamps, past the Short Stop and vacant lot full of weeds, and across the freeway overpass. The whine of cars below filled my ears like a siren going off in my head. I ran fifteen blocks past sleeping households to the sanctuary of Mary's home.

Mrs. Hernandez shifts from one foot to the other and looks up at the judge over the rims of her glasses. "Your Honor, Laura left home to stay with the Shannons. After a confrontation with her father, she called our office to step in."

Father knew immediately where to find me. He and Uncle Boua showed up a few hours later. I tried to explain, but he only became more irrational. I had never heard him so angry. He demanded Mr. Shannon let them take me home. Father made terrible threats, caught up in the fury of his helplessness. The whole time I was sobbing and begging him to stop. The police arrived and warned Father and Uncle they would have to take them to jail if they did not leave.

"Given the unstable nature of Laura's father, the Shannons petitioned the court for temporary custody of Laura and a restraining order on Mr. Lee, pending a hearing on the case. This was granted by Judge Owen." Mrs. Hernandez turns to the next page of her notes. "A week ago Tuesday, Dang Moua, the young man Laura's parents wish her marry, and several of his friends made an attempt to kidnap Laura on her way to school. In the Hmong culture, if a young man takes a woman to his home and keeps her there for three days, she is considered his wife. Luckily, Mr. Shannon drove by and stopped them. There is now a restraining order on Mr. Moua as well."

Mrs. Hernandez describes the two meetings with my family, which only antagonized Father more. "Laura is a very bright and dedicated young woman. Her teachers at school report she has worked hard and has an excellent academic record that will enable her to attend a good college with a full scholarship. She has a promising future. Surely her parents must realize what she risks losing."

The judge nods and thanks Mrs. Hernandez as she sits down.

My attorney steps forward and explains that the Shannons have offered to assume full custody until my eighteenth birthday.

The judge turns to my father. "Mr. Lee, I have reviewed the facts in this case and find it very troubling. The court does not wish to take children from their families. But legally, you cannot insist that your daughter marry against her wishes." He stares at him for a moment. "Do you understand?"

Father stands up, his shoulders squared with tattered pride. "I am head of family. I decide what is best for my daughter. Dang will be good husband."

I think of how others must view my father--a small and spare man in a worn jacket, speaking imperfect English, an unreasonable person. And I ache for him. I want to explain that he has been a loving parent, a source of strength in our unstable, shifting life. They cannot see both sides as I do. These people can't understand how hard it is for Father to accept a system that will not recognize his authority over his family. My parents lost their relatives and friends, their village and homeland, now bit by bit America is tearing away their Hmong existence, luring their children down another path.

"But do you understand you cannot force your daughter to marry against her will in this country?" the judge asks.

"Yes, yes, but I am her father. In Hmong culture, elders decide what is best."

The judge sighs. "Mr. Lee, I cannot allow you to take Laura back into custody unless you guarantee the court you will not try to marry her."

Father puts his hands behind his back, feet apart. "She is disobedient daughter who brings her family great shame. Marriage is the only way to save the family."

"I will find you in contempt of court and place you in jail if you do not comply. Is that clear?" The judge's voice grows more impatient.

"How can you tell me what to do with my own daughter? What kind of American freedom is this?"

The judge rubs his forehead and leans back in the chair. After a long pause, he turns back to me. "Miss Lee, I am going to give you the choice. The Shannons have agreed to provide you with a home for the next year. I am ready to grant them custody, if that is what you wish. Or you can go home with your parents and a court order that you are not to marry without your written consent. Do you feel your parents' will adhere to the court's terms?"

"She is *my* daughter," Father yells.

I turn to my father, my heart breaking. "I love my parents and I don't want to hurt them." I repeated the sentence in Hmong to Mother. "But as you can see, nothing will change my father's mind. For him this is about saving face and family honor. That is more important to him than my future. He gives me no choice. I will stay with the Shannons." The words fall from my mouth like heavy stones.

The judge nods. "Mr. Lee, I regret this decision. I understand there are cultural issues involved, but your daughter has a right to live her life as she wants. I hereby grant the Shannons custody of Laura Nou Lee until her eighteenth birthday. Mr. and Mrs. Lee, you may have visitation rights under the Shannons' supervision, which can be worked out by Child Protective Services. I am also extending the restraining order on Dang Moua, and I suggest this young man stay clear of Laura or face charges."

Uncle explains the outcome to Mother, and she lets out a low howl. Father staggers toward the courtroom door, Uncle holding him up, my mother following behind.

I call out to them, "Please, I'm sorry."

Father slowly turns around. "You are no longer my daughter." And he slams out the door.

EPILOGUE

 I hurried from the library and across campus as the carillon rang the noon hour. Sunshine streamed down from a dazzlingly blue sky, but a chill touched my shoulders the moment I passed under the shade of the sprawling oak trees. The university was oddly quiet. With the semester almost over, many students had already gone home. I turned on Shattuck Avenue and gazed down the hill past the expanse of buildings spilling onto the shore of the glistening bay. In the distance a thick bank of fog hung over the hills of San Francisco and towers of the Golden Gate Bridge. Even after four years, the view never failed to amaze me.

But I needed to get home. Blia and her daughter May, now five, would be arriving within the hour. I climbed uphill past tiny cottages painted rainbow hues with neat, tidy gardens lush with tangled thickets of climbing roses, dahlias, lavender, lobelia, and dark-eyed pansies. At last I reached my bright yellow duplex. Behind the picket fence that framed the front yard, my tomatoes, long beans, squash, lemon grass, Chinese broccoli, and bitter melons flourished. I knew May would have fun wandering through the rows to hunt for caterpillars and sow bugs, and I had a glass jar ready for her collection.

We were sharing a special celebration for Blia's birthday, her graduation from junior college the week before, and my graduation from Berkeley the following week. For four years I struggled to balance my studies with part time work to supplement scholarships and loans. I had made it. In the fall, I would start at Hasting law school in San Francisco. But it was Blia's determination that I admired. After finishing continuation high school, she worked and saved for two years before enrolling in junior college. She had managed a heavy load of classes, worked full time, and raised her little girl with her parents' help. I had balloons, streamers, sodas, chips, and a chocolate cake to mark the occasion.

I dropped my book bag next to the desk in my bedroom. The answering machine flashed with two messages. The first was from Mary. *Nou, where are you? Call me as soon as you can. Josh and I are going out to dinner tomorrow night with a friend of his from L.A. I thought maybe you'd like to come. This guy is really cute. It's just dinner. Call me!*

I laughed. She never stopped trying to fix me up. Even though we lived across the bay from one another and talked on the phone at least three times a week, we were lucky to get together once a month. Now she was engaged to Josh. There had been no one significant in my life since Pete and I broke up at the beginning of our junior year in college. For over two years, we trekked back and forth on weekends between Berkeley and Stanford to be together. But with only our past to hold us together, we drifted apart. That last summer, Pete traveled with friends to Europe, while I worked at Macy's during the day and waitressed evenings. The disconnect between our lives became too glaring. As junior year began, the phone calls and visits became as perfunctory and strained as our lovemaking. The end came naturally, a mutually agreed upon parting, without surprises. All that remained was a lingering emptiness and sorrow for feelings that had faded away.

The second message was Blia. *Hey cuz. We're going to be about twenty minutes late. Sorry, but you know how hard it is for me to get out of here. May is so excited to see you. And we have a really big surprise for you.*

230

It didn't matter if they were late. I needed the extra time to straighten up and fix lunch. I retrieved the sweatshirt I had tossed across a basket of journals and hung it in the hall closet. My roommate had moved out the week before so the living room was nearly bare. I had arranged enormous blue and green pillows on the hardwood floor along the left wall. Shelves, made of bricks and boards, ran along the opposite wall with my inexpensive stereo system, CDs, rows of books, and four framed photos. In the dining room, two chairs and a stool surrounded a card table, and a TV tray against the wall held the blue tea pot with matching cups Mary had given me last Christmas.

I selected a CD of classical guitar music and turned up the volume. In the kitchen, I filled the electric rice cooker, pulled out the pot of soup, made that morning with fresh garden vegetables, and set it on a low burner, then assembled the ingredients for green papaya salad. Humming along with the music, I chopped and diced and tossed the salad. The drinks were cold, the table set, and streamers and balloons hung from the overhead light fixtures. I blew up five more balloons for May to play with and tossed them in the corner. I turned down the music and peeked out the front window. There was no sign of Blia's car, only Mrs. Wilcox from down the street walking her cocker spaniel.

I lighted the blue, square candle that sat next to sticks of ginger incense in a bowl of amber sand and a picture of my family Blia had taken at the last New Year's celebration. These rested on a black runner edged with embroidery, cross stitch, and reverse appliqué in bright colors, which I had made last winter. Here at this makeshift altar, I prayed to my ancestors and spirits. Another piece of my *paj ntaub* in red, green, and white interlocking lines that formed the family pattern was framed and hung above the book shelf. Ironically, I found sewing relaxed me after a long day of school and work. There was something reassuring in controlling the needle to create tiny stitches and mixing bright colors of thread. I liked to improvise on traditional patterns, to create something unique.

I studied the family photo as I often did. My sisters, brothers, and cousins were all at least a foot taller now, their faces thinner, more mature. But I would know them anywhere. There were several new babies I had never met. Mother and Father appeared weary and somber, old beyond their years. Father looked thinner than ever, drowning in his clothes. The skin on his face hung in loose folds. I missed them all every day, an ache that never diminished.

Since that day in court five years before, I had been banished from the Lee family as if I had never existed. Senior year I had spoken occasionally to Mee at school, but even she distanced herself. If I asked about my parents or siblings, she shifted uncomfortably and made excuses why she had to go. Then one day shortly before my high school graduation, Blia walked into the drug store where I was working. She said she had thought about me a lot and realized how unfair the situation had been. She understood. The relief and joy of having one of my family reach out to me, even if it was the most unlikely person of all, reduced me to tears. She hugged me and said no matter what our crazy family thought, she wanted to see me. It started with lunches every few weeks. May's presence helped bridge the awkwardness and distance. A friendship blossomed. She and May had been visiting me weekends in Berkeley whenever they could for the last four years.

As we grew closer, I finally gathered the courage to ask Blia what had happened right after I left. She said it had been hardest on my mother. She had slipped in and out of her dark periods for months. My sisters were devastated, angry with our parents and then with me. My young brothers kept asking for me not understanding what had happened, thinking I was coming back. My parents continued to work hard and do their best. I could not help but wonder if they had wiped me from the slate, no longer giving me a thought. Did they ever feel regret?

I went to check on the soup and filled a bowl with chips. The doorbell rang and I raced back, flinging the door open, ready to scoop May into my arms. At first, all I saw was a tiny woman in a navy blue dress with a double row of white buttons down the front, a red bead necklace and earrings, and graying hair swept up on top of her head. She stood very still, clutching a package. I thought she must be one of the religious ladies who walked the neighborhood handing out pamphlets.

"Hello, Nou."

My brain finally registered what I never could have expected, and my hand flew to my mouth. "Mother."

She gave me a tentative smile. "I surprise you. I come in?"

"Please." I reeled back, my mind spinning as she stepped into the room. "But how…"

"Blia bring me," she answered before I could finish my question. "She took May to park," she added as I glanced out front.

My heart beat wildly. It was impossible to comprehend. "You're speaking English."

A grin spread across her face as she put her head to one side, like a shy schoolgirl. "I learn for almost two year. Your brother and sister help."

She placed her package on the floor, leaning it against the bookshelf. "For you, later."

"I can't believe you are really here. How are you?"

"I am happy now."

"And Moa and Houa and all the children."

"Everyone is fine."

"And Father?"

Her lips pulled together in a tight, hard line. "He is the same."

I stared at her with a million questions. Why had she come? Was she still angry? Did she want an apology? Or would she offer one? Did she still love me? I longed to throw my arms around her and tell her how much I missed her. But then again, I wanted to ask how she could have abandoned me, how she could have waited five years for this moment. Instead, I grabbed a chair from the dining room and asked her to sit down.

"You can show me your apartment maybe."

"Of course." I took her on a tour of the black and white tile bathroom and two small bedrooms--one empty as I waited for my new roommate to move in--then the kitchen with its ancient appliances and covered back porch.

"Everything nice. I wonder for long time how you live." She paused to inspect the simmering pot of soup. "Smell good."

In the living room again, she stood by the front window. "Good garden. You do this?"

"Yes. I like fresh things." While I was growing up, she had rarely said anything complimentary. It could not be easy for her to do it now.

She nodded her approval and turned to my shelves, inspecting my books and CDs. She picked up the frame that held a photo of me with four other girls and ten boys, all Hmong, having a picnic in Tilden Park. I noticed the frame shaking in her hands and became aware that my own hands were trembling as well.

I answered her puzzled look. "Those are friends from the Hmong Student Union here at Berkeley. We get together and talk about school and things." I didn't mention how many of my friends had to balance family demands and cultural restrictions as I had, or that two of the girls in the picture had gotten married and dropped out of college. "Last semester we sponsored a Hmong culture day with an exhibit in the student union building."

"Blia told me." She put the picture down and brushed her hand over the black embroidered runner. "Who made this?"

"I did. And the piece up there and this." I held out the embroidered belt I had tied through the belt loops of my jeans. I sounded like a little girl asking for her approval as I had years before. "My stitching still isn't very good, but I like doing it."

Her face fell slack and her eyes filled with tears as she stared at the family photo with everyone but me. She turned her back as she wiped her eyes.

I wanted to reach out, touch her shoulder, but it was all too new, too uncertain. "You look so nice in that dress," I said at last.

Mother took a deep breath and faced me smiling. "I bought for today. Only ten dollar."

The sound of footsteps racing onto the porch filled the room. May burst through the front door and ran into my arms to squeeze me tight. I wanted a little girl just like her some day.

234

Blia walked in and gave me a hug. "So, were you completely blown away?"

"I still can't believe it." I looked at Mother, unsure what to do next. Silence filled the room.

"Mommy says I can have soda," May said in her sweetest voice. "Do you have any soda, Auntie Nou?"

We all laughed. "Only for very special girls like you. I'll get us drinks."

Blia followed me into the kitchen with an anxious expression. "Soooo?"

"Why didn't you tell me she was coming?" I whispered.

"I was afraid if you had too much time to think about it, you might say no. I didn't want her to be disappointed."

"I would never have said no."

"She's wanted to come for a long time."

"Why didn't she then?" I found myself feeling defensive. What had kept her away?

Blia scrunched her mouth to one side for a moment. "She was afraid to go against your father." She put her hand on my arm. "How do you feel about it?"

I sighed and gathered myself together. "Good."

The trees along the familiar streets have grown taller, looking spindly now with their leaves lying in golden-red piles in the gutter. As I drive through the Shannon's neighborhood, I notice some houses have been remodeled, others painted new colors. I went to visit Mary and her parents first this morning as she and Josh are home for the weekend. I needed their strength and encouragement to bolster me for the afternoon ahead. Mary and I retreated to her old bedroom while I changed into the traditional Hmong outfit that Mother and I worked on together. We laughed like teenagers again, helping to ease my frayed nerves.

In September Mother invited me to the family New Year's celebration. A new year, a new start, she said. I have no idea what kind of reception I'll receive. I expect my cousins and siblings to be friendly, or at least polite. Mother insists that Auntie Yer and

Auntie Kia can't wait to see me. But I have not heard any mention of Father or my uncles, whether they are ready to welcome me. At least Father agreed to allow me to join them. Mother and Blia seem so confident and optimistic about the reunion. I want to believe them.

I am gripping the wheel so hard my hands ache. I feel slightly claustrophobic wrapped in layer after layer of embroidered cloth, my sash and apron tightly wound around my middle. But my clothes are like protective armor, good luck charms. I cross the freeway and approach our street for the first time in over five years. On the rare occasions I visited Sacramento with Mary, I avoided coming anywhere near my family's apartment.

I am fifteen minutes early, so I park on the street in front of the vacant lot, out of sight behind the oleander bushes that now tower twenty feet in the air. My heart is pounding and I cannot seem to catch my breath. I put an icy hand on my forehead and close my eyes. Perhaps this is a terrible mistake.

Since our reunion in early June, Mother has come to visit me four times. One Saturday in July she arrived with Blia, May, and my three sisters. The girls were awkward around me at first, but their uncertainty eased as the day wore on. They stared wide-eyed as we walked around campus and wandered through shops on Telegraph Avenue. Over lunch they offered snippets of their life at school and with friends. Houa is planning on going to junior college.

Since then Mother has taken the Greyhound bus by herself and stayed overnight one weekend each month. Cautiously, we are nourishing a relationship as two adults, two equals, in a manner I never imagined possible. We are becoming friends, companions, and sometimes mother and daughter. One Saturday, we played tourists in San Francisco, gliding over the hills in a cable car, browsing in China Town, and visiting the De Young Museum. On other days we tried a new Thai restaurant in Berkeley, then my favorite Italian place in Oakland. A child-like quality of awe and delight reshapes her face with each new discovery. All the while she chides me for spending too much money.

I love our quiet times shopping and cooking at home. She insists I am too thin. I don't know how to feed myself properly. What man would want a skinny girl like me? She cooks huge pots of chicken and vegetables infused with lemon grass and cilantro and steaming bowls of pork with mustard greens and peppers so hot they scorch my mouth. We eat in my dining room with cloth mats and napkins and candles. In the last light of evening, we sit on my back porch with cups of tea and chocolate chip cookies that I baked myself.

Sometimes it is enough to simply be together, sewing clothes for the New Year and listening to music. Occasionally she shakes her head and grabs my fabric, correcting my stitches. But more often she forces herself to hold back and let it be. Either way, it makes me laugh. She gossips about the family and discusses problems with my sisters and brothers, even asking my advice on how to deal with Noa's rebellious behavior. I have discovered my mother is funny and thoughtful. There is a depth to her I never recognized before.

There are subjects we still do not broach. I have never mentioned Pete. We do not acknowledge the cause of our split, the court hearing, or the decisions we all made in the midst of the turmoil. We talk of the intervening years as if I have been out of reach, away on a long vacation in Berkeley. Mother never raises the topic of my father. I have no idea what she tells him of her visits.

Some things never change. She questions me about my social life. Why am I am not dating a nice Hmong man? What is wrong with the men in the photo of the Hmong Student Union? I tell her they are either married or too young. I haven't offered that I dated one of them for a few months, but he was too jealous and domineering. On her last visit, she mentioned a nice man who works with Father at the Hmong Center. I could meet him some time when I come to Sacramento. Wasn't it surprising that a handsome man, already twenty-six years old, has never married, she said. Nothing I say dissuades her.

The more time we spend together, the deeper my desire to learn about our former life in Laos, about the village I barely remember. Like the bombed-out houses with gaping holes in the roofs and walls that we left behind, important pieces of my past are missing, obscured by time. Mother is hesitant to reopen old wounds, but slowly she has unearthed memories and emotions that span from her early life to the days when she married Father and war and tragedy took over. She tells me of her childhood with a mother she never understood, a woman she felt never loved her. She recounts her first blissful years of marriage and the birth of my brothers. And then there were years of war and killing and brutality, never knowing when the enemy might appear or a bomb might drop. Guilt and remorse weigh on her for secrets she has never shared with anyone before. Her confessions break my heart. There was a day when Pathet Lao soldiers raped and beat the other women in the village, while she hid in a corn crib, untouched.

"What could I do? How could I have helped?" she asked me, tears streaming down her face.

Many times she said, "I have forgotten these things. These are memories I try to bury, but it is important for you to know."

And all I can answer is, "I never knew. I didn't understand." The stories wrap our hearts together like the threads weaving in and out of cloth, binding patterns into a whole piece.

It is time. I walk from the car down the street and into the parking lot. The apartment building appears unchanged except for a fresh coat of dark brown paint and white trim. There are new rose bushes along the right side. Three small children who I don't recognize play in the side yard, staring at me with curious eyes. I climb the metal stairs listening to the happy murmur of voices coming from my parents' apartment through an open window. I wonder if the entire family is gathered and if they will fall into silence when I enter. Who will speak to me. Who will ignore me. And Father. Please let him forgive me. Let us be family once more.

I hold my hand in the air, ready to knock on the door.

The End

AUTHOR'S NOTE

 While *Across the Mekong River* is a work of fiction, the story is based on events during the 1960–1973 civil war in Laos, part of the wider second Indochina War, the communist takeover of the Lao government in 1975, and the exodus of up to one third of the Laotian population to refugee camps in Thailand and other countries. For those interested in learning more about the history of Laos, the Hmong/Laotian refugee experience or Hmong culture, I recommend the following resources:

Organizations

Legacies of War: http:// www.legaciesofwar.org

Hmong National Development: http:// www.hndinc.org

Hmong Archives: http://www.hmongarchives.org

Hmong Studies Center: http://www2.csp.edu/hmongcenter/

Hmong Cultural Center: http://www.hmongcc.org

Books/Articles:
Branfman, Fred, *Voices from the Plain of Jars: Life under an air war*. Vientiane, Laos: Cluster Munition Coalition, 2010 (second edition); originally published New York: Harper and Row, 1972.

Chan, Sucheng (edited by), *Hmong means free: Life in Laos and America*. Philadelphia: Temple University Press, 1994.

Conboy, Kenneth, with James Morrison, *Shadow War: The CIA's Secret War in Laos*. Boulder, Colorado: Paladin Press, 1995.

Donnelly, Nancy D., *Changing lives of refugee Hmong women*. Seattle: University of Washington Press, 1994.

Evans, Grant, *A short history of Laos: The land in between*. Crows Nest, Australia: Allen and Unwin, 2002.

Faderman, Lillian, with Ghia Xiong, *I Begin My Life All Over*. Boston: Beacon Press, 2005.

Fadiman, Anne, *The Spirit Catches You and You Fall Down*. New York: The Noonday Press, Farrar, Straus and Giroux, 1997.

Hamilton-Merritt, Jane, *Tragic Mountains: The Hmong, the Americans, and the Secret Wars for Laos, 1942-1992*. Bloomington and Indianapolis, Indiana: Indiana University Press, 1999.

Haney, Walt, "The Pentagon Papers and the United States involvement in Laos". In Noam Chomsky and Howard Zinn, eds. Vol. 5. *The Pentagon Papers, Gravel edition: Critical essays*. Boston: Beacon Press, 1972.

John Michael Kohler Arts Center, *Hmong Art Tradition and Change*. Sheboygan, Wisconsin: Sheboygan Arts Foundation, Inc. 1985.

Khamvongsa, Channapha and Elaine Russell, "Legacies of War: Cluster Bombs in Laos," *Critical Asian Studies,* Vol. 41, No. 2, June 2009, pp. 281-306.

Long, Lynellyn D., *Ban Vinai, the Refugee Camp.* New York: Columbia University Press, 1993.

Mote, Sue Murphy, *Hmong and American.* Jefferson, North Carolina: McFarland & Company Inc., 2004.

Moua, Mai Neng (edited by), *Bamboo Among the Oaks: Contemporary Writing by Hmong Americans.* St. Paul, Minnesota: Minnesota Historical Society Press, 2002.

Pholsena, Vatthana, "Life under Bombing in Southeastern Laos (1964-1973) Through the Accounts of Survivors in Sepon," *European Journal of East Asian Studies.* Vol. 9, No.2, 2010, pp. 267-290.

Russell, Elaine (forthc.), "Laos -- Living with Unexploded Ordnance: Past Memories and Present Realities." In: Vatthana Pholsena & Oliver Tappe (eds.), *Interactions with a Violent Past: Reading Post-Conflict Landscapes in Cambodia, Laos, and Vietnam.*

Quincy, Keith, *Harvesting Pa Chay's Wheat: The Hmong and America's Secret War in Laos.* Spokane, Washington: Eastern Washington University Press, 2000.

Stevenson, Charles, *The end of nowhere: American policy toward Laos since 1954.* Boston: Beacon Press, 1972.

Stuart-Fox, Martin, *A history of Laos.* Cambridge: Cambridge University Press, 1997.

Vang, Chia Youyee, *Hmong in Minnesota.* St. Paul, Minnesota: Minnesota Historical Society Press, 2008.

Warner, Roger, *Back Fire: The CIAs Secret War in Laos and Its Link to the War in Vietnam*. New York: Simon & Schuster, 1995.

Yang, Dao, "Hmong at the Turning Point," *The Journal of American-East Asian Relations* Dec 22, 1994,; Vol. v3, No. n4.

Yang, Kao Kalia, *The latehomecomer: a Hmong family memoir*. Minneapolis : Coffee House Press, 2008.

Films:
"Gran Torino" Warner Brothers, directed by Clint Eastwood, 2008. Drama

"Bomb Harvest" Lemur Films, directed by Kim Mordaunt, 2008. Documentary. Distributor: TVF International, 375 City Road, London EC1V 1NB United Kingdom. Website: http://www.bombharvest.com/contact.html

"The Betrayal (Nerakoon)" Pandinlao Films, directed by Ellen Kuras, 2008. Documentary. Distribution: Cinema Guild, Ryan Krivoshey, 115 West30th Street, Suite 800, New York, NY 10001. Website: http://www.thebetrayalmovie.com/contact.htm

"The Most Secret Place on Earth" Gebrueder-Beetz-Filmprodukion, directed by Mark Eberle, 2007. Documentary. Gebrueder Beetz Filmproduktion Köln GmbH & Co. KG, Im Mediapark 6a, 50670 Cologne, Germany. Website: http://www.gebrueder-beetz.de/engl/index.htm

"Bombies" Bullfrog Films, directed by Jack Silberman, 2002. Documentary. Distributor: Bullfrog Films, PO Box 149, Oley, PA 19547. Website: http:// www.bullfrogfilms.com/contact.html

"The Split Horn," Alchemy Films, produced by Taggart Siegel and Jim McSilver, 2001. Documentary. Distributor: Independent Television Service (ITVS) 651 Brannan Street, Suite 410, San Francisco, CA 94107. Website: http://www.itvs.org/films/split-horn

ABOUT THE AUTHOR

Elaine Russell is the author of fiction for adults and children, including short stories and the middle grade adventure series *Martin McMillan and the Lost Inca City* and *Martin McMillan and the Secret of the Ruby Elephant.* Her novel *Across the Mekong River* was a finalist in the Carolina Wren Press 2010 Doris Bakwin Award, the Maui Writer's Conference 2003 Rupert Hughes Prose Writing Competition, and the Focus on Writers 2001 Friends of the Sacramento Library Awards. The book won four 2013 independent publishing awards She has written articles and spoken at conferences on the history of Laos and the aftermath of the second Indochina War. She currently lives with her husband in Sacramento, California, and on Kauai in Hawaii.

Visit her website: www.elainerussell.info